It took effort, but Jenna managed not to fall prey to Buzz's crooked smile and flashing eyes.

"Maybe I'm just a sweet guy?" Buzz cocked his head to one side.

She shook her head. "Sweet? No. Infuriating, yes."

"Why am I infuriating?" He waited.

"I've already told you. It's like you're...up to something." She reached for the lamp switch. "What do you want, Buzz?"

His fingers wrapped around her wrist. "You know what I want. Another kiss." He turned her hand over and pressed a featherlight kiss to the inside of her wrist. "I'd like to think you want that, too."

The gruff edge to his voice seemed to mute the rational part of her brain. Her gaze wandered from his thumb caressing the inside of her wrist, up the wall of his chest, to the most knee-weakeningly gorgeous face she'd ever laid eyes on.

If she admitted he was right about her wanting his kisses—and so much more—there'd be no turning back. And even though she knew giving in to Buzz Lafferty would likely end in heartbreak, she found herself moving closer to him.

What harm could one last kiss cause?

Dear Reader,

I'm so glad you've chosen to return to Granite Falls. If you've read previous Texas Cowboys & K-9s books, you've met Buzz Lafferty before. If you haven't, you are in for a treat. Not only is he a super charming and handsome veterinarian, he's funny. And while he's vowed to stay kidless and carefree, he hadn't planned on meeting Jenna. Meeting her mid-kitten rescue instantly earns Buzz's respect—and grabs his attention. He can't wait to see her again.

Until she walks into his clinic with four kids in tow. Jenna and the kids totally rock Buzz's world. I loved writing them and I hope you will love reading their love story. Plus, the kids are pretty adorable, too.

Happy reading,

Sasha Summers

The Rancher's Full House

SASHA SUMMERS

Recycling programs for this product may not exist in your area.

ISBN-13: 978-1-335-72404-5

The Rancher's Full House

For questions and comments about the quality of this book, please contact us at CustomerService@Harlequin.com.

Harlequin Enterprises ULC
22 Adelaide St. West, 41st Floor
Toronto, Ontario M5H 4E3, Canada
www.Harlequin.com

Printed in U.S.A.

Sasha Summers grew up surrounded by books. Her passions have always been storytelling, romance and travel—passions she's used to write more than twenty romance novels and novellas. Now a bestselling and award-winning author, Sasha continues to fall a little in love with each hero she writes. From easy-on-the-eyes cowboys and sexy alpha-male werewolves to heroes of truly mythic proportions, she believes that everyone should have their happily-ever-after—in fiction and real life.

Sasha lives in the suburbs of the Texas Hill Country with her amazing family. She looks forward to hearing from fans and hopes you'll visit her online: on Facebook at sashasummersauthor, on Twitter, @sashawrites, or email her at sashasummersauthor@gmail.com.

Books by Sasha Summers

Harlequin Special Edition

Texas Cowboys & K-9s

The Rancher's Forever Family
Their Rancher Protector
The Rancher's Baby Surprise

Harlequin Heartwarming

The Cowboys of Garrison, Texas

The Rebel Cowboy's Baby
The Wrong Cowboy
To Trust a Cowboy

Visit the Author Profile page at Harlequin.com for more titles.

Dedicated to those who welcome everyone
into their family—blood or not.

Chapter One

"What in the Sam Hill?" Buzz Lafferty leaned forward to peer out the windshield, slowing his crew cab diesel pickup truck and pulling onto the edge of the farm-to-market road. He'd thought today would be like any other day, without any surprises to shake things up. The woman crawling around on all fours on the side of the road told him that wasn't the case. He rolled to a complete stop several feet back from the bright red minivan, watching the woman with mounting curiosity.

He'd never spied the minivan or, from what he could see of her, the woman before. Granite Falls was small enough that everyone was familiar. Not best friends, necessarily—but acquainted. So, a stranger, especially one crawling around on the side of the road, stood out.

"Any ideas?" He turned to find Roscoe and Scooter, his canine companions, just as curious as he was. Roscoe, a large black-and-white Great Pyrenees-Labrador mix, had his head cocked to one side.

Scooter, a blue heeler, had both pointed gray ears perked up and his stubby tail was wagging as he looked back and forth between Buzz and the woman. He whimpered, his tongue lolling out the side of his mouth, and rested a paw on Buzz's arm.

"I know. I know. I'm going." Buzz chuckled, adjusting his cowboy hat. "Don't you worry." He rolled down the windows so the dogs wouldn't get hot in the truck, turned off the engine and climbed down. "Stay put." He closed the truck door, knowing full well both Scooter and Roscoe would be leaning out the passenger window to watch what happened next.

As Buzz walked closer, he could hear her talking.

"Come on," the woman crooned. "I won't hurt—ouch—you." She shifted on the ground, shaking her hand, before planting it and scooting forward.

Still a way back, Buzz squatted, scouring the thick underbrush of thistles, ryegrass and enough goathead stickers to make him wonder what or who she was talking to. He didn't see a thing so he stood, pushed his cowboy hat forward to scratch the back of his head and walked closer.

"I know you're scared." She was using a singsong voice, pitched low and soft. "But I'm not scary." She pulled up her hand again. "Ouch," she hissed.

He was within earshot now. "Ma'am?"

She glanced back over her shoulder but he couldn't make out much beyond a tangled mass of brown curls. With a puff of air, the curls lifted long enough for her eyes to be visible. Big eyes. But that was about all he saw. "I need help." She kept her voice soft. "There's a kitten..." She pointed into the underbrush. "It's hurt, I think."

"Hurt?" Buzz stopped beside the woman, glancing back at his truck. As the only veterinarian in Granite Falls, he'd made it into a mobile medical unit of sorts. If he could get to this kitten, he might be able to help it. "Did you hit it?"

"Me?" Somehow, she managed to sound outraged without ever raising her voice. "No. But it was limping when it crossed the road and I couldn't just leave it out here."

"I wasn't blaming you." Buzz crouched beside her. "Animals dart out and, sometimes, there's no missing them. Especially on a two-lane road like this one." It happened all the time. Living in the country meant wildlife encounters—of all sorts. "It's back in there?" he asked.

She nodded. "Under that bush, there." She pointed.

That's when he saw the ant on her arm. "Ma'am." He swiped the bug aside, his gaze sweeping the ground. A few feet from where she crouched, there was the telltale hole of a fire ant mound. "Those are fire ants." He stood, offering her his hand. "Too many bites and you'll be in a world of hurt."

"You don't have to tell me." She flexed her hand. "Mean little things." But she didn't take his hand. "If the bites hurt me, that little guy is in even more trouble than I thought." She scooted forward.

"Hold up." It came out a little sharper than he'd intended. "You put your hand down on that and the fire ants won't seem so bad." He pointed at a small clump of newly grown prickly pear cactus.

"Killer plants and bugs?" The woman sat back. "What have I got myself into?" The last was so soft Buzz couldn't be sure he'd heard right. "I can't just leave the poor little thing. It's…it's a jungle out here."

Buzz had a hard time swallowing back his laughter. A jungle? Cactus and fire ants were just part of Texas. A native would know that and keep an eye peeled for both. Lucky for her, she hadn't encountered a scorpion or a rattlesnake—both were common in the Hill Country.

"What do I do?" she asked, sounding deflated. "We do?"

"I've got a catch pole in my truck." Not that he'd caught sight of the cause of all this. "Let me get it and we'll get the little thing out and I'll take him to my clinic and give him a thorough assessment."

"A catch pole?" She peered up at him, pushing the hair from her face and giving him his first good look at her. "What sort of doctor are you?"

Buzz found himself momentarily speechless. The kitten rescuer was pretty. Real pretty. Even red-cheeked and sweaty from the heat, he could see that. Finally, he shook his head and cleared his throat before answering her. "Veterinarian."

"You are?" Her delighted smile revealed dimples. "Isn't that a touch of fate?" She winced, flicking an ant from her forearm.

"I guess." He offered his hand again. "Best get out of their path. People have wound up hospitalized from too many bites."

She took it and scrambled to her feet. "Thank you."

"Any more?" he asked. "You might want to shake out your clothes a bit—while I get the catch pole."

As he was walking back, catch pole, small crate, and thick leather gloves in hand, he saw her shaking out her shirt, stomping her feet and tugging up her pant legs. "How many is too many?" she asked him, tugging up her pant leg to reveal an angry red grouping of bites above her ankle.

He frowned, noting the welts on her arm and other hand, too. He didn't feel too good about the number of bites. Those were just the ones he could see. Likely, there were more under her clothes. "Best get this kitten rescued." The sooner the better.

She nodded. "It's there." She pointed. "Under that little rock ledge, behind those vines."

Vines, he noted, that looked a whole lot like poison oak. He'd point it out later—after the kitten was safe and she was, too. He knelt, sweeping the underbrush with narrowed eyes. There, in a sliver of sunlight, he spied a patch of tawny fur. "Got it." But if he missed, the kitten would have to bolt past them and wind up running out onto the road again. He whistled and tugged on his leather gloves. "In case I need backup." He put the crate by his feet and opened the front, ready to transport his patient to the clinic.

The woman stepped back as Roscoe appeared. His size made him intimidating but he wagged his tail in greeting. Scooter ran around her once in a circle but both dogs wound up at his side. He gave them the hand signal for "herd" before setting the catch pole and moving it slowly, carefully, into the brush toward the tiny ball of fur.

In a flash of an eye and an explosion of leaves and fur, Buzz looped the kitten with the catch pole and carefully pulled the thrashing creature from its prickly hiding spot. It tired quickly, its sides heaving as it gave up the fight and sat, wide-eyed and panting.

"Huh." He didn't reach for the kitten. "That's

no kitten, ma'am. That's a baby bobcat." A bobcat whose right back leg had a large gash and was so swollen Buzz knew the wound had to be infected. "But you're right about the limp. Probably hurts something fierce to put any weight on that leg." As carefully as possible, he drew the catch pole close and reached out one gloved arm. From the looks of it, the little thing didn't have much fight left in him. "I got you now." He used his calming voice. "Nice and easy." He gripped the bobcat by the scruff of the neck and lifted it, keeping it at arm's length, before lowering it into the crate.

It growled and hissed and aimed one pathetic swat Roscoe's way but didn't fight Buzz. The bobcat went into the crate without a struggle. "The little critter is plum tuckered out." Buzz closed the door and lifted the crate to get a better look at the animal.

"Can I?" she asked.

He held the crate forward, watching the woman's entire face light up.

"Aren't you the sweetest thing?" She glanced up at Buzz, smiling. "I'm sure it would thank you for coming to its rescue if it could."

"I don't know about that." Buzz chuckled, setting the crate on the ground to tug off his gloves.

"Well, I thank you." The woman sighed. "For saving me from the ants and the cactus—"

"And the poison oak." He tucked his gloves through his belt and nodded at the vines.

Her eyes went round. “Poison oak? Like poison ivy?” She rubbed her forearm.

“Yup. You should get that looked at.” He didn't like how red the blotches were on her arm. “The sooner the better.”

“I have some Benadryl in my purse,” she offered.

“Even so.” He shook his head. “I'd feel better knowing you'll get checked out by a doctor.”

She nodded, studying him. “Thank you again, Mister…? Rather, Doctor…?”

He held his hand out. “Buzz Lafferty.”

“Buzz?” Her brows rose but she shook his hand. “Thank you, Dr. Lafferty.”

“You're welcome, Missus…?” Not exactly subtle.

“Miss Jenna Norris.” She smiled.

“You're welcome, Miss Norris.” He let go of her hand. “There's a good doctor close by in my hometown. Granite Falls?”

“I know it.” She nodded. “I just moved there, actually. I'm the new sixth-grade science teacher at the middle school.”

Meaning this wasn't the last time he'd get to see Miss Norris. “Then I'll see you around town.” He gripped the handle of the crate. “Feel free to stop by and see the patient anytime you like.”

“Really?” Jenna asked. “I'd like that.”

Buzz wouldn't mind seeing that smile again. “Other than the fire ants and cactus and injured bobcat, it was nice to meet you." He reached up and tipped his hat at her.

"You, too, Dr. Lafferty." Her gaze swept over his face.

"I best head back into town and get this little guy looked at." He paused. "And let you get those bites taken care of."

She nodded, waved and headed back to her minivan. Buzz stood, Roscoe and Scooter flanking him, and watched the red minivan pull away.

"That was something, wasn't it?" he asked, holding up the crate. "You're one lucky critter."

The bobcat kitten's growl was weak.

Not a good sign. "We'll get you fixed up." He slid the crate onto the front passenger seat and let the dogs load up into the back seat. "All good?" Roscoe barked, and Buzz closed the passenger door and headed round to the driver's side. He climbed in, turned on the AC and pulled out onto the road. He chuckled, shaking his head over the newest addition to Granite Falls. "So much for today being like every other day, eh, boys?" Not that he was complaining. He could use a little excitement in his life and something told him Jenna Norris might be just that.

"I'm fine." Jenna resisted the urge to scratch the bumps covering her arms, legs, stomach and back. "Really."

Her pronouncement was met with open disbelief by her younger siblings.

"You all wed." Five-year-old Frances frowned. "Bumpy and wed. Wed wed wed."

"Does it hurt? It looks like it hurts." Eight-year-old Garrett pushed his glasses back up his nose.

Yes. "Nope." She grinned. "But it itches a little." *A lot*. "That's why the cream." Other than mild irritation, she was fine. But they'd all been through so much that she knew little things like bug bites could set off a panic. Still, this was a teaching moment and, as a teacher, she knew she had to use it. She might not know much about mothering, but teaching? She had that down. "We didn't have this kind of ant in Kansas so you'll want to avoid them." She resisted the urge to scratch. "You see them, you stay far, far away."

"'Cuz they're bad?" Frances asked. "Weally bad?"

"Yes. No." Jenna paused. "I don't think they're bad, not really. They're just...doing what ants do, I suppose." *Which was bite the crap out of you and make you swell up like a balloon.*

Thirteen-year-old Monica dabbed a little more calamine lotion onto Jenna's back. "I think that's all of them. We could probably connect all the dots to make a picture."

Jenna frowned. "Ugh. Lovely."

"I wanna make a pitchew, Jenna." Frances grinned. "I wanna see."

"I was kidding, Frannie." Monica tickled her sister until the little girl was giggling with pure glee.

"What do you guys want for dinner?" Jenna asked, opening the refrigerator. "I guess we need to go shopping." She nibbled on the inside of her lip.

"Ice cweam." Frances made her excited face—her eyes and mouth taking on a perfect O and her nose squishing up. "Ice cweam, ice cweam."

"We can't have ice cream for dinner, Frannie." The mix of condescension, disappointment and tolerance was way more dad-voice than eight-year-old voice but Garrett had never acted his age. "Ice cream is for dessert."

"Or pawties," Frances argued. "Or boifdays."

Garrett pushed his glasses back up and gave a long-suffering sigh.

"You can go to the store," Monica suggested. "I can stay here with Biddy."

Jenna was determined not to burden Monica with Biddy, their fourteen-month-old sister. "How about we all go? Biddy will be up from her nap soon." She swallowed, trying to picture all of them at the store together. She was pacing herself with this whole motherhood thing. Not that she was their mother. She was and always would be their big sister. But since their mother's death, she was now *also* their guardian.

"Can I get mosh-mel-lows?" Frances asked. "Little ones." She held up her hand, using her fingers to show the right size.

"Maybe." Up until four months ago, Jenna had been the cool older sister who showed up, showered her siblings with candy and cookies and presents, took them to movies or parks or on sleepovers and adventures, giving them kisses and fun and a break from the constant sadness of their mother. Jenna had tried to do more—she'd even offered to move home and help out with her siblings on more than one occasion. Every time she offered, her mother got upset, they'd argue and Jenna would drop the subject until her next visit. Now that her mother was gone, she'd replayed those arguments, over and over, and wished she'd pushed harder to come home. If anything, she might have been more prepared to take on this new *parenting* role she had to play. As it was, she felt like she was pretending. An imposter. Any minute, someone was going to call her bluff and CPS or the state or someone was going to take away her siblings because she wasn't up to it. She swallowed. *I'm up to it. I've got this.* So far, so good. All she could do was take it minute by minute. "We can get some yummy fruit."

"Cheese sticks?" Garrett would happily live on cheese sticks and pretzels if Jenna let him.

"Maybe." *Maybe* had become Jenna's go-to word. Telling them *no* was hard, especially after everything they'd been through. Telling them *no* felt wrong—even when it was the right thing to do. But saying *no* was part of parenting. It taught boundaries and, as hours of in-service classes and a semester or two of educational and child psychology classes had insisted, kids needed those. "How about we make a list together?"

Bridget, Biddy to everyone, woke up the minute they'd all gathered around the table, pencil and paper at the ready.

Jenna rested a hand on Monica's shoulder to keep the young teen from jumping up and assuming diaper-and-baby duty. From what Jenna had gleaned, Monica had been playing mother to her youngest sibling since Biddy's birth. It made sense, in a way. Their mother had been consumed with depression since Jenna's stepfather, her siblings' biological father, had lost his fight with prostate cancer two years ago. "I've got it." She gave Monica's shoulder a gentle squeeze. "Go ahead and start the list."

She left the kitchen of their new-to-them home and walked down the hall to Biddy's room. "Hello, Biddy-boo." She flipped on the overhead light. "How's my little ball of happy?"

Biddy held on to the side of her crib and bounced up and down.

"I see you. You're standing up, like a big girl. Did you have a nice nap?" She tapped her little sister on the nose and scooped her up. "As soon as we get you cleaned up, we're going on an adventure. Okay?"

Biddy smiled.

"Excellent." Jenna nodded, laying Biddy on the changing table. "I know you've got all sorts of things to tell me, Biddy-boo. I bet there are so many more words just waiting to bubble up and out, aren't there?" No matter how hard she coaxed her little sister, Biddy kept her words to a minimum—even for a fourteen-month-old. "And once you start talking, there will be no stopping you." At least, that's what Jenna hoped for.

Biddy blinked her big light brown eyes.

"You'll never guess what happened to me," Jenna went on, chatting through the whole diaper change. "I met a real-life handsome cowboy. I didn't think they were real, Biddy. I mean, I know Lizzie is married to one, but how many real-life handsome cowboys can there be? But there he was, in a cowboy hat—which cowboys wear." She paused. "His name is Buzz Lafferty and he's a veterinarian. That means he is an animal doctor."

Biddy blinked again. She didn't seem all that impressed.

"Anyway, I thought it was lucky he was the one that stopped. He was just who *needed* to be there today." She lowered her voice. "He saved that little tiny bobcat and he kept me from getting tangled up in poison oak and cactus and...and who knows what with those damn fire ants." She paused, wincing. "Oops, forget that word, Biddy. That's not a good word." Jenna could envision Biddy clearly enunciating her first word, *damn*. Jenna shook her head. "He did say we could come and see him and the bobcat—"

"Are we going?" Garrett's voice startled her so much she almost knocked the box of baby wipes onto the floor.

Jenna turned to find all three of her siblings standing in the doorway. "Since when did you three develop a stealth mode?" She went back to changing Biddy. "Or eavesdropping."

"It's not really eavesdropping when the baby monitor is on." Monica joined Jenna at the changing table. "Is it, Biddy?" She made a face at the baby, earning a bright Biddy smile.

"I guess not." Jenna couldn't exactly argue with that logic.

"How handsome is handsome?" Monica asked. "Lizzie's husband, Hayden, is way handsome."

Jenna couldn't argue with that either but she wasn't sure it was okay to tell her thirteen-year-old sister that Buzz Lafferty was hella handsome. "*Handsome* handsome," she murmured, shrugging.

"He saved you fwum the fiwe ants?" Little Frances looked afraid. "Do fiwe ants shoot fiwe?"

"Are they really called fire ants?" Garrett followed up.

Jenna sighed. “Yes. They are.” Why did the insect have to have such a menacing name? It sounded like something out of a cheesy horror or sci-fi movie. “But don’t worry, Frannie, they don’t shoot fire.”

“Then why they called fiwe ants?” Frances asked, looking up at Garrett—who normally had an answer for everything.

Jenna decided telling Frannie the bites burn like fire might worry her little sister too much so she shrugged instead.

“I’ll research it, Frannie.” Garrett was the king of research. If there was a question that needed answering or something he didn’t know, he was always quick to rectify that.

“Okay, Gawett. Thank you.” Frannie smiled up at her brother.

Garrett nodded before turning back to Jenna. “Are we going to meet him? The cowboy veterinarian?”

“No.” Jenna shook her head. Not that the idea wasn’t appealing. It was. *Very.*

“We should thank him, Jenna.” Monica watched as Jenna snapped up Biddy’s onesie. “You always tell us to thank people when they do something nice for us and he did. We could even make him cookies or a pie or something. He saved you from—”

Garrett cut in, ticking off the list with his fingers. “Poison oak and cactus and the da—”

“Okay.” Jenna scooped up Biddy. “Okay. Let’s not repeat that part.” She bounced the baby. “How about we go to the store and buy what we need to make cookies? We can take them to him tomorrow?" Maybe then she wouldn't be covered in pale pink patches of dried lotion that kept her bites from itching to high heaven. "Sound like a plan?"

"Yep." Frances grinned.

Garrett nodded.

"I guess." Monica shrugged. "Can we make oatmeal chocolate chip cookies? Everyone loves those."

Jenna nodded, the cell phone in her pocket vibrating. "Everyone get their shoes on and we'll go." She watched the three of them scatter and pulled her phone from her pocket. "Let's see who it is, Biddy." Seeing Lizzie's name scroll across the screen made her answer right away. "Hey, you, what's up?"

"Skylar called and told me what happened. Are you okay?"

"Fine. Covered in calamine lotion so I look like a walking patchwork quilt, but fine." Jenna bounced Biddy in her arms. "Who is Skylar?"

"Skylar is Buzz's vet tech. She's also my sister-in-law." Lizzie giggled. "You'll get to know everyone in Granite Falls, don't worry. What did you think of Buzz? He's a character, isn't he?"

"As far as I'm concerned, he's a knight in shining armor." Jenna headed for the kitchen, carrying Biddy with her. "Seriously, Lizzie, if I'd known nature was so dangerous in Texas, I'm not sure you'd have talked me into coming here."

"It's not so bad. You just have to know what to look for." Lizzie paused. "You and the kids should come over for dinner tomorrow and we can talk through them all."

"I'll think about it. If I'm not all calamined up." She slid her purse strap up and onto her shoulder. "Right now, I have to brave the grocery store with the whole gang to get ingredients for Buzz's thank-you cookies."

"Thank-you cookies?"

"The kids reminded me it's a thing. A thing I started." She made a face at Biddy.

"I'm sure Buzz will love them." Lizzie chuckled. "Let me know if you need anything, will you? I'm sure it's…a lot. Settling in and the kids and… everything. I'm here, for whatever you need. Anytime, day or night."

"Thanks, Lizzie." She waved the kids out the front door. "We should make you thank-you cookies, too. You're the one that helped me find this job and this house and everything, really." She locked the door, Biddy on her hip, her phone sandwiched between her shoulder and her ear.

"Ever stop to think I just wanted you closer?"

"Aunt Lizzie gets cookies, too?" Frances skipped down the path to the waiting red minivan.

Jenna gave her the thumbs-up.

"Yay." Frances clapped. She loved baking or,

as Garrett put it, she loved making a mess in the kitchen. “Baking pawty.”

“I hear Frannie.” There was a smile in Lizzie’s voice. “I hope you’ll come tomorrow night. I know the girls and Weston would love to meet them.”

“No promises.” Jenna wanted to make a good first impression—not a speckled one. “I should go.”

“Gotcha. Have fun shopping. Give the kids a hug from me. Bye.” Lizzie hung up.

By the time Jenna had Frances and Biddy buckled into their seats, she was sweating. It was hot, ridiculously hot. So hot her calamine lotion patches were giving way to the dewy condensation forming on her skin. Great. Hopefully, she could make it through the grocery store before she started clawing at her bites. She climbed into the van and immediately blasted the air conditioner, worried about the kids in the heat. *Shouldn’t it be cooling down now that the summer months were wrapping up?* It felt like they should be in swimsuits, headed for a pool or lake or something. Instead, she’d be starting her new job at the middle school next week. So far, Jenna wasn’t sold on Texas. From the heat to the bugs to the vegetation, it felt like everything was out to get her. She could handle herself but the kids? She didn’t want to think about it. She shuddered, glancing in the rearview mirror at her four precious siblings. No, she’d read up, she’d take precautions—she'd do whatever she needed to keep them safe.

Fire ant bites aside, the high point of their Texas relocation so far was meeting Buzz Lafferty. And, once the bites were better and the cookies were made, she'd be all too happy to visit with the handsome knight in shining armor of a cowboy again.

Chapter Two

Buzz looked up from the chart he was reviewing to find his veterinary technician leaning against his office door. He glanced at his watch and sighed. "We have a walk-in?" It had been a long day and he was more than ready to head home, warm up some chili and put his feet up for a while.

"Sort of." Skylar was grinning ear to ear.

Buzz scratched the back of his head. "Is it Kyle? Is he pranking me?" He shook his head and stood. "Your husband needs to accept defeat. He can't out-prank me." Skylar's husband was one of his oldest friends. He and Kyle Mitchell had been pulling pranks on each other as far back as Buzz could remember.

"I'll make sure to tell him that when I get home." Skylar rolled her eyes. "But it's not Kyle. It's a woman? Asking about the bobcat? Jenna Norris."

Buzz stood. The chili could wait. "She's here?"

Skylar paused, her brows rising. "Yes. She mentioned something about you inviting her to visit the bobcat?"

"I did." He'd hoped she'd take him up on his offer but he'd been too busy to ponder it much in the day and a half since he'd watched her minivan drive away. He smiled. "I did."

Skylar crossed her arms over her chest, watching him.

"What?" He mimicked her posture.

"Nothing." Skylar waved a dismissive hand.

"That's not a nothing look." He frowned.

"Oh, and Cassie is here, too." Skylar shrugged.

"Wonderful." He mumbled. "Don't start with that or anything." He shot Skylar a narrow-eyed look. As much as he loved his sister, Cassie, she was a lot to handle. He brushed past Skylar and headed into the waiting room. Where he came to a hard stop.

Jenna was animated, her hands moving as she talked to Cassie. All dimples and smiles and big eyes. She was lovely, no doubt about it. That part was good. Fine.

It was the kids that caused concern. A baby, a teen and two more in between. This wasn't just one. Or two. This was a *lot* of kids. He knew they didn't belong to Cassie or Skylar so that meant they belonged to—

"Jenna's here." He heard the amusement in his sister's voice. "She came to check on her bobcat."

"I see that." He tore his gaze from the kids and looked Jenna's way. She was prettier than he remembered. Which surprised him. He was sure she was the prettiest thing he'd ever seen as it was. He'd wanted to see her again and, now, here she was. With kids. "This is a surprise."

"They couldn't wait to see the bobcat." Jenna bounced the baby on her hip, smiling at the little girl. "Isn't that right? Oh, and they wanted to meet you, too, of course."

They wanted to meet him? He swallowed, hard, all sorts of internal warning signals blaring. Buzz liked to consider himself easygoing. Hell, he was easygoing. Not many things got under his skin or ruffled his feathers and he was proud of that. That applied to dating, too. When it came to dating, he didn't have many deal-breakers. Except one: kids. He had a good reason, too—one that'd left an ache that had never fully healed. And now here's Jenna with *four* kids. She was too young to be the teen's mother—likely the boy's, too. So, he needed to know where, exactly, these kids fit into Jenna's life.

"If it's not a good time, we can come back later," Jenna suggested, absentmindedly bouncing the baby on her hip, her smile fading the longer she studied him.

Cassie, Skylar, Jenna and all the kids were staring at him. Waiting.

"We made cookies." The little girl stepped forward, holding out a tin. "See all the animals? We picked it since you'we an animal doctaw." She smiled up at him.

"I should have called first," Jenna murmured.

"No, not at all." Cassie was all smiles for Jenna—before shooting a death glare his way. "This is lovely. My brother, Buzz, loves cookies. Especially homemade."

Right. He swallowed again. They were here. They'd made him cookies. They'd made him cookies? *Snap out of it.*

"Thank you, Doctaw, for saving her from the fiwe ant meanie monstahs." The little girl was plum adorable. Her wide-eyed and solemn declaration made Buzz answer her.

"You're welcome." He took the tin. "It's the least I could do."

"See all the animals?" the little girl asked, standing on tiptoe to point. "A doggy and kitty and piggie, too." She giggled. "Even a boid."

"A bird," the little boy explained, pushing up his glasses.

"That's what I said, Gawwett." The little girl stuck her tongue out. "I said it wight."

"Frannie." Jenna's voice was soft but firm. "Dr. Lafferty, these are my siblings. Monica, Garrett and Frannie." She bounced the baby, who smiled. "And this is Biddy."

Siblings. That made sense. There was a faint family resemblance. Siblings that were close; he'd picked up on that right away. Like he and Cassie were close. *I can work with siblings*. The momentary panic eased up. "Nice to meet you all." Sibling rule number one: If they didn't like him, he wouldn't stand a chance with Jenna. *Better turn on the charm.* "And thanks for the cookies." He winked at Frannie.

"Oatmeal chocolate chip," Frannie said. "And wegular chocolate chip cookies." She held up two fingers. "Oh, and peanut buttah ones, too." She held up a third finger.

"That's a lot of cookies." Buzz grinned.

"We do really appreciate you taking care of Jenna," Monica said, holding out her hand. "We just wanted to thank you."

Buzz shook the girl's hand.

"Yes, sir, thank you." The boy stepped forward, pushed his glasses up his nose and held out his hand. "We also wanted to see the bobcat, too."

Polite siblings at that. He was pretty sure he and Cassie were pushing each other around and full of sass at their age. "Of course." Buzz shook hands with the boy. "He's in the back, healing up. We can go see him."

"Do I shake his hand, too?" Frannie whispered loudly, looking at Jenna for guidance.

"You gave me the cookies. You don't have to shake my hand, if you don't want to," Buzz whispered back.

"You hoid that?" Frannie whispered back.

"Everyone heard that." Garrett nudged her.

Buzz didn't miss the look Jenna shot Garrett before she said, "It's very sweet that you're using your manners." Jenna smiled at Frannie. "It makes me proud. Of all of you."

Frannie's little chest puffed out from Jenna's praise.

Buzz watched the interaction, amused. He and Cassie were so close in age they'd been inseparable growing up. He couldn't imagine having such a wide age gap between them—or how different their relationship would have been. "How about I show you the kitten your sister was trying to save?"

"A kitten?" Garrett looked disappointed. "I thought it was a bobcat."

"It is. But your sister thought it was a kitten *and* a baby bobcat is called a kitten." Buzz saw the boy's brows rise.

"They are?" Garrett asked. "Cool."

"He is pretty little—it's easy to see why she thought it was a kitten. Come see for yourself." He waved them back, holding the door wide for Jenna and the kids. But when Cassie and Skylar looked ready to follow, he held his hand up. "You two tagging along, too?"

Cassie shot him another look. "I'm thinking about it. You locked up like a deer in the headlights."

Buzz sighed but he didn't argue. She was right and he knew it.

But her expression softened as she placed a hand on his arm, offering him a reassuring squeeze. She knew him better than just about anyone. Likely, she knew he was struggling with the memories he kept boxed up, locked away, deep inside. "You good?"

"I'd be better if you two stopped trying to cramp my style." Better to tease than acknowledge what she was asking.

Cassie rolled her eyes. "Right. I'm out. I've got a date with a hottie superhero movie and some brownie fudge ice cream." With a fluttery wave, she walked back out of the exam room.

"I guess I'll close out the chart on the spay from earlier." Skylar glanced into the recovery ward where the Norris family had gathered. "That's a lot of kids." She grinned. Buzz had no doubt she'd tell Kyle everything that happened—and he'd hear all about it later. "And then I'll head out, too. If you're sure you don't want a hand?"

"I'm sure. Sounds good. See you in the morning." He followed the Norris family into the exam room.

Garrett and Jenna were reading over the canine anatomical poster, engaged in conversation.

"What's that?" Frannie stood behind Monica, one little finger pointing up at the surgical light mounted on an adjustable arm. "Is that a wobot? Fwum outa space?"

"I tried to tell her it's not a robot, Jenna." Monica reached back and took the little girl's hand. "But she's scared, anyway."

"It looks like the wobot fwum Gawwett's comic book." Frannie peered around Monica. "Scawy."

"Nothing to be scared of, Frannie. Monica is right. It's not a robot. Though, come to think of it, it does sort of look like one, doesn't it?" Buzz grinned at Frannie's quick nod. "It's a light." Buzz reached up and turned it on. "I need it when I'm taking care of animals. See how bright it is? Now watch." He moved the light, turning it several different directions. "It helps me see from all angles." He turned it off. "Pretty cool, huh?"

Frannie nodded, no longer hiding. "Pwetty cool."

"How about we go see your bobcat?" Buzz asked.

But Garrett stopped by a large kennel near the exit. Inside was a large stray dog, shaggy and dirty and wary of people, that had come into the clinic a couple of days ago. "Who does he belong to?" the boy asked, kneeling to peer into the cage.

"Is he sick?" Monica asked.

The massive dog curled in on himself, dropping his head low and whimpering.

"Careful, Garrett." Jenna placed a hand on her brother's shoulder. "Remember what I told you."

"Don't touch an animal unless you know its owner gives you permission." Garrett sighed.

"She's right," Buzz agreed. "Better safe than sorry." He glanced at the dog. "He's a stray dog. A utility worker pulled him out of a drainage ditch a few days ago. His front paw was all tangled up in plastic netting. We've been giving him food and water and a whole lot of care. He'll be back onto his feet before long." He saw their concerned faces and added, "And he'll be good as new."

"Powah puppy," Frannie moaned. "Powah thing."

Jenna rested her hand on the little girl's shoulder.

"Where will he go after he's better?" Garrett's gaze never left the dog.

"Oh, I don't know." Buzz shrugged. "I'm working that out. If I don't find him a home, there's always room at my place." He already had his own menagerie; one more wouldn't hurt. "I guess you could say I take my work home with me now and then."

Jenna laughed—and Buzz was instantly pulled in by the sound. And he didn't mind one bit. The way her cheeks flushed when their gazes met and held had him smiling from ear to ear. He liked thinking he was the reason for the rosy red blooming in her cheeks.

"The bobcat?" Monica murmured, her gaze bouncing between him and Jenna.

"Right this way." Buzz nodded, waving them through another set of doors. "He's back here. Now that he's had some medicine and fluids, he's feeling more like his ornery self." He led them to the cage and stepped aside. "Much better than when your sister found him." He nodded at the cage. "He's cute, but don't let him fool you. He's got claws and teeth and knows how to use them."

"But he's so pwetty." Frannie's expression was all wonder and delight as she stared into the cage.

To Buzz, all babies were cute—even the human kind. This little guy was no different. But, cute or not, a bobcat was a wild animal.

"Remember, Frannie, pretty can be pokey." Jenna crouched, balancing the smallest sibling on her knee as she spoke. "Just like a rose."

"Oh, wight." Frannie frowned. "Wose hoit me."

Buzz glanced Garrett's way for interpretation.

"A rose hurt her," Garrett whispered, quiet enough that no one else would hear. "A thorn."

Buzz gave the boy a covert thumbs-up. "Your sister is right. The bobcat kitten might be cute but it wouldn't make a good pet, he'd bite or claw you if you tried to pet or cuddle him." He squatted by the cage. "But you can look all you want." He glanced up to find Jenna studying him. As gung ho as he was over getting to know her, she looked…skeptical. Meaning he'd have to work a little harder to win her over. *I can do that.*

As far as Jenna was concerned, Dr. Buzz Lafferty was one smooth character. Charming. Handsome. Kind—with kids and animals and strange women crawling around on the side of the road. He had the sort of smile that left her dazed. It was weird, in a good way. Here he was, taking time out of his day to give them all a personal tour and spend time answering their questions. He seemed, by all accounts, like a good guy.

But that didn't add up. A good guy—one as handsome and outgoing as Buzz Lafferty—wouldn't be single. As much as she hated the way her mother had worded it when talking about single men with potential, Buzz did appear to be *quite a catch.* So far. *Really, Jenna, you've known the man for a total of an hour.* It was a little early to start making grand character assumptions.

It's just… Well, he was unexpected.

She'd never been one to get flustered over a man. Attraction was the result of friendship and common goals. The whole rapid pulse, tight lung, wobbly knee, warmth thing she'd read about in books or seen on television had been just that: fiction. But there was something about Buzz Lafferty, his cowboy hat and his slightly crooked smile that made her think he could turn fiction into reality.

"Let me show her?" Monica reached for Biddy.

"Let me know if she gets too heavy." Jenna watched as Monica sat next to Garrett on the floor, cradling Biddy in her lap.

"Look, Biddy." Monica pointed. "Bobcat." Biddy clapped her hands. "You like that?" Biddy grinned up at Monica and clapped again. "Me, too." Monica giggled.

"He has big feet." Garrett leaned forward, staring into the cage.

"He does." Buzz nodded. "For climbing and burying food."

"He buries his food?" Garrett asked.

"Sure does. Or it might get taken." Buzz pointed at the kitten. "A bobcat is a predator. That means he eats mice and squirrels and rabbits—he could even get a smaller deer if he wanted to."

Jenna watched her younger brother metabolize this new information.

"Wow." Garrett looked impressed.

Garrett was hardly ever impressed.

"Unless he goes wandering into mountain lion territory, he doesn't have much in the way of enemies," Buzz explained. "But coyotes and other bobcats, owls, that sort of thing, will be all too happy to take his prey."

"Mountain lion?" Monica stopped bouncing

Biddy and glanced up at Buzz. "There are mountain lions in Texas?"

Jenna was on the verge of assuring her sister that there were no lions in Texas when Buzz said, "Yep, sure are. They used to be all over Texas but, with people moving in, there's been less and less over the years. But we still have them in the hills here. Not that you'll see them. You might hear one, if you're in the country at night. They're mostly nocturnal." He shook his head. "There's nothing like hearing one after dark, let me tell you." He chuckled.

"Noctoonal?" Frannie repeated.

"They come out at night," Garrett explained.

"Like monstahs?" Frannie asked. "A lion is like a monstah. It has big teeth and claws and can eat you."

Buzz chuckled. "No mountain lion attacks on humans in these parts, Frannie. Not a one. Don't you worry." He pointed at the wall. "Texas is home to all sorts of critters. You can see. This is only some of the wildlife in the area. And a few of my patients."

The kids all hurried over to stare at the photos, but Jenna was still processing the whole mountain lion thing. She'd brought her sisters and brother from a safe, quiet small town to *this*. Then again, they couldn't have stayed where they were. Their safe, quiet community had been shrinking so much that they'd cut back on the number of teachers they needed. Jenna was one of six teachers who had been let go.

"I didn't mean to worry you." Buzz's voice was low.

She'd been too lost in her own thoughts to realize he was standing at her side—close. And, up close, his blue eyes were startlingly blue. Bright. Vibrant. And examining her.

"I mean it, about the mountain lions." The corner of his mouth kicked up. "They are more scared of us than we are of them."

"I wouldn't bet on that." She wrinkled up her nose. "But I guess I'll take your word for it. You're the one wearing the white doctor's coat, after all."

"The coat does make everything I say true." He nodded.

She laughed—she couldn't stop herself. "Everything?" When he smiled, the corners of his eyes creased exactly the right amount.

"Well, most everything." He shrugged, those eyes locking with hers.

So blue.

"How are the bites?"

"Pardon?" She blinked.

"The ant bites?" That crooked grin grew.

"Oh." She held up her arm. "Frannie said I look like a Dalmatian. All my spots."

"That's a fair bit of calamine lotion." His gaze wandered along her arm.

"And that's just one arm." She sighed. "They're all over. I'm sure you can imagine how the rest of me looks." But as soon as the words were out of her mouth, she hurried to say, "I mean, not that you would. Why would you. I just meant—"

"That you have a lot of bites." He nodded, those blue eyes crinkling just right again. "What else would you mean?"

The eye crinkling and crooked grin made it impossible for her to answer.

"Is this a zebra?" Garrett asked.

Jenna sucked in a deep breath and tore her gaze away from Buzz. "A zebra?"

"There are a few ranches hereabouts that keep exotics." Buzz walked to the wall covered in photos.

"Is a zebwa a swiped hoise?" Frannie asked. "Looks like it is."

"Sort of." Buzz took one of the zebra pictures down and handed it to Frannie. "It's more closely related to a donkey, but they're all part of the genus Equus."

"What's that?" Frannie's face squished up as she passed the photo to Garrett.

"Science stuff," Garrett answered, studying the image.

There were times Jenna worried about her brother. He was so serious, so intense. When she'd been his age, she'd been climbing trees, collecting bugs in mason jars and reading adventure novels. *Okay, so I was a dork.* But she'd been a carefree dork. Then again, she'd had both parents and a pretty idyllic childhood. Garrett, all of them, had spent the last couple of years in less than idyllic circumstances. And Jenna was partly to blame for that.

"Garrett loves science," Monica told Buzz, shifting Biddy to her other hip. "He's the smart one."

"You're *all* geniuses," Jenna countered, scooping up Biddy. "Each and every one of you." She made a face at Biddy, who grinned. "Garrett just loves science the most."

"Science is cool," Buzz agreed.

Garrett looked up at Buzz then, wearing an expression Jenna had never seen before. "The coolest."

"I love baking. And cooking. I love that most." Frannie nodded.

"Baking and cooking has science in it, too." Buzz bent forward. There was the eye-crinkling smile again. "And it's delicious."

Frannie grinned.

"Jenna teaches science." Monica winked at her. "And math."

What did that wink mean? Her sister's rather mischievous grin didn't help. Jenna wasn't sure what Monica was up to, but she was up to something.

"I knew she was a teacher." Buzz straightened to look at her. "Science and math, huh? I don't remember those being anyone's favorite class, back in the day. You're a glutton for punishment."

Jenna had to laugh. "Not really. I think a lot of people struggle with math and science because of the teachers they had. My goal is to make both subjects *fun*."

Buzz was smiling at her. It was a very nice smile.

"She's really good, too." Monica jumped in. Jenna couldn't help but notice the way her sister's gaze kept bouncing back and forth between her and Buzz. "One of my best friends back home had her for chemistry and they said they only understood it because Jenna gets so excited and is such a good teacher."

Wait. Was Monica doing what Jenna thought she was doing? Talking her up, to Buzz? Jenna couldn't decide if this was sweet or sad. *My thirteen-year-old sister is trying to play matchmaker—so more sad than sweet.* Definitely, something they'd need to talk about later. *I can't wait.*

"If she's half as enthusiastic and determined as she was when I first met her, I'm sure her class is highly entertaining and educational." There was no missing the amusement in his tone.

"Is that a camel?" Garrett was back to inspecting the wall of photos.

"It is." Buzz pinned the zebra photo back in place, explaining the differences between a dromedary, one-hump camel, and a Bactrian, a two-hump camel.

But Monica's throat clearing and not-so-subtle wave to Jenna had her walking away from the photos and back to the bobcat.

"Why do I get the feeling this isn't about the bobcat?" Jenna asked, making a silly face at Biddy. "What's Monica up to, eh, Biddy?"

"You're way right, Jenna. Dr. Buzz is so, so cute." Monica grinned. "You two should totally go on a date."

I was right. "I said he was cute, that's all—"

"Whatever." Monica crossed her arms over her chest, looking so much like their mother Jenna was momentarily speechless. "You're young, Jenna. You're just as pretty as he is. And you haven't had any interest in a guy since you and…you-know-who broke up." Maybe it was the pose or her expression, but Monica even sounded like their mother when she said, "You need to live your life to the fullest, Jenna."

"Not you, too." Jenna sighed, but she draped an arm around Monica's shoulders.

"Mom's not here to make you do stuff but I am." Monica rested her head on Jenna's shoulder.

"I've kind of got a lot going on right now, kiddo." She rested her head against Monica's. "I'll get around to being single and stuff…eventually." Not that she had any idea how that would work with her four siblings in tow.

"I'm going to remind you that you said that, you know? We're not the only ones starting over. You are, too." Monica sighed. "Not to sound mean but I'm glad Hugh is gone. He was sort of a…jerk."

"Jenna, Jenna, look!" Frannie's shrill cry had Jenna spinning.

"What? What's wrong?" Jenna was already heading across the room, scanning her younger siblings for any sign of injury or concern.

"Doctaw Buzz whestled an alligatah." Frannie offered her a photo.

A nervous laugh bubbled up. "Oh." She took the photo. "Look at that." Buzz, in a skintight white T-shirt, atop an alligator. "That looks dangerous." She frowned, noting the large teeth and Buzz's well-muscled but completely unprotected arms way too close to said large teeth.

"He had fishing line tangled around his snout so tight it was cutting into him—and he couldn't eat." Buzz shrugged. "If we'd left him that way, he'd have starved. He didn't put up much of a fight so I'm thinking he knew we were there to help him."

"Powah alligatah." Frannie made her mournful face again. "Doctaw Buzz, you take cawe of all the animals."

"That's my job." Buzz grinned. "Helping animals."

"And people." Garrett had been studying the alligator photo, but he handed it back to Buzz now. "My sister. You helped her."

Buzz grinned. "I'd never seen someone crawling around on the side of the highway before, Garrett. And then I heard her talking to herself—at least, that's what I thought until I realized what she was doing."

"Getting bitten by fire ants and about to crawl into poison oak?" Jenna rolled her eyes. "Trying to coax a baby bobcat into coming with me?" Only now did she see it from Buzz's eyes. And it wasn't exactly a flattering picture. "I'm surprised you stopped."

"I was thinking more along the lines of doing whatever was necessary to rescue an animal in need." Buzz chuckled. "But I guess the other stuff is true, too."

"Both of you awe animal hewoes, then." Frannie clapped her hands.

"And you both love science." Monica nodded, taking Frannie's hand and turning to look at Garrett. He frowned at her, rubbing his arm when Monica nudged him with her elbow. "Go on," Monica whispered.

"And..." Garrett pushed up his glasses. "And you both like cookies."

Jenna was mortified. Were the three of them in cahoots on this Buzz thing? This was bad. And not in the least bit subtle. The only option? Retreat. Quickly. "Which I hope you'll enjoy," Jenna murmured, unable to meet Buzz's gaze. "Thank you so much for showing us around, Dr. Lafferty. We won't take up any more of your time." She took a deep breath and hurried on, "Thank you, again, for everything." She started herding her brother and sisters to the door. "It's been very educational."

"Do we have to go?" Garrett asked.

"Yes, we do." Jenna used her teacher voice. "Say thank-you to Dr. Lafferty."

"Thank you," the three of them chanted in unison.

Jenna kept them moving, breathing a little easier when they were standing at the clinic door.

"I'm glad you all stopped by." Buzz reached past her to open the door. "And thanks for the cookies. You all make sure your sister doesn't scratch those bites."

That had Jenna smiling and looking his way. "As long as I don't run out of calamine, I should be fine." She bounced Biddy, acutely aware of the many—many—distractingly handsome details of the man holding the door for her. "Just a little spotted."

"I'll keep an eye on hew," Frannie said, waving.

"I bet you will." Buzz chuckled, nodding his goodbyes to Monica and Garrett. "I am glad you stopped by, Jenna." Those blue eyes met hers.

"Cookies have that effect on people." Why did she sound so breathy and weird?

"Pretty sure I'd enjoy visiting with you just as much without the cookies, Miss Norris." The corner of his mouth kicked up.

Jenna shook her head, more than a little off-kilter from those blue-blue eyes of his. "Have a good evening, Dr. Lafferty. Goodbye." She followed her siblings out and onto the sidewalk. "To the van." She pointed down the block to their waiting red minivan.

"Give me a call if you find any more animals in need of rescue," Buzz called out.

Jenna glanced back over her shoulder. He was there, smiling, watching and far too handsome. As far as she was concerned, he was more handsome than Lizzie's cowboy hubby. Not that she'd admit as much to Monica—or Lizzie. Nope, she was going to keep her opinions and thoughts on Buzz Lafferty to herself. Between her siblings, her new job and making Granite Falls home, Jenna's hands were full, anyway. She didn't have time for distractions of any sort. Buzz Lafferty? He had distraction written all over him.

Chapter Three

"A PowerPoint presentation?" Buzz scratched his head. "Don't you think that's a little overkill?" He wiped the sweat from his neck with a bandanna.

"I do what I'm told." Kyle Mitchell chuckled.

"And he was up all night doing it." John Mitchell, the youngest brother, yelled down from the roof, rubbing his hands on his jeans. "We good?"

"Lemme check." Hayden, the eldest brother, held up his hand and used his knees to steer his horse along the house.

"Looks good to me," John called out.

"Of course, it does." Kyle tipped his cowboy hat forward to shield his eyes and peered up at his brother, laughing. "You're up on the roof."

Hayden moved closer, inspecting the new gutters they were installing. "Hold up. There's a gap here."

"Hope you didn't screw anything in place," Buzz called up to John. He wasn't sure why he'd agreed to help the Mitchell boys repair the gutter and screens on one of the vacant bunkhouses—especially now that the temp was climbing into the triple digits. But, triple digits or not, Kyle had asked for his help. If Kyle, or any of the Mitchells, asked for his help, he was there. It's the way things were, the way things had always been. And, now that the brothers' hard work had the ranch flourishing, there was a sense of urgency to getting the place habitable for the new ranch hands they were hiring.

"Dammit," John grumbled. "Let's get a move on. I'm baking up here." He wiped off his face with a sweat-soaked bandanna.

"Yep. Nothing like working in the heat of the day." Hayden gave Kyle a long pointed look. "If someone had gotten up on time, we'd have been long done by now."

"How many times does a man have to apologize for oversleeping?" Kyle frowned.

"It's not his fault." Buzz came to his friend's defense, sort of. "He was up making the PowerPoint presentation for Skylar?" He chuckled, angling his cowboy hat for shade from the blazing sun. "Happy wife, happy life. Or something like that?"

"Go on and laugh it up." Kyle pointed at him. "Your time will come."

"I'll buy tickets to that one." Hayden Mitchell stood up in the stirrups, handing the caulking gun up to John. "See it? The hole, right there?"

"Yep." John stooped, his posture awkward due to his bum knee. Not that he let his limited range of motion slow him down. But then, as their mother, Jan, liked to point out, those Mitchell boys are a stubborn lot. "Good?" John asked, waiting for Hayden's thumbs-up to hand down the caulking gun. "I'm with you, Hayden." John Mitchell gave Buzz a head-to-toe sweep. "Buzz is awful high-maintenance." He made his way to the ladder propped alongside the house.

"Whoa, whoa." Buzz held up one hand. "What is this? Gang-up-on-your-buddy time?"

"You started it." Kyle started coiling the all-weather extension cord up. "We're sure we're good to clean up?"

"We're good." John sighed, climbing off the bottom rung of the ladder and heading to the truck parked beneath the tree. "Because I'm down and I'm not going back up."

They all laughed.

"Kyle should go up, anyway," John pointed out.

Buzz shrugged. "He *is* the one that made us all late."

"See, there you go again." Kyle shook his head, chuckling. "Some friend you are."

"All I know is we'd better hurry." Hayden slid off his horse and helped clean up the tools, pieces of cut gutters, plastic, chalk line and all into the open toolbox of the large work truck. "Don't want to be stuck out in that." He nodded at the dark clouds on the horizon.

"Or be late for dinner. Mom'd be fit to be tied," John agreed, pulling a clean wet towel from the ice chest and ringing it out over his head. "Whoo-ee, that's cold." He sighed, smiling.

"Hey, you got a little something red right there." Hayden pointed at John's face. "All of that." He waved his finger around. "You get a little overheated up there?"

"No shit." John threw the wet towel at Hayden.

It hit the eldest Mitchell brother square in the chest.

"Thanks." Hayden caught the towel before it hit the ground. "I needed that."

That was something else Buzz loved about being here—being part of the family. He and Cassie were close, but they were all the family they had. Sometimes, he enjoyed being part of a big family. Talking over each other, laughing, telling stories and everyone lending a hand.

"Mom likes it when we're all under one roof—but she won't tolerate us being late for dinner."

Hayden wiped off his face with the towel and threw it back at John, who caught it. "Oh, remind me to tell Bobby the farrier is coming out next week."

"Will do." John nodded. "He'll want to wear his horseshoe suspenders."

They all laughed at that. Bobby Doherty was the Mitchell ranch foreman. His wife, Eileen, bought him suspenders for every birthday and holiday. Not just any suspenders, either. Bright colors and patterns and themes, the more outlandish the better. Bobby wore them with pride.

"I'll head back." Hayden mounted his horse. "See you in a few."

"Don't waste time." Kyle pointed at the sky, before climbing into the rear passenger seat of the club cab work truck.

Hayden nodded, nudged his horse into a trot and disappeared over the hill.

Buzz climbed into the passenger seat, turning to look back at Kyle. "You owe me a beer. Or two."

"I'll make it a six-pack," Kyle responded.

"Glad we brought the truck instead of riding." John climbed into the driver's seat, started the truck and turned on the air. "Most saddles don't come equipped with air-conditioning."

Kyle's phone pinged a few minutes into their ride, his soft chuckle drawing Buzz's and John's attention.

"From the sound of that chuckle, it's Skylar."

John glanced in the rearview mirror. "Yep. It's Skylar. Look at that sappy smile."

"Just like the one you wear when you're talking to Nat?" Kyle snorted. "Don't even get me started over how bad you are over your baby girl."

Buzz saw the instant softening of John's features. "My wife's hot. And my baby girl is perfect. What's not to like?"

"All you Mitchell boys are married men—with kids." Buzz laughed. "You realize what this means, don't you? You're old."

"I guess now is a good time to remind you that I'm younger than you." John was smiling. "Sounds to me like you're jealous."

"Nah." Kyle leaned forward over the back of the seat. "Who needs a wife and kids when you've got fifty or so animals to keep him company? That's enough to make any man content."

"I am, actually." Buzz didn't take the bait. He'd come awful close to tying the knot once. Once was enough. There was no way in hell he'd ever open himself up for that sort of hurt again. "So, who is this PowerPoint presentation for? Skylar doing some sort of program for the school or something?" Considering Skylar worked with him eight hours a day, five—sometimes six—days a week, he was surprised this was the first he'd heard about this.

"Nah, it's more of a welcome to the Hill Country with a few *watch out* sort of things thrown in for good measure. One of Lizzie's friends just moved to Granite Falls and I guess she mentioned something about wishing she knew more about what to watch out for." Kyle paused, flicking Buzz on the back of the ear. "Oh, wait. *You* know her. Lizzie's friend. It's Jenna."

Jenna? Buzz was smiling as he held up his hand to cover his ear. Jenna was friends with Hayden's wife, Lizzie?

"Oh-ho, look who's smiling now." John chuckled.

"I'm not saying she's not something to look at." Buzz shrugged. *And she's all kinds of feisty.* Not that he was against the idea of taking the lovely Jenna Norris on a date. That, he could get on board with. "This PowerPoint presentation is for her?"

"I guess she told Lizzie she's ill-equipped for the dangers of Texas living, or something like that. And Lizzie told Skylar, and they both had all these facts and pics but no time… And somehow I wound up with all of them making a PowerPoint." But Kyle didn't sound inconvenienced. "Now she's coming out for dinner tonight to watch it."

Dangers of Texas, huh? Like fire ants and bobcats and poison oak and mountain lions? Buzz was smiling.

"I wouldn't miss Mom's pot roast and Lizzie's rolls." John sighed. "I don't give a lick about the PowerPoint. Except to point out your mistakes, that is."

"Of course—" Kyle flicked Buzz's ear, harder this time "—I bet we could make room for one more? For dinner, I mean?"

"Dammit." Buzz leaned forward, rubbing his ear. "What are you, five?"

"Mom makes a mean pot roast." John slowed as they reached a dip in the limestone road. "And don't even get me started on Lizzie's rolls."

"Hungry, little brother?" Kyle chuckled.

"Hell, yes." John nodded. "Starving. All that working under the blistering sun will do that to a man."

Buzz chuckled, relaxing against his seat. Pot roast and rolls did sound good. But pot roast and rolls with Jenna Norris sounded even better. Besides, a man's got to eat. "Only if you're sure it's no trouble."

"No trouble," Kyle said, flicked his ear again, then burst out laughing.

"And we're going to use our very best manners?" Jenna asked.

"We always do." Frannie frowned up at her. "We awe good kids, Jenna."

"I know." Jenna hugged her little sister. "I know you are, Frannie. I'm sorry. Of course, you are."

"That's wight, we awe," Frannie murmured.

"You're all tense." Monica took Frannie's hand. "Why?"

Sort of. She was tired. There was a teeny leak in her bathroom and the constant drip-drip had kept her from getting a good night's sleep. *And* she still didn't feel all that confident taking all four of them out on her own. She knew they were good kids, that wasn't what she was worried about. Tonight, she'd be surrounded by women who were *actually* mothers—they were bound to notice she was treading water. What if she was doing even worse than she thought? Would they judge her silently or take pity on her and offer advice? Jenna would take all the help and advice she could get. For now, she'd *try* to relax and have a good time. "No, I'm not." She smiled, unbuckling Biddy from her car seat and lifting her out. "Not in the least." She tapped her baby sister's nose, balancing Biddy on her hip. "I'm excited. Are you?"

Biddy grinned.

Garrett stared at the sprawling ranch house. "Are they real cowboys?"

"Do they wide hoises?" Frannie asked.

"Do they wear spurs?" Garrett pushed up his glasses. "If this a cattle ranch? What sort of cattle do they raise?"

"All questions that we can ask. Sound good?" Jenna loved Garrett's inquisitive mind but he could be tireless in his pursuit of knowledge. "But, pace yourself, okay? We have plenty of time to find out."

"And you don't want to overheat someone's brain with all your questions." Monica giggled.

"Overheat yaw bwain?" Frannie regarded Garrett's head. "Weally?"

"No, not really." Garrett took Frannie's hand in his.

Jenna led the way, with Biddy on her hip. Behind her, Monica and Garrett had Frannie between them, holding her hands. The large wooden front door swung open long before Jenna reached it.

"Jenna," Lizzie squealed, hurrying onto the porch to hug her. "You're here. I'm so excited." She drew back. "Look at you guys! You're all getting so big." She hugged them all—even a reluctant Garrett. "Come in, come in. The heat's just awful, isn't it?"

Jenna nodded, following Lizzie inside the massive wood-and-stone ranch house. "It is." Kansas got hot but this was a whole other level. Here, it was warm before nine in the morning and stayed that way long after nine in the evening. "But I guess that's why we have air-conditioning."

"Amen." A man, holding a baby a little younger than Biddy, said. "John Mitchell."

"Hello. I'm Jenna. This is Biddy." She turned. "Monica, Garrett and Frances."

"Fwannie," Frannie announced.

"Got it. Frannie, it is." John smiled and nodded. "Nice to meet you all."

As it turns out, there were a lot of Mitchells.

From the look on her siblings' faces, they were just as overwhelmed by the number of people and names as she was.

"Doctaw Buzz!" Frannie announced with glee. "You hewe? You wiv hewe, too?"

He was here? Yes. Jenna swallowed, hoping she didn't look as excited as she felt. From the cleft in his chin to the dimple in his cheek to the teasing spark in his blue eyes, thoughts of Dr. Buzz had become a regular occurrence for Jenna. When she'd been looking over her lesson plans or washing dishes or having a wine glass when the kids were all tucked into bed, he'd spring to mind and derail any and all of her thoughts. Now he was here, in the flesh, not in her imagination.

"He's an adopted Mitchell," Mrs. Jan Mitchell—Jan, she insisted—who seemed to be everyone's mother or grandmother somehow or other, said. "We love Buzz."

"We do, too. He is a hewo." Frannie nodded.

"That's nice to hear." Buzz grinned, his gaze locking with hers.

Oh, my. Her throat grew tight. *This* was what she'd been afraid of. She hadn't imagined it. His too-handsome-for-his-own-good looks and all the charm were bad enough. But he had a sort of…magnetism that drew her in. *What?* No. That's ridiculous. There will be *no* drawing in. *No* staring or internal combustion or light-headedness. She cleared her throat and took a deep breath. "Dr. Lafferty." She nodded in acknowledgment.

"Buzz, please. I figure we're over the formal stuff. I'm your hero *and* you made me cookies and all." The eye crinkles appeared.

Okay, a little internal combustion was okay. *Breathe. Shake it off.* "Dr. Buzz, then."

"Or just Buzz," he suggested, his voice smooth as velvet. "I hear we're going to be enjoying a PowerPoint this evening? Some recreational learning?"

"I hear the same thing." Jenna had asked for a list of things she needed to warn the kids off of, but this was even better. Garrett would be over the moon—and likely full of follow-up questions.

"Jenna, Jenna, can I go play?" Frannie was tugging on her jeans. "See? There awe kids to play with."

"Yes, Frannie. That's Mya and Brynn—my Kyle and Skylar's girls. They're about your age." Jan waved the twin girls over. "Mya, Brynn, this is Frannie."

The girls' initial awkwardness lasted for five seconds before they went running off to find Mya's dolls.

"Do all those dogs belong to you?" Garrett asked Mrs. Mitchell, pointing to the mass of dogs sprawled across the tile floor on the far side of the room.

"Oh, they're all a little mine." The older woman

smiled. “But most of them belong to my sons. Two of them are Dr. Buzz’s, too.”

“You have two?” Garrett stared up at Buzz, wearing that same awestruck face he’d worn earlier.

“With me.” Buzz chuckled. “I’ve got a whole lot more at my place.”

“Buzz has his own little animal sanctuary,” Lizzie offered. “I keep telling him he could charge people to come visit.”

“Wanna meet them, Garrett?” Buzz was watching the boy.

“Okay.” Garrett pushed up his glasses, a slow smile building. “Sounds good.”

“I think I’ll go, too.” Monica followed, wearing the mischievous smile that had Jenna’s throat tightening all over again.

It would be okay. She and Monica had talked. They had. As soon as they’d put the little ones to bed, she and Monica had sat at the kitchen table to work on a puzzle and talk. Rather, Jenna talked and Monica nodded a lot. At the time, Jenna had assumed all the nodding meant her little sister was agreeing. But maybe the nodding had been to mollify Jenna—and cut the talk short. *Something I’m pretty sure I did a lot of at her age, come to think of it.*

“If you want to put little Biddy down, I can get a play mat out? Don’t worry about the dogs—they’re used to little ones and wouldn’t hurt a fly.” Jan took one of Biddy's hands. "Or are you walking yet, little girl?"

"She's pulling up but, for the most part, I think she's content to let everyone else carry her around." Jenna bounced her baby sister, making a face. "And, of course, we're all too happy to do just that."

"That was so John." Jan nodded, pointing at John. "My baby." She leaned forward, smiling at Biddy. "Let me get you that mat."

"Only if it's not a bother—"

"No bother at all," Mrs. Mitchell assured as she left the room.

"She loves taking care of people." Lizzie held her hands out. "Can I hold her?"

Surprisingly, Biddy leaned forward. "I'll take that as a yes." Jenna eased Biddy into Lizzie's arms.

"She knows you need a break." Lizzie's tone was pure sympathy. "How are you doing?"

"Other than the fire ant bites, which itch so much, I'm fine." Jenna offered up her arms. "I've gone through a whole bottle of cream already. Oh, and there's some leak in my bathroom. Not as soothing as you'd think. But, fine, overall. Really."

"I'm so glad you're okay." Lizzie turned her arm, inspecting the spots. "People get hospitalized from fire ant bites."

"Lovely." Jenna sighed. "I have to say, it's way more Wild West than I thought it would be." From the corner of her eye, she saw Garrett sitting on the floor. He was smiling, really smiling, surrounded by dogs and loving every minute of it. Monica sat beside him, laughing at all the doggy kisses and wagging tails.

"It's not all bad." Lizzie used a silly voice and Biddy laughed. "There's some gorgeous country and beautiful views."

Jenna's gaze shifted to Buzz. He stood, watching Monica and Garrett. "True."

"I was referring to the land sort—not the cowboy-hat-wearing-veterinarian sort." Lizzie laughed. "I so saw that, so don't even try to deny it."

"I didn't mean..." She held up both hands. "Fine. I won't." But she'd better shut down the Buzz talk before it went any further. "I should probably go change Biddy."

"Right." Lizzie rolled her eyes. "Using a diaper change for escape. Like I've never done that before. Thank goodness Weston is out of diapers." She pointed. "The nursery is down the hall, second door on the left."

Jenna took Biddy, grabbed her diaper bag and headed that way. "Don't look at me like that."

Biddy was staring at her with wide eyes.

"I know, I know. You're fine. And it's wrong to tell stories. But I couldn't come up with anything else to say." She sighed, turning into the nursery. "Look at this, Biddy. Giddyap. Look." She pointed at the horseshoes and cowboy hats stenciled around the room. "I'm betting this is Weston's room." She chattered through the whole diaper change, straightened Biddy's pink-striped onesie with tiny flower appliqués and snapped it into place. "Now you're good."

But Jenna lingered, sitting in the rocking chair and letting Biddy crawl around on the floor.

"All clear?" Buzz asked. "Garrett warned me to keep a safe distance. Just in case. He said something about potential biohazard diapers."

"All good. That sounds like Garrett." Jenna laughed. "What else did he mention?"

"He wants a dog." Buzz seemed to be waiting for her response.

"I'm not surprised." She watched as Biddy crawled across the floor to the board books stacked on the floor. "He's wanted one for a while." And she wanted to get one for him—anything that would make her little brother smile was a good thing. "It's just, right now, things are still getting worked out."

"Sure." He nodded. "I'm sure your parents wouldn't appreciate you taking them back home with a dog. I imagine their house is pretty full and all sorts of busy. Just felt like I had to say something. You know, we science guys have to stick together."

Back home to my parents… It was a natural assumption: her siblings were visiting her. Back to school hadn't started yet, it was summer break, so why not stay with the older sister and have fun? Logical enough. *But nowhere near the truth.* She swallowed, her throat tight. This was the awkward part. Part of her had hoped Lizzie had told everyone her situation, so she wouldn't have to. But, if Lizzie had told everyone, Buzz hadn't heard. "Busy, yes… but my parents… No." She smiled, trying to keep it light. "It's just me and my brother and sisters."

"Oh?" He looked wary, his posture stiffening somewhat. "What does that mean?"

"My parents are dead and I'm their custodian." She spoke quickly, getting the words out as fast as she could. "So, it's me and the kids. Here. Together. A family."

"Oh." He wasn't leaning against the door anymore. If anything, he seemed…braced. Ready to run. He looked…flustered.

It was the look of panic that tipped Jenna off. She'd seen that look before on Hugh's face. Hugh, her almost fiancé and future father to her children. It was the look on Hugh's face as he'd explained that he was too young to become the father to four kids that weren't even his. She hadn't blamed Hugh or argued with him or tried to stop him. "They are my responsibility. Twenty-four-seven," she murmured, watching Buzz.

"Right." Buzz looked downright alarmed now. "Family. Yeah." He pulled at the collar of his shirt. "Well… I should see if Hayden needs a hand with…

needs a hand." He touched the brim of his cowboy hat and disappeared.

"And that's the end of that, Biddy." Jenna sighed, helping her little sister stand. "It's okay. If Buzz Lafferty prefers animals to kids, especially kids as amazing as you all, that's his loss." She pressed a kiss to Biddy's cheek, hurt nonetheless. "Assuming he was interested..." Which was a pretty big assumption. "It doesn't matter. We've got each other, don't we? We don't need anyone else." But, deep inside, there was a part of her that wanted someone else. Someone to share her day with, have adult conversations with, drink wine or watch a horror movie or cuddle up with. Maybe, someday, she'd find that someone. "But now I know Buzz Lafferty isn't on the list."

Biddy grabbed her face with her little hands and gave her a big kiss.

"Exactly. This is a time-saver, isn't it?" Jenna laughed. "Who needs a hunky cowboy?" *Not me.* Not at all. Want? Well, that might be a different story.

Chapter Four

Smooth, Buzz. Real smooth. Could he have handled that better? No doubt. But it was over and done with and there was no undoing it. He'd locked up and made an ass of himself and she'd noticed. How could she not? He'd all but tripped over his own boots. Now he was taking four times longer than necessary to wash his hands in the guest bathroom… All to avoid making things worse. Thankfully, Kyle hadn't seen that whole exchange. If he had, Buzz would *never* hear the end of it.

There was no way he could cut and run, make excuses and leave. If he tried, everyone would know something was up. He couldn't even fake a veterinary emergency because Skylar was there and would insist on going with him. All he had to do was pretend that that hadn't just happened and enjoy the rest of the evening. *Easy enough.* He glared at himself in the mirror as he wiped his hands on the towel. What had that been about, anyway?

Hell yes, he was disappointed and he wished her situation were different but it wasn't the end of the world. The longer he thought about it, the more relieved he was that he'd found out now—before things had a chance to start. Just because he'd never ever date her, didn't mean they couldn't be friends. Kids or no kids, friendship was fine. But not dating…

It still hurt to think about Cameron and Lisa—he'd loved the two of them with all his heart. They'd been like his own kids. Their mother had been all too happy to let him step in, leaving the kids with him when she had night shifts at the hospital or something came up. The time he'd spent with them had made him excited about his future. He couldn't wait for them to be a bona fide family… But it hadn't turned out that way. Losing them… Well, when they were no longer a part of his life, he'd never hurt that way. *No.* He couldn't, wouldn't, do that again.

Friends is good. He was fine with that. Good with that, even. By the time he'd wandered back into the great room, he was calmer.

Kyle stopped trying to untangle the ball of cords

he was holding. "Make yourself useful." He thrust the cords at him. "What got your tail feathers in a twist? Something happen? You were fine five minutes ago?"

Buzz shook his head, pulling one cord free. "I *am* fine."

"Uh-huh." Kyle picked up his longneck beer. "Suit yourself, don't tell me."

"There's nothing to tell." Buzz sighed, pulling another cord loose.

"What did you do to Buzz, Kyle?" Skylar asked, offering Buzz a beer. "What did you say?"

"*Me?* Nothing." Kyle shook his head.

Kyle's outrage was so comical Buzz had to laugh.

"Then why is Buzz all *pinched*-looking?" Skylar pushed. "You know, sometimes you tease each other a little too much."

"I didn't say a word." Kyle held up his hands, one still clasping his longneck. "All I did was ask him why his tail feathers were in a twist."

Skylar didn't look convinced.

"That's it," Kyle added.

"He didn't do anything." Buzz glanced between them, still smiling. "To set the record straight, my tail feathers aren't in a twist and I'm not pinched. Not that I don't appreciate the concern." He finished untangling the cords. "Here."

"You could have at least tried to make that look difficult." Kyle took the cords.

Skylar hugged Kyle close, laughing.

"Doctaw Buzz, Doctaw Buzz." Little Frannie came barreling across the room to grab his hand. "Scootah gave me a kiss."

"Scooter loves to give kisses." Buzz wasn't sure what was cuter, the way Frannie stared up at him with wide-eyed excitement or her mispronunciation when it came to *r*'s. Likely, it was a toss-up. Either was pretty damn adorable. Which was *bad*. Frannie Norris was the sort of irresistible cute he'd do well to avoid. "And he likes tummy rubs."

"He does?" Frannie seemed to consider this. "I can do that." She let go of his hand and went sprinting back to the pile of kids and dogs taking up a good portion of the floor.

"That's a picture." Kyle nodded in the direction Frannie had gone in, draping his arm around Skylar's shoulders. "I don't know who's happier, the dogs or the kids."

"Please." Buzz snorted, carrying his beer onto the back porch. He didn't need to look. The less cuteness, the better. And he certainly didn't need anymore questions from Kyle or Skylar. He needed a minute to himself—to clear his mind.

He was disappointed, that was all. But his level of disappointment seemed a little high, considering he barely knew the woman. It had been a long time since anyone caught his eye the way Jenna had. A long time. There's no point pondering what can't be. Starting now, he'd be wise to keep his thoughts Jenna Norris–free.

He stared out over the rolling hills of Mitchell ranch, enjoying the natural beauty of the land he loved so much. The sun was on its way down, casting long shadows on the hills and kicking off the nightly cricket serenade. He stood, confident that everything would be fine—

Until he saw Garrett Norris crouching along the fence line, intently studying something in the grass. Buzz couldn't get over how much Garrett reminded Buzz of himself. Always investigating. Always making mental notes. *Always getting into mischief.* Buzz hesitated, then set his longneck on the porch railing and headed across the yard. He scanned the grass for whatever had Garrett so entranced.

And then he saw it.

"Garrett." He spoke softly. "Listen up. I need you to back up, slowly."

"What is it?" Garrett asked, cocking his head to the side. "It's not a rattlesnake. It's not making noise."

He wasn't sure what it was, not yet. But he wasn't going to risk it. "Garrett, now, don't touch it." He did his best to keep his voice level. If he panicked, Garrett might panic and that wouldn't help.

"I'd never touch a snake." But Garrett wasn't moving.

"That's a good rule. One to keep." He was almost to the boy. "Don't panic, now, but I need you to step back. Slowly." The snake was coiled up, the brown, tan and black pattern down its sizeable body indistinguishable. Without seeing the head, Buzz couldn't confirm which type of snake it was. "Pretend you're in slow motion and step back to me." His tone was a little sharper than he wanted but it got results.

"Okay." Garrett stood slowly and took one step back—then another.

Buzz grabbed the boy around the waist and lifted Garrett up and into his arms. "You good? You didn't get bit?" He held him back, giving him a once-over.

At the sudden movement, the snake moved. The head lifted.

"We're good." Buzz could breathe. He set the boy on his feet. "All good."

"Is it a poisonous snake?" Garrett whispered.

"It's not." Buzz nodded, eyeing the snake happily sunning itself on a rock. He took a deep breath, offering Garrett a reassuring smile and ruffling his brown hair. "Didn't mean to scare you but it's better to be safe than sorry with snakes."

"Makes sense," Garrett agreed, eyeing the snake. "What kind is it?"

"That's a Texas rat snake. Useful critters on a farm and ranch." He crouched.

“I guess they eat rats?” Garrett glanced at him, grinning.

“Yessir.” Buzz chuckled. “Pretty much any rodent. And birds and eggs. He’s a constrictor so he might rear up at you and hiss to scare you off but, for the most part, he’s harmless.” He hurried to add, “Not that you want to go poking at him.”

Garrett nodded.

The slight squeak of the back door was followed by Jan Mitchell yelling, “Dinner,” from the porch. “What are you two looking at?”

“A snake,” Buzz answered. “A beauty of a rat snake.”

“Only you would put it that way,” Jan called back, laughing. “You two hungry?”

“I’d say so.” Buzz glanced at Garrett.

Garrett nodded again.

“Garrett is, too.” Buzz steered the boy back toward the porch. “About that rule of yours? The no-touching-snakes rule. I’ll say it again, that’s a good rule. Everyone should have that rule.”

Garrett grinned up at him.

“You go on and wash up, Garrett, honey.” Jan Mitchell waited for the boy to run inside before saying, “I get the feeling that boy has a case of hero worship.”

Buzz stared at the woman, confused. What was she talking about?

“Buzz Lafferty.” Her sigh was all disappointment. "That little boy has decided you're something special."

"Me?" He shook his head and laughed. "Well, I am, aren't I?"

She shook her head, smiling. "And modest, too."

"Always." Buzz winked, holding the door for her. "Need a hand with anything?"

"Nope. We're getting the food on the table. I hope you brought your appetite." Jan headed for the kitchen without waiting for his response.

Buzz marveled at the arrangement of tables and chairs—like a massive jigsaw puzzle complete with high chairs and booster seats.

"It's a lot." Lizzie stopped by his side. "But, somehow, it works." She nudged him. "Bet you can't wait to have a big family of your own one day."

He glanced her way. "Don't you start, too." He crossed his arms over his chest. "Just because all of you've paired off and are happy doesn't mean us single folk aren't just as happy being single." He shrugged. "I've no interest in being tied down or worrying over schedules or bedtimes or answering to anyone but myself. I have just the right amount of responsibilities—I don't want more. I'm happy just as I am."

"I get it." Lizzie laughed. "Fine. You should probably sit over there." She pointed. "Away from the kids."

Buzz headed in the direction she pointed, all too

happy to be seated between John and Kyle. That is, until he looked up from the roll basket being passed and straight into Jenna's eyes. She was seated exactly opposite him. And even though there were a dozen or more children plus adults between them, Buzz found himself looking her way—again and again—throughout the meal.

Jenna cut up some carrots from the pot roast and put them on Biddy's high chair tray before wiping butter from Frannie's cheek. In the time that she'd been their full-time guardian, dinnertime had been about making sure all the kids were taken care of. She'd feed Frannie and Biddy, make sure Monica and Garrett ate and then it was straight into the bath and bedtime. Afterward, she'd poke at leftovers as she packed them away and cleaned up the kitchen. In time, it would get easier—she hoped.

Not that she'd ever made a pot roast that smelled this divine. Or made from scratch yeast rolls that were light and fluffy and perfectly golden. The very idea of making *anything* from scratch felt impossible.

Almost as impossible as not glaring at Buzz Lafferty. It'd been kind of funny, and a teeny bit sad, to see him bolt after she'd explained the whole guardianship thing to him. But then his speech? It had been too pointed for her to misunderstand—she'd been standing right there. He was telling her, Jenna, *not* Lizzie how happy he was as a carefree bachelor. *As if I'd somehow misunderstood his rapid exit earlier that day.* Message received. Loud and clear.

"You want another roll?" Lizzie asked, offering the bread basket to Frannie.

"Yes, please." Frannie nodded, lighting up as she made her choice.

"Jenna? Want one?" Lizzie offered her the basket.

"Thank you." Jenna took one and put it on her plate, vowing to keep this one for herself and not break it into bites for Biddy. "They smell delicious."

"They taste even better," Lizzie gushed. "Here, Frannie." She spread a dollop of butter on the little girl's roll. "Eat up those yummy carrots, too."

"Yes, ma'am." Frannie frowned at the carrots, her least favorite vegetable. She poked at one with her fork, then leaned close to Lizzie. "But the wolls are my favowite."

Lizzie laughed. "They're Hayden's favorite, too. That's why I make them."

All through dinner, the love and devotion amongst the Mitchells was obvious. Gramma Jan adored her grandchildren. John and Nat, Kyle and Skylar, and Lizzie and Hayden all managed to be blissfully wrapped up in one another while showering attention and love on their offspring. While Jenna wasn't one for feeling sorry for herself, she couldn't help but think about how much easier it would be to have a partner.

Buzz laughed at something, drawing her gaze. The moment his blue eyes found her, she turned her attention to Biddy. She wasn't angry with him—there was no point. But allowing herself to stay googly-eyed and swoony over a proud bachelor *was* a good reason to be angry with herself.

"I think Biddy might be done." Lizzie pointed at Biddy, laughing. "At least, that's what Weston used to do when he was done."

"Oh, Biddy." Jenna grinned at her baby sister who had mashed carrots into the wispy brown swirls of hair atop her head. She was using her little fingers to mash up the bites of soft vegetables Jenna had put on the tray, happily preoccupied. "She likes to make art with her food. Finger painting."

"Oh?" Lizzie perked up, peering at the tray. "Let me see that, little miss. I'm a trained professional, after all."

It was Jenna's turn to laugh. Lizzie was an amazing artist, art teacher and in charge of the entire Fine Arts Department for the Granite Falls brand-new, state-of-the-art high school campus. It was there that Lizzie had heard about the sixth-grade science position that had opened up—right about the time Jenna had needed it most.

"I'll keep an eye on Garrett, if you want to clean those two up?" Lizzie offered. "My bathroom is kid-friendly and full of bath toys and bubbles and stuff, you can't miss it. Down the hall to the right, second door on the left."

"Thank you." Jenna scooped up her goo-covered little sister in one arm and took Frannie's hand in the other. "Let's go, girls." Lizzie was right, the large bathroom looked like a toddlers' playground. "Goodness. How did you get carrots there?" Jenna unsnapped Biddy's diaper to find carrots stuck to her tummy. By the time cleanup was all over, Biddy had been stripped and washed and dressed in clean clothes while Jenna was left in a damp and carrot-stained pale pink button-up blouse.

"You got a mess wight thewe." Frannie pointed at the stain, her head tilted up so Jenna could wash her face.

"I know." Jenna patted Frannie's cheeks dry. "And I'm the only one I didn't bring extra clothes for."

"Why not?" Frannie frowned. "You bwing clothes for all of us."

"That's a good question, Frannie. I guess I should, just in case." Jenna sat back, taking in her scrubbed-clean sisters. "I think we're safe to go back out and play."

But when she entered the great room, what she heard sent a chill down her spine and had her frozen in place.

"It was a big snake." Garrett pushed up his glasses as he added, "Big and brown."

Lizzie's eyes went round and she glanced Buzz's way. "Oh?"

"He had some pretty markings, too." Buzz nodded. "He was likely getting in some sunbathing before the sun went down."

"I've never seen one like that, up close." Garrett was excited, animated and smiling as he spoke.

Jenna knew the look in her little brother's eyes and it didn't bode well. Whenever Garrett latched on to something new, he went all in. She could almost picture his new bedroom wall—papered in snake posters and his desk stacked high with every book on snakes he could locate in the library. "I guess I've never seen a snake that big alive in real life before. Well, except at the zoo."

That big? Jenna swallowed, hard.

"I wouldn't be surprised if that was the first of many snake sightings. They're shy creatures so keep your eyes open. You handled today well." Buzz patted Garrett on the back—and her little brother practically glowed from Buzz's praise.

It was Buzz's far-too casual tone that thawed Jenna out. *Handled today well?* What did that mean? What, exactly, had happened? And why was she finding out about it now? This way? Any fear she had gave way to anger. "A snake?"

Lizzie, Garrett and Buzz all looked her way.

Lizzie was all sympathy and concern.

Garrett was too excited to pick up on her mood—not yet, anyway.

And Buzz? After those blue eyes inspected the spot on her still-damp shirt, he had the nerve—the nerve—to give her one of his most knee-weakening smiles. "Yes, ma'am."

Ignore the smile. Ignore the blue eyes. Ignore... him. She drew in a deep breath, plucking at the hem of her shirt. "When did this happen? Just now? While I was washing up the girls?" She glanced out the glass panes of the French back doors, already knowing the answer. Outside, it was pitch-black.

"Before dinner." Buzz ruffled Garrett's hair. "Garrett's got a healthy dose of curiosity."

He's also a child. "Yes," she managed, her throat feeling hot and tight. "Frannie and Garrett, why don't you go play with the dogs? Lizzie, will you take Biddy for just a minute?" Her brother and sister hurried in the direction of the dogs.

"Come here, sweet thing," Lizzie said, reaching for Biddy. "Look at you, pretty as a picture. Not a bit of carrot left in your little curls."

Jenna took another deep breath before she asked, "Dr. Lafferty, may I speak with you for just a minute?"

That was when Buzz seemed to realize things weren't quite right. "Sure."

"Outside, maybe?" She was out the back door before she heard his answer.

The back door closed and Buzz asked, "Why do I get the feeling I'm about to get sent to the principal's office?"

Jenna waved him forward—too irritated to find him remotely amusing.

Buzz stepped forward, his brows dropping and his forehead creasing.

"What, exactly, happened?" she asked, trying not to let her anger and irritation and fear bubble up.

He hesitated, like he was trying to figure things out. "I came out and found Garrett squatting over there." He pointed at a fence post on the far side of the yard. "I walked over and saw the snake, moved him back—for safety. But once I saw it was a rat snake—which are nonvenomous—and there was nothing to worry about, he had questions and I did my best to answer them."

"Right." No harm was done. Not really. But… "And you didn't think this was something I should know?" Her voice was low, but there was no denying the snap to her words.

He blinked, wary.

"As you said, Garrett is curious. It's his nature. But he's a child and this—" she waved her hand around to include the sweeping views of Mitchell ranch, her voice brittle and high "—this place is full of all sorts of unknowns. For him and for me." She took a deep breath, doing her best to lower her voice again. "I'd appreciate it if you *didn't* encourage his curiosity when it came to potentially dangerous things like *snakes*." Her voice broke.

He was staring at her, his eyes sweeping over her face and the muscle in his jaw tightening. "I wouldn't put that boy, or anyone, in harm's way."

She gripped the railing with one hand. "And what happens if he comes upon a snake and you're not there to tell him what's dangerous or not? What happens when his curiosity overtakes caution and… and—"

"Jenna, no offense, but that boy isn't the risk-taking type." He crossed his arms over his chest.

"I'm so glad that, after two hours, you've come to this conclusion." She knew she'd said enough but she was upset—about everything. He didn't know a thing about her, her siblings, their life or what they'd been through. He had no right to be making statements on any of them. Or making decisions about what was or wasn't potentially dangerous for Garrett. "You don't know Garrett or how tenacious he is or how he won't let go until he's learned each and everything he can on whatever he takes an interest in. Now, you've made snakes far more interesting than they need to be."

He didn't say anything. In fact, she wasn't sure he was listening to her. He was still looking at her, but his focus had shifted and he was entirely too focused on her mouth. He must have taken a step closer to her while she'd been ranting because now

Jenna was certain the space between them was closing in. It had to be; her lungs were aching for air and every nerve was pulled tight.

A new wave of churning heat and anger flooded in her stomach. She was angry. More so now that—even full of anger and frustration—she was equally aware of his lips and how close they were. Her hand was tightly gripping the porch railing now. “Can’t you see?” she whispered.

Move. Go inside. It was clear he didn’t see and he wasn’t going to apologize so the faster she removed herself, the better. All sorts of internal alarms were blaring and they were all warning her away from one thing: Buzz Lafferty.

Letting go of the porch and closing the space between them was a terrible idea.

The shudder she felt from his warm strong and fierce arms pulling her close and crushing her against his chest didn’t change that. Or the soft groan that escaped his mouth right before their lips met. Or the toe-curling delight, something she’d never experienced before, of the press of his lips against hers. When he cupped the back of her head, Jenna gave in. Terrible idea or not, she didn’t want this—any of this—to stop. Hot and demanding, he coaxed her closer until she wasn’t thinking or feeling or aware of anything but his kiss.

Chapter Five

This was bad.

This was good. So damn good.

Here he was, standing on the Mitchells' back porch, kissing Jenna like his life depended on it. This woman had reached for him and that was it—there'd been no hesitation. Sure, he'd wanted to kiss her since he first laid eyes on her but this wasn't what he imagined.

This was white-hot, catching him off guard and knocking him off balance. One minute, he'd been downright offended and the next, he couldn't get close enough to her—couldn't get her close enough. Now, his arms didn't want to let her go. His lips were more than willing to keep kissing her until…

Well, he didn't know. He was in no hurry to find out, either.

It was over just as quickly as it had started. He'd have held on if he'd known she was letting go—but it was too late now. Jenna stood, breathing hard and wide-eyed, holding on to the porch railing and just out of his reach. All it would take was one step. He knew, deep down, that if there wasn't so much damn space between them, she'd wind up right back in his arms.

"That..." She paused, drawing in an unsteady breath. "That won't happen again."

What? Where had that come from? He'd been thinking the exact opposite of that. More like, that needed to happen again—starting now.

"I'm not interested in a relationship..." She waved her hand again, her face turning a deep red. "And I don't have casual relations. This..." She pointed between them this time. "No."

As much as he respected what she was saying, he didn't like it. That kiss? He was going to have one hell of a hard time walking away from that. He'd like to think she would, too. "You almost make that sound like a challenge, Jenna."

She tore her gaze from his. "No challenge. I'm simply stating facts." There was a fire in her voice again. "And Garrett—"

"I won't encourage him," Buzz cut in. "I meant

no harm." If anything, he'd thought he was doing something good.

Jenna glanced his way. "I guess we should go inside." She ran a hand over her hair, straightened her shirt and headed for the back door. "You coming?"

He nodded. "In a minute." If he went in there with his heart pounding or remotely out of sorts, the Mitchell brothers would know—and there'd be no end to the teasing.

"Okay." She slipped inside, the quiet of the evening disrupted by the layers of conversation and laughter happening inside. The door shut, the sound grew muffled and he was left to enjoy the night serenade of cicadas, crickets and an occasional owl.

A gust of hot summer wind lifted the hair from his forehead but did nothing to put out the fire Jenna Norris's kiss had ignited. Then again, he hadn't expected to damn near combust like that. It made sense he didn't know how to shake off the feelings the woman had kicked up. *Touching her, kissing her, was like tossing a match on gasoline.* He shook his head. And if he didn't shake off these feelings, he was likely to get burned. He shook his head again. "No, thank you." She said she wasn't interested; maybe that was true. There was no way he was going to get sucked into something that had disaster written all over it. *Been there, done that.*

The back door swung open. "I know it's a pretty view and all but you best get in here if you want dessert." Nat, John's wife, leaned out. "John and Kyle have already put a dent in the third pie."

"Hell, Nat, why didn't you say so earlier?" He pushed off the porch railing and crossed the wide-planked deck. "I'm not missing dessert."

"Don't worry, Jan set aside a piece for you." Nat laughed. "Unless the brothers got to it already."

The great room was in the middle of a transformation. Chairs and sofas and big floor pillows had been turned toward the large television mounted over the fireplace. The dogs, Garrett, Weston and Kyle and Skylar's twins were already comfortably propped on the pillows.

"We watchin' a movie," Frannie announced as she ran around the chairs to flop on the floor, between a pillow and a canine.

"A movie?" he asked, doing his best to locate Jenna just so he could make sure there'd be no accidental looks or touches.

Lucky for him, Jenna was sitting in a rocking chair, a sleepy-eyed Biddy in her arms.

"Skylar says we're watching something about Texas?" Monica carried a dessert plate to him. "This is for you. From Miss Jan."

"Thank you. And Miss Jan." He took the plate, the scent of warm apple pie an irresistible temptation.

"A movie? Please tell me this isn't about the list I asked you to make," Jenna asked Lizzie, her tone concerned enough to draw his gaze.

Lizzie shrugged. "Well...maybe. It's just, you were so upset and I felt responsible for what happened so... Skylar and I—"

"Hold up." Kyle stopped connecting cords into the television. "I think I should get a little credit here. I'm the one that worked on it until the wee hours of the morning."

"You did?" Jenna's mortification was obvious. "Lizzie, I didn't mean to cause any trouble."

"You didn't know?" John started laughing. "About this?"

"No. I don't even know what, exactly, *this* is." Jenna glanced at the television, then back at Lizzie and Skylar.

"It's the teacher in me. I knew you'd appreciate it. Garrett, too." Lizzie winked at Garrett. "I thought some pictures and bullet points and fun slides—"

"Don't worry, it's not as boring as it sounds," Kyle murmured. "I didn't want anyone dozing off."

"Here." Jan crossed and held her hands out to Jenna. "I'll take little miss here and you eat. I've a plate warm in the oven, just for you."

Once again, Jenna looked mortified. "But—"

"No buts." Jan took the baby, speaking to Biddy when she said, "You tell your sister I'm an old pro at babies and she needs to take care of herself, too."

Biddy grinned and clapped her hands—earning a smile from Jenna.

He forced his attention away. It was hard enough

forgetting what had just happened on the back porch. If he got too caught up in one of her smiles, he might just wind up pulling her up out of that rocking chair and—

"You should eat," Monica echoed, still standing beside him. "She didn't. She never does. She's always taking care of us." She murmured this last part, just for him.

Was he supposed to say something here? Monica was looking at him—expectant. "You should never skip a meal."

"I agree." Monica nodded. "I bet she'd eat if she went out now and then. You know, where she wasn't having to juggle Biddy and Frannie and Garrett."

Buzz nodded. Everything the girl said made sense. But he wasn't sure how feasible it was to leave a houseful of kids. Unlike the Mitchells, Jenna didn't have a huge family network to come running at a moment's notice.

"You should take her to dinner."

Buzz almost dropped his dessert plate. He should not take her to dinner. He should do his damndest to stay as far away from Jenna as possible. "I don't know—"

"I do," Monica cut in. "She likes you." She shrugged. "She likes that you have science in common, too. You'd have things to talk about."

He wasn't worried about the talking. He was worried about what might happen instead of talking. "Still—"

"Or, maybe, there's someone else you think might be better suited?" Monica asked. "Jenna's so pretty and sweet and funny. And super-duper smart. It's not fair she doesn't get to have any fun. Because of us."

There was the slightest hint of something in the girl's voice. Guilt? Concern? Something. Something Jenna likely wouldn't want her little sister feeling. "Jenna looks happy to me." He didn't look at her. "I'm sure she's happy to have a big loving family. Who wouldn't be?"

Monica perked up, then. "Right. Who wouldn't be? So, you'll think about it?"

"Think about what?" He frowned, sifting through what was said to catch up.

"Taking her out?" Monica leaned forward to whisper, "I think she really likes you."

It would have to be that moment that his gaze would slam into Jenna's panicked eyes. She was sitting at the wide kitchen bar, a bite of food paused midway between the plate and her mouth, staring at them. There was no hint of the earlier redness in her cheeks. At the moment, she was looking a little pale.

Interesting. "What makes you say that?" He shouldn't ask. He shouldn't care. He *should* stop looking at Jenna. He didn't.

Monica's smile widened and she whispered, "She

said you were handsome. Like *really* handsome. In a way that, you know, totally says she likes you. Even if she didn't say it, exactly."

He kept on watching Jenna squirm on her stool. *She said that?* There was no stopping his grin.

"Everyone ready?" Hayden asked, his gaze sweeping the room. "You know, there's a lot of people in here." He started laughing.

"Isn't it wonderful?" Jan asked, sitting with Biddy in her lap.

"I'm going to go sit." Monica moved to the floor, sitting at the edge of the kids and dogs—not quite a kid, not quite an adult.

But, apparently, old enough to try to fix her sister up. He carried his dessert to the bar and set it on the wide marble countertop. Without acknowledging Jenna, he pulled out the stool and sat beside her.

"Handsome, huh?" he asked, scooping a big bite of mostly melted ice cream and freshly baked pie.

Jenna ignored him, chewing her food.

"I said, handsome?" He looked at her. "Monica said you think I'm handsome."

Jenna stopped chewing and closed her eyes.

"She's a good sister, you know that? Reminds me of Cassie." He took another bite. "Always worrying about me—trying to find ways to make me happy, that sort of thing."

Jenna sighed. "What else did she say?"

"Oh, nothing." He didn't want to get Monica in

trouble but he couldn't resist. "Except I should take you out for food—since you never get to eat."

Jenna closed her eyes once more.

"Here we go." Hayden pressed a few buttons and the mega-sized television screen sprang to life.

Jenna turned, her plate on her lap, to stare at the television.

"Welcome to Texas," a voice said.

"Who's that?" Skylar asked.

"It's me." Kyle nodded. "I used this voice thing on my phone."

"To make you sound like John Wayne?" Buzz asked.

"Yup." Kyle grinned. "Cool, right? Just wait for it." And then music began, the sort of epic swelling music that most big-budget films had.

Buzz laughed. "Move over Martin Scorsese." From the corner of his eye, he saw Jenna looking at him and met her gaze head-on. "So, handsome?"

That was enough to put the red in her cheeks. "You know you're handsome." She shook her head. "I get the feeling you've been told that plenty of times. You don't need to hear it from me."

"Texas is the home to a wealth of natural beauty and Granite Falls is just about the prettiest Hill Country town you'll ever see." Kyle's John Wayne–voice went on.

"Now, hush, Kyle and Skylar and Lizzie went through all this trouble. I'd appreciate it if you'd stop distracting me so I can watch." She went back to eating, her eyes glued on the television screen.

Buzz ate his pie, laughed at Kyle's surprisingly entertaining video endeavor and found his attention wandering back to Jenna, over and over. Each time, he hoped he'd feel less...well, less. But things weren't working out the way he'd hoped. If anything, it was getting harder and harder not to think about how she felt in his arms or how to resist dragging her off her stool so he could kiss her one more time. She wouldn't appreciate it. She'd made it clear she had no interest in something casual and, with him, that was the only option. *It had to be.* Since his big break-up, he'd never broken his no-kids rule, he wasn't going to now—no matter how tempting she was. No kiss, no matter how good it'd been, was enough to open himself up for that kind of heartbreak again. *I'd best remember that.*

That's why, when the movie was over and his dessert was gone, he made quick goodbyes and all but ran from Mitchell ranch. It was over and done and, if necessary, he'd go out of his way to avoid Jenna Norris and her adorable siblings.

"Alonzo's dad is single." Monica rinsed off the last dinner plate and put it in the dishwasher. "His parents have been divorced for a while but they're totally still friends so you wouldn't have to worry about an evil ex. Plus, she has a boyfriend."

Jenna popped the lid on the plastic storage container full of spaghetti. "How do you know all of this?" This was the second week of school and, every night, Monica would share whom she'd met and what they'd talked about—but this was the first time her sister had mentioned single dads. She'd hoped the whole Buzz disaster had taught Monica a lesson. *I guess not.*

"He's so cute, Jenna. Alonzo, I mean." Monica shrugged. "We ate lunch today—well, me and some friends, and he came over. It wasn't like just the two of us or anything. That'd be way weird."

Jenna smiled. *"Way."*

Garrett, who was doing his homework at the kitchen table, laughed softly.

Monica rolled her eyes. "Whatever. Anyway, like I was saying. Alonzo is cute so maybe his dad is cute. The open house thing is tomorrow so, you know, you'll probably get to meet him."

"The middle school is across the street from the high school, Monica. There's no reason for him to stop by the school—"

"Maybe he will." Monica shrugged.

"Maybe?" Jenna turned her sister to face her. "Or he *will*?"

Monica smiled sheepishly. "He...will."

Garrett's sigh was all disapproval.

"Monica." She hugged her sister. "What am I

going to do with you? I mean it when I say I'm one hundred percent happy as is. I don't need a guy—"

"If it wasn't for me, you'd still have a shot with Dr. Lafferty." Monica cut her off before Jenna could argue. "I know you liked him, Jenna. I *heard* you. If I hadn't been all dorky and, I don't know, made things way awkward, he might not have disappeared." Monica's arms tightened around her waist.

"None of that was your fault. I told you that, kiddo. He's…cute but he's…not my type." At least, that's what she's been telling herself every night for the last week and a half. "He's a little too full of himself." She kissed the top of her sister's head, glancing at her brother. She'd come to terms with the whole Buzz thing but she suspected Garrett hadn't. *If it wasn't for the I-want-to-kiss-him-until-my-lungs-collapse thing, we might have managed to be friends.* But there was no way they could be friends as it was. "You didn't have anything to do with him disappearing." Buzz might be attracted to her but he wasn't up for taking on all of them—not many men would be. "And while I appreciate you looking out for me, I'd really rather pick the guy I date next, okay?"

Garrett stopped tapping his pencil against his papers long enough to say, "Besides, it's weird, Monica."

"It's not. We know her best. So why can't we help—if there's a guy we think she'd like?" she shot back, frowning at Garrett. "Okay. But after the open house, because Alonzo's dad is totally stopping by to see you." Monica eased out of their embrace. "And if you don't, you know, click, I'll stop." She held her hand up. "I promise."

"I'm holding you to that." Jenna nodded at the table. "Now, homework time."

"Who gives this much homework this early in the school year?" Monica grabbed her backpack off the side table and slumped into one of the kitchen chairs. "It's not cool."

"Um..." Garrett flipped through the worksheets he had stacked up. "I have homework."

"That's because you're a genius and your brain needs work or it'll starve." She nudged him and laughed as she set her backpack on the table. "It's like these teachers don't want us to like them or their classes." She glanced at Jenna. "I bet your students don't have homework."

"A little." So far, she'd done a lot of getting-to-know-you assignments. Sixth grade was the first year in middle school, the first year away from elementary school, so she wanted to make the transition as easy as possible. "Things are different now, Monica. You're a freshman." Jenna had a hard time believing it herself. Like Garrett, Monica was smart for her age so she'd skipped a grade and was younger than her classmates by a year. But, unlike Garrett, Monica had an ease with people and making friends that kept her from dealing with any issues with her peers.

"Phone," Monica and Garrett said in unison as soon as the first ring started.

"Thanks." Jenna headed for the charging station for her phone. "Hello?"

"Jenna?" The voice, a woman, paused. "It's Skylar. Kyle's wife? From dinner. And the veterinarian clinic. I don't know if you remember me? There were a lot of people there—"

"I remember. That was such a wonderful evening and movie." She'd been in awe of the production value and obvious time Kyle had put into their welcome to Texas, but she'd so appreciated it. "How are you?"

"I'm good. I wanted to see if you needed anything? Jan and Kyle have the girls and I'm running errands and figured, if I could pick something up for you, I'd be happy to do it."

"Oh. Wow." Jenna opened the refrigerator. "Are you sure?"

"Yes, ma'am." Skylar laughed. "I know how daunting grocery trips can be when you have more kids than hands."

"That is so true." Jenna laughed. "Milk? If you don't mind."

"Nothing else?" Skylar asked.

Even though she was out of almost everything, Jenna didn't have the heart to ask the woman to shop for her. "Milk would be fabulous." She had enough to put off a marathon grocery shop until after the open house tomorrow. Depending on how late it went, maybe the day after that.

"Will do. I'll bring it by in a bit. And I'll text so no one gets woken up." Skylar said her goodbyes and hung up.

"Who was that?" Garrett asked, looking hopeful.

"Skylar Mitchell." Jenna noted the disappointment on her little brother's face. "Who did you think it was?"

"No one." Garrett went back to his homework.

Twenty minutes later, Skylar arrived with the milk.

"Thank you, really." Jenna took the gallon jug and headed into the kitchen. "Do you want a drink? Some water?" Which was basically all they had. "Or some milk?"

"I'm fine." Skylar laughed. "Homework? Already?" she asked, peering over Monica's shoulder.

"Right?" Monica nodded, looking horrified. "So not cool."

"Not at all," Skylar agreed.

"It's not that bad." Garrett shrugged.

"A can-do attitude. I like that." Skylar smiled at him. "I wish I had more time but I can't stay."

"No, of course." Jenna walked her back to the door.

"I was wanting to ask you something." Skylar hesitated. "If you have a minute?"

Jenna nodded.

Skylar spoke softly then, almost a whisper. "The dog? The big dog at the clinic? Buzz hasn't been able to find him a home and, well, I know Garrett really wanted a dog so I thought I'd see…" She broke off, shrugging.

"I don't know." Garrett's mention of a dog had gone from once or twice a week to once a day. "It's a lot of responsibility. And I already have my hands full." Biddy and Frannie were in bed, the kitchen was clean, the other two were doing homework and she hadn't a minute to herself. Adding a dog to that?

Skylar nodded. "Of course. I just figured, since the dog's better and Garrett had asked about him, I'd check with you."

"I'm glad the dog is better." Jenna remembered the sad-eyed, too-skinny dog. "He's a big dog." Big enough for Frannie to ride. "And I bet he'd need training?"

"You don't have to explain a thing to me, Jenna. I get it, I do." Skylar smiled. "Forget I even mentioned it."

Deep down, Jenna knew that wasn't going to happen. "Thanks again, for the milk." Jenna smiled. "It was a huge help." She paused, then said, "You know… Let me think about it. The dog, I mean." It would be Garrett's dog, not hers. She had no doubt, not a one, that Garrett would take exemplary care of him. And it would make her brother so happy.

"Great." Skylar reached into her jeans pocket. "I was hoping." She offered her a business card. "Here. This is the number for work. Sometimes, I don't hear my cell in the clinic. Dogs, cats, all the noise."

Jenna laughed and took the card. "Thanks." If she called ahead, then Buzz would have plenty of time to make himself scarce. *At least, I hope he will.*

"But it really is okay if it's not a good time." Skylar glanced into the house. "If you ever need a hand or a break or…anything, you can call. I know how hard it is to do this on your own. It's hard. But you've got Lizzie and me. And Jan is always up to help out."

Jenna hugged the woman. At first, Skylar went all stiff. *Because I'm basically a stranger hugging her.* But a second later and Skylar relaxed and hugged her back. "Thank you. Really."

Skylar's arms tightened. "Anytime, Jenna. You're not as alone as it may feel. Okay?" She let go. "I'll check in soon."

Her throat was too tight to speak so she nodded and waved, closing the front door behind Skylar Mitchell and turning to find Garrett and Monica standing in the kitchen doorway. "What?"

"Sound travels, like really bad, in this house." Monica shrugged.

"It's like a whisper tunnel. You stand in one place but someone can hear you someplace else. Acoustics, you know?" Garrett shrugged. "Just like the Whispering Gallery in Grand Central Station in New York."

"How do you..." Jenna broke off. Garrett knew all sorts of things. Why was she surprised he knew about the Whispering Gallery in Grand Central Station? "Okay. Now I know." She wandered back into the kitchen and sat at the table, her siblings trailing after them. "Let's talk."

Garrett carefully stacked his paperwork up, set it aside, and rested his arms on the table, his little hands crossed.

"Are we getting a dog?" Monica sat on the edge of her chair, far less restrained. "Garrett really wants one. I'd like one."

"I don't know," Jenna answered honestly. "I don't want to get ahead of things, so this is what I'm proposing. I think we should go spend time with this dog before we make any decisions, okay?"

"That sounds fair." Garrett smiled. "When can we go see him? Tomorrow?"

Tomorrow was already nonstop. First thing, she had to drop off Biddy and Frannie at their fabulous in-home day care with Klara Cruz. She would leave Monica and Garrett in her classroom while she went to a morning faculty meeting. She'd then send Garrett and Monica off to their respective classes, would have a full day of her own classes, after-school prep work and cleanup for that evening's open house. Afterward, she, Garrett and Monica would pick up Biddy and Frannie, and they'd all have a couple of hours before her open house. Klara had kindly volunteered to watch the girls at home that night, so that helped, but trying to fit in a dog visit?

"Please." Garrett blinked, that smile never wavering.

"Okay." Jenna nodded, covering his hand with hers. At some point, she was going to have to learn to tell them no. *No* was a good thing. *No* was part of life—it taught boundaries and self-respect. But right now, she couldn't do it. "But it will have to be quick. Tomorrow is—"

"The open house," Garrett finished for her. "We will go for a short visit tomorrow and a longer one the next day. There's nothing Wednesday, is there?"

Jenna shook her head. "If tomorrow goes well and if we're all in agreement, we will go back and visit again on Wednesday."

Garrett was up and around the table before Jenna realized it. His arms slid around her neck for the longest sweetest hug Garrett had ever given her. Since her eyes were pressed closed, she was surprised when Monica joined in. Jenna wrapped them both up, her heart so full of love. She knew she was making mistakes, but they were doing okay. She might always be hungry and feel slightly rumpled but there were worse things—like being without love. “I love you, guys,” she said, giving them an extra squeeze.

Chapter Six

"Jenna?" Buzz ran a hand along the back of his neck. "When will she be here?"

"Any minute now." Skylar didn't look up from the computer chart she was working on.

He sighed. Today had been one of those days he wished he'd gone into accounting or history. One of their long-time patients, an ancient calico cat named Gingham, had passed away. It wasn't unexpected, the poor cat had been fighting cancer for years, but that didn't make it hurt any less. Gingham's owners, Ricardo and Uma Fernandez, were beside themselves and, truth be told, Buzz was pretty torn up over it, too.

"I figured you'd want to make yourself scarce."

There was a hint of amusement in his veterinary tech's voice.

"Why would I need to do that?" He shot her a look before going to his office and closing the door behind him. He didn't need the teasing. Not today. He downed a bottle of water, opened the patient database on his computer and clicked through tomorrow's patient load.

Did he hear the digital doorbell announce Jenna's arrival? Yes. Did he hear Frannie's cheery voice? There was no missing it. And Garrett—even he sounded excited.

Buzz glanced at his office door, holding his breath as their shadows moved past the frosted glass pane that took up the top half of his door.

"Whewe's the doctaw?" Frannie's question was loud and clear.

"Oh, he has so much work to do," Skylar explained. "I know he'll be sad he missed you."

He leaned back in his chair, glaring at no one in particular, and felt like an ass. It wasn't like he'd see Jenna and lose control. He wasn't that far gone. *I'll never be that far gone.* He'd managed to convince himself that all the current and spark between him and Jenna was like a lightning strike—rare, isolated and one-off. It wouldn't happen again. At least, the chances of it happening again were one in a million, or thereabouts. If he was ever alone with Jenna again, that pull wouldn't be there. And if it was, he knew it wouldn't be as strong. Not that he was planning on testing his theory anytime soon but…

Besides, what he was hearing right now had nothing to do with him and Jenna. Those were happy kids, here to do a good thing and right now, he could use some happy. "Fine." He stood, walked around his desk, opened his office door and, before he could change his mind, headed back to the surgical bay where the Norris family was gathered.

"Doctaw Buzz!" Frannie squealed, running across the room and hugging him around the knees. "We came to see the poowah puppy but he's all bettaw."

"Hello, Frannie." He patted her back. "He is all better. And I bet he's happy to have visitors." He ignored the surprise on Skylar's face and marched straight over to the kennel—where Garrett waited. "What do you think?" he asked the boy.

"You did good." Garrett beamed up at him. "You fixed him up, all right."

"Skylar, here, might have helped." Buzz shrugged. "Maybe." He winked at Garrett. "You want to meet him?" The dog was still timid but he didn't cower in the corner anymore. Garrett was standing close to the kennel front and the dog was stretching out his neck, sniffing the air with interest.

"He looks different." Garrett watched as Buzz opened the kennel door. "Healthy."

"He is. His leg's got a scar, but there's no long-term worries. After too many baths to count and a whole lot of patience, my sister, Cassie, worked out all the matting and brambles from his fur and gave him a nice haircut." Buzz crouched. "Come on out."

The dog's tail, long and fluffy, turned into a small wind turbine—wagging with force—as he stepped out of the kennel.

"Hi." Garrett sat on the floor, radiating with barely repressed anticipation. "You look like you feel better."

Buzz watched as the dog took small steps closer to Garrett, his head lowered and his tail wagging faster than ever.

"You have a name yet?" Garrett asked, smiling as the dog dropped and did a semi-army crawl across the floor until his head was almost in the boy's lap.

"We've been calling him Shaggy," Skylar said.

"Shaggy, huh?" Garrett turned his hand over so the dog could smell him. "You like Shaggy?"

As if in answer, the dog rolled onto his back and offered Garrett his tummy.

Garrett laughed and leaned forward, rubbing the dog's tummy. "I think it's a good name."

"Can I pet the big dog, too?" Frannie asked, tugging on Buzz's pants leg. "Please, oh, please."

"I don't see why not." Buzz smiled at the little girl. "You see how Garrett's doing it? Being gentle and soft with him?"

Frannie nodded, her expression serious. "I can do

that, too, Doctaw Buzz. I can, weally." She turned. "Can I, Jenna?"

"If Dr. Lafferty says so, then I'm sure it's okay. You, too, Monica," Jenna agreed. "Just be gentle. There's a lot of you and only one of him. It might be overwhelming for him. You don't want to spook him."

It might have been Buzz's imagination but, from the corner of his eye, he thought Jenna glanced his way when she said that. On further inspection, though, she appeared entirely caught up in her siblings and the adoring dog they were all fawning over. Beautiful, soft and entirely too tempting for his liking. The way she was smiling tugged at a place he'd done his damndest to box up inside years ago. An empty, hollow place that longed to be filled.

"He sure is sweet natured." Jenna stepped closer to the dog, little Biddy on her hip. "Aren't you?"

The dog lay, content to have his belly rubbed by the three Norris siblings.

"You think he'd be okay with babies?" Jenna asked Skylar.

"I'd think so." Skylar nodded at the kids.

"Best way to know is to find out." Buzz stepped forward. "Let's let Shaggy—it is Shaggy?" He paused, waiting for Garrett's nod. "I think you four have already made friends, don't you? Let's see if Shaggy and Biddy can be friends, shall we? But as long as you're giving him a tummy rub, he won't move."

All three of them stopped rubbing Shaggy's tummy and sat back. Shaggy rolled over, his tail still wagging and his tongue lolling out the side of his mouth.

"Be a good boy, Shaggy." Garrett patted the dog on the back.

"Here." Buzz stood beside Jenna and whistled. Shaggy stood, his head cocked to one side as he waited on Buzz. "Come on, Shaggy. Come here for a sec." He patted his thigh and Shaggy trotted to him. "He knows a few things, too. He's smart." He held his hand up, palm out. "Stay." Shaggy stopped, ears up and eyes fixed on Buzz. "Sit." The dog sat. "Good boy." He dug a treat from the pocket of his white jacket and fed it to the dog.

"What a good boy." Jenna turned Biddy around as she spoke. "See that, Biddy?"

Once Biddy saw the dog, everyone in the room knew it. With a squeal and coo, the toddler was a wiggling ball of glee.

"Oh, my goodness, Biddy." Jenna chuckled. "Are you excited over the puppy? That's Shaggy."

The dog tilted his head one way, then the other, his tail never slowing.

"Come on." Buzz patted his thigh and Shaggy trotted right up to Biddy and did a thorough sniffing of her bare wiggling feet. "What do you think of that?"

"You're a good boy, Shaggy." Jenna's hand ran over the dog's head and scratched the dog behind the ear. "And trained. That's a bonus." She was smiling when her gaze locked with his.

"I'd say so." He cleared his throat but the sudden lump didn't budge. Damn, but he didn't want this to happen. She was pretty. Fine. But he'd seen plenty of pretty faces in his time. A pretty face was just as capable of telling lies and destroying dreams. He knew that. Hell, he'd lived it. So why did this one, with four kids, have to be the one to shake the ground beneath his feet? He wanted to deny that she had his pulse tripping. He'd prefer to ignore the vise slowly squeezing the air from his lungs. And if there was any way to pretend he wasn't on fire for her, he would. He was a damn fool, through and through. And the longer he stayed, drowning in her eyes, the higher the chances he'd do something foolish, right here and now.

Biddy squealed, Jenna blinked and Buzz managed to force his attention away—specifically, to the tile beneath his feet.

"Biddy's right." The rasp in Jenna's voice didn't help. "We have to go."

Good. He drew in an unsteady breath.

"Now?" Skylar asked.

"Open house," Jenna murmured. "Students. Parents. All that."

"And don't forget Alonzo's *dad*," Monica piped up. "He *really* wants to meet you."

Jenna sighed. "Thank you for the reminder."

"Alonzo's *dad*?" Skylar turned to Monica. "Is Alonzo one of your friends?"

"Yup. And his dad is single. And so is Jenna." Monica shrugged. "Alonzo's cute so maybe he will be, too. And then he and Jenna will be all in love and all that stuff. You know?"

Why was Skylar smiling like that? What if this man, whoever the hell Alonzo's father was, was some jerk?

"Monica is determined to get me paired off with someone," Jenna murmured.

"You don't sound all that enthusiastic about it." He hadn't meant to say a thing—not one word. But the words were coming. "Are you?"

"I don't..." But Jenna shifted Biddy to her hip, frowning right back at him. "Maybe I am. For all I know, he's a delightful man."

"Alonzo's dad?" Buzz asked, hands on hips. "Is that his legal name?"

The corner of Jenna's mouth twitched. "I'll ask to see his driver's license and let you know."

Stop staring at her mouth. Stop looking at her. *Stop aching for something you can't have.*

"We can come back tomorrow, though, right?"

Garrett was on his knees, hugging Shaggy. "We can come back and visit?"

"Of course," Buzz answered, finding it impossible to look at anything but Jenna. More like Jenna's mouth.

"Maybe." Jenna's voice was raspy again, the sound sending a jolt straight through him.

"I'll put Shaggy away," Garrett offered. "If you want?"

"I normally walk him first," Skylar said.

"Oh, that's nice," Garrett mumbled.

The boy's disappointment gutted him. And, for reasons he wasn't about to analyze, he came up with an idea that suited his—er, everyone's purposes. "Why don't you let Garrett stay?" he offered. "We can take Shaggy for a walk and I'll bring him up to you before the open house ends? It won't take long."

"Please, Jenna, please." Garrett was immediately on board. "I promise I won't cause any trouble."

She shot him a death glare before turning to her brother. "It wouldn't be right to cause any inconvenience—"

"If it was inconvenient, I wouldn't have offered," Buzz cut in, determined now. "If you're thinking about Shaggy joining your family, it can't hurt for Garrett to walk him. It'd help me and Skylar out." He glanced at Skylar. "Wouldn't it?"

Skylar looked confused. "Um...yes?"

"See. It's all settled." Buzz placed his hand on

Garrett's shoulder. "I'll bring him up in a half hour or so. If that's not too late?"

"No, it's not too late." Jenna shrugged, too rattled to argue with him. "Okay. If you're sure."

"Yep." Buzz nodded.

"I guess we'll see you later." The way Monica was studying Buzz made him uncomfortable. There was no reason why. It's not like a thirteen-year-old girl would figure out this wasn't just about Shaggy and Garrett. Or that he'd agreed to this whole dog-walking, drop-off-later scenario just so he could meet this Alonzo's dad. He hadn't needed any further evidence that he wasn't thinking straight when it came to Jenna Norris. But now, this, well—when it came to Jenna, Buzz didn't know what he was going to do next.

Jenna was in the middle of putting on light makeup when Klara arrived to take care of the little girls. She glanced at the time, tried not to panic, finished getting ready and ran for the door, calling out her goodbyes as she went. Monica's music blasted from the speakers as soon as Jenna turned on the ignition but she didn't mind. Instead of letting stress put knots in her stomach, she turned up the radio and sang along all the way to the school. She parked in the teachers' parking lot, turned off the ignition and slid the strap of her leather messenger bag onto her shoulder, hurrying across the parking lot.

Don't forget you have a geometry test tomorrow, Jenna texted Monica. Then followed it up with a red heart emoji.

Monica's response was a string of thumbs-up, hearts and kissy-face emojis.

I guess that means she's got it covered? She put her phone in her bag and headed for her classroom, relieved to see a handful of parents. *I'm not late. I'm good.*

Jenna appreciated that tonight had a schedule. The campus had arranged seven fifteen-minute sessions—time for each of her classes' parents to cycle through, following their students' schedule. It kept her from being overwhelmed with all her parents at once and made sure they didn't linger too long. While she'd had her fair share of unwelcoming experiences since her arrival in Texas, the people of Granite Falls didn't fall into that category. She was surprised, again and again tonight, by how genuinely warm they were. They didn't just want to know about what their students would be learning, they wanted to know about her and if there was anything they could do to help her settle in here in Granite Falls. Before the evening was over, Jenna was feeling a little more at home.

"Is this Miss Norris's class?" a man asked, his printed student schedule in his hand.

Jenna turned. "Yes. I'm Miss Norris. If you want to take a seat, I think we start again in two minutes?" She shrugged. "Whenever they ring the bell, that is."

He smiled, stepping aside as more parents arrived. She greeted each new arrival, had them fill out their contact information on her neatly printed spreadsheet, but the man didn't sit or budge. He stood there, awkward by now, as if he had something to say.

"I'll try to cover everyone's questions," she said to him. "If you want to take a seat?"

He opened his mouth but the bell rang and she shrugged.

She turned to her projector and began her presentation. She did a little bio of herself, pictures of her siblings and then dove right into her class expectations and what she'd cover over the year.

"If any of you have questions, now is the time to ask." Jenna smiled, turning to the audience. A few questions trickled in before the final bell and the night was over.

That was when she spied Garrett in the back corner—smiling and waving. What on earth was the strange brown streak down the middle of his chest? Considering one parent was still lingering, she decided not to dwell on the stain until this was over. Buzz was here. *Great.* And now Buzz was talking quietly to the one remaining dad—the one who never sat down. From the looks of it, the two of them knew each other.

"You did great." Garrett gave her a thumbs-up.

"You did." Buzz nodded, looking dangerously handsome in his pale blue button-up and straw cowboy hat. Of course, he'd been equally as easy to look at in his white doctor's coat. "Had me thinking fondly of my grade-school years."

For goodness sake, he's not that good-looking. Jenna ignored Buzz and the fact that she'd just told herself an outright lie and turned to the man who'd been waiting. "I'm so sorry. Was there something specific you needed from me?"

"No." He held his hand out. "Not exactly. I'm Luis Benavidez."

"It's nice to meet you." She shook his hand, mentally scrolling through her student lists, but it was too early in the year to know who was who. "Which class is your student in?"

"AP Physics. Over at the high school." He chuckled. "I'm—"

"*This* is Alonzo's dad, Jenna." Buzz crossed his arms over his chest.

Oh. Oh, no. He came. *He's here.* Monica's friend's father.

Luis took in her expression. "I'm sorry. I thought you were expecting me. Alonzo assured me Monica had set this up?"

"Oh." Jenna nodded, recovering. "She did. She

mentioned you might be coming but… I'll be honest, Mr. Benavidez—"

"Luis, please."

"Luis, I didn't think you'd actually come. I've had friends try to set me up before and…well, they were no-shows." She shrugged. "So, forgive my slightly stunned reaction."

Luis chuckled. "No problem."

"Turns out I know Luis." Buzz pointed at the man. "You've got a pair of rescue dogs, right?"

Luis nodded. "I do."

"That's nice," Garrett chimed in. "There are a lot of animals that need a home."

"This is my brother, Garrett. As you can tell, he is a genius." She knelt in front of Garrett. "But what on earth do you have all over your shirt?"

"Chocolate ice cream." Garrett grinned.

"Oh, really?" Jenna had already made such a *terrific* first impression on Luis Benavidez she didn't want to make an outright fool out of herself because of Buzz Lafferty. "Shaggy's treat?"

"Dogs can't eat chocolate, Jenna." Garrett sounded oh, so disappointed. "It'll make them sick. Really sick."

"Sounds like you're a regular dog expert." Luis smiled. He had a nice smile. "I'm guessing you have a few yourself?"

Jenna stood. "Well, we're thinking about it.

Dr. Lafferty has a big sweetheart of a dog that Garrett's pretty much set on."

Garrett nodded. "I am. He's a real good dog."

Jenna laughed—so did Luis and Buzz. "We're going to see him tomorrow, remember?" She squeezed her brother's shoulder. "Let's take it one day at a time."

"She's right. Don't want to rush into anything, Garrett. Owning a dog is a big responsibility," Luis agreed.

Jenna smiled her thanks. Being cautious wasn't a bad thing. Chances are Shaggy would come home with them by this weekend but she didn't want to rush into this. She didn't want to rush into anything. Up until now, most of her decisions had been made out of necessity—especially the last year or so. Between her mother and her siblings, losing her job and this move… One monumental and essential thing, one after the other. Now that her choices were less life altering, she wanted to make sure they were the right ones before committing one way or the other. "There's no rush." She risked looking at Buzz, then. "Is there? Do you have another family interested in Shaggy?"

Buzz's blindingly blue eyes were waiting for her. "Nope. Just you."

Why was he looking at her like that? Why was he staring at her mouth? Was he doing this on purpose? And *why* was her heart launching into the stratosphere? “Buzz.” She’d meant to sound assertive and just the slightest bit irritated. Instead, she sounded all breathless and weird. “Dr. Lafferty, thank you for bringing Garrett here.” Out of the way—and not in the least bit convenient.

Buzz nodded but made no move to leave. “My pleasure.”

It wasn’t just the way he was looking at her now—it was the way he said that. *My pleasure.* Loaded with all sorts of innuendo and…heat. She swallowed, hard.

“Well, I guess I should head out.” Luis was glancing back and forth between the two of them. “It was nice to meet you.”

Jenna turned, giving the man her full attention. The poor guy had been forced to sit through her open house lecture and then endure all this weirdness. “It was nice to meet you. I’m just sorry you had to sit through my parent–teacher talk.”

“I didn’t mind.” Luis grinned. “You can always tell when someone enjoys their work and you, Miss Norris, definitely enjoy your job. Your students are lucky to have you.”

Did Buzz just snort? It didn’t matter. “Jenna, please. And you’re right, I love my job.” She was thankful that, even with all the change they’d faced, she’d landed a better job than the one she lost. “And it helps to be in a school where the parents are so involved. I’m still settling in here in Granite

Falls but I'm finding something new to like about it every day."

"I'm glad to hear that." Luis glanced at Buzz before saying, "I'd be happy to take you to the falls, with your brother and sisters, maybe? It's cold water and good for swimming."

"That sounds fun." She ruffled Garrett's hair. "Don't you think so?"

"I guess." Garrett didn't sound the least bit interested.

Luis chuckled. "You think about it. The offer is open-ended. I'm sorry about before. The other fix-ups being no-shows. That's not right. But…it was their loss." And with that, and another very nice smile, he left.

Buzz let out a whistle. "Huh. Who knew old Luis had game?"

"It was a very nice thing to say." Jenna began straightening her room. "Who doesn't like a genuine compliment now and then?"

"How can you tell when a compliment is genuine?" Buzz followed her. "Luis doesn't strike me as the spontaneous sort. In fact, he probably has a pack of index cards with a selection of compliments and, right before he goes out, he draws one and uses it."

Jenna paused long enough to stare at him. "I can't tell if you're trying to be funny or mean?"

Buzz grinned and shrugged.

That grin and the eyes and the crinkles and all

the warmth… *No.* “Give me a minute to pack up, Garrett. I know you’re tired.” She packed up her leather messenger back, sprayed everything down with disinfectant spray and flipped off the lights. She led Garrett into the large hallway, with Buzz trailing behind. “Was there something you needed?”

“Nothing else pressing, I guess.” He shrugged. “Figure I’d walk a lady, and her brother, to her car. You know, be a gentleman, and all that?”

“That’s not necessary.” The sooner he left, the sooner she could get home and have a big glass of wine. With any luck, the wine would make her sleep well—without any Buzz Lafferty dreams.

“I’m gonna get some water.” Garrett ran down the hall.

Jenna flipped open her bag. “My keys. I’ll be right there, Garrett.” She opened her class door and hurried to her desk, flipping on the desk lamp to see.

“You need a hand?” Buzz asked.

“No, Buzz, I don’t.” She rifled through the neatly stacked papers on her desk. “I don’t understand why you’re here, honestly. I appreciate you giving Garrett the time with Shaggy. It’s sweet of you but I don’t understand why you’re doing it.” She spun. “There.” She grabbed her keys from atop her filing cabinet and turned to find Buzz perched on the edge of her desk.

It took effort, but Jenna managed not to fall prey

to his crooked smile and flashing eyes. No matter how charming he was, she didn't want to play this game. Whatever this game was.

"Maybe I'm just a sweet guy?" Buzz cocked his head to one side.

She shook her head. "Sweet? No. Infuriating, yes." Infuriatingly handsome. Or maybe she was so infuriated because of the way *she* reacted to *him*. Until Buzz, she'd never been one to daydream or linger over memories or what-ifs. Now, she spent far too many minutes each day mulling over that kiss and the still-lingering burn inside her. For him. This man, sitting on her desk, smiling like he didn't have a care in the world.

"Why am I infuriating?" He waited.

There was no way she'd admit to him anything about the daydreams or the aching or wanting. No way. Instead, she said, "I've already told you. It's like you're...up to something." She reached for the light switch. "What do you want, Buzz?"

His fingers wrapped around her wrist. "You know what I want. Another kiss. May I?" He turned her hand over and pressed a featherlight kiss to the inside of her wrist. "I'd like to think you want that, too."

The gruff edge to his voice seemed to mute the rational part of her brain. It was the only explanation for her total lack of resistance or restraint. Her gaze wandered from his thumb caressing the inside of her wrist, up the wall of his chest, to the most knee-weakening, gorgeous face she'd ever laid eyes on. *That was the truth.*

But she pressed her lips tight, refusing to let the other far more alarming truth slip free. If she admitted he was right about her wanting his kisses—and so much more—there'd be no turning back. And even though she knew giving in to Buzz Lafferty would likely end in heartbreak, she found herself moving closer to him. What harm could one last kiss cause?

Chapter Seven

Buzz pulled, gently, until Jenna was pressed close against him. He didn't want to admit he was nervous, but he was.

"It's that simple? A kiss? You want me, I want you and that's it?" Jenna whispered, her voice wavering.

He nodded. "Couldn't have said it better myself." Had she just said she wanted him? Or was she on her way to making a point he'd likely not want to hear.

The ghost of a smile she'd been wearing faded as she said, "There is nothing simple about this—for me." Her shirtfront was beating in time with her heart—racing almost as fast as his was.

"Maybe you're overthinking this." His hands held hers. "We don't need to name what's happening between us—or put expectations on it. We could enjoy each other and see where things go?"

"Are you wanting to date me, Buzz?" She drew in a deep breath. "Or are you talking about sex?"

Buzz was almost too stunned to respond. "There's a chance we could work each other out of our systems?" He hoped like hell it would. And, like it or not, *this* was all he could offer her.

"Are you serious?" She stiffened, her eyes boring into his. "I guess the *you're overthinking it* speech might be enough for a lot of women, but I'm not like a lot of women. I can't be sweet-talked into your bed and discarded shortly thereafter. I won't be. Not by you or any man. I told you I'm not interested in a relationship with you… Or anything else." But her gaze wandered, and stayed, fixed upon his mouth.

And the way she was looking at his mouth made it hard for him to say a thing. But, dammit, there were things to be said. He shook his head. "You're telling me you're fine walking around, burning for me?" He cradled her cheek in his hand. "That's how I feel, Jenna. Every time I see you, I want you more. To touch you." His thumb traced along her cheek. "And kiss you." He stroked the full swell over her lower lip and hungered all the more when she quivered from his touch. "I want to spend hours mapping every inch of you, so I can trace you in my mind when we're apart." He leaned forward. "I want you so much it hurts." Finally, his lips sealed with hers.

His hands came up, cradling her neck as his tongue traced the curve of her lower lip. She swayed into him, her breath hitching, before she opened for him. He moaned, pulling her closer to fully explore the wet heat of her mouth. He wanted more. He wanted her.

But Jenna pushed against his chest. "Buzz," she whispered. "I can't." She pulled back, breathing heavily. "It's not about wanting you, obviously." Her hand tightened in the fabric of his shirt before she pushed again. "But, it's not enough… Not the right time… I can't." She smoothed his shirt. "I'd appreciate it if you—we—don't do this again." There was that ghost of a smile again, sadder now. "As much as I like to think I'm a strong, independent and smart woman, you test that."

It was the flash of desperation on her face that stopped him from arguing. He'd never wanted anyone the way he wanted Jenna but he wasn't an outright bastard. No meant no. He got it. It was that easy. He'd no way of knowing what she'd been through but he wasn't the sort of man to exploit her vulnerability to get what he wanted. If there was no compromise to be had, then he'd do as she asked—for both their sakes. It wouldn't stop the wanting, but it would damn well stop him from acting on it.

"If I led you on—"

"No." His hands eased from her, to rest on his thighs. Gripping his thighs. "You didn't." Buzz shook his head, giving her a smile. "I… I see you and I can't help but hope is all."

Her gaze fell from his and she stared at the keys in her hand. "Maybe… No, there are no maybes about this." She took another deep breath. "It's best if we don't see each other."

No. That's not right. He'd looked for her every day for the last week and a half. Not seeing her hadn't been easier. But he'd had hope then… Now, he didn't. "I don't get a say here?" Just thinking about not seeing her put a razor-sharp lump in his throat.

She swallowed, then shook her head. "I'll call Skylar before we come over tomorrow to visit with Shaggy."

"And I won't be there." He pushed off the desk, trying his best to sound nonchalant. "Easy enough." Which was bullshit. He wouldn't push her but, damn, giving up went against his every fiber.

"Right," she said again. "Easy."

He walked with her to the classroom door, waited for her to close it and headed down the hallway. He'd been rejected before but this was different. There was no way for them to meet in the middle—no compromise to be made. Now he was supposed to go without seeing her. It didn't sit right.

Garrett was down the hall near the water fountain, pointing at something in one of the cases that lined both sides of the entryway. "What is that?" he asked.

Buzz paused and peered into the case. "That's a horned lizard—a Phrynosoma. The little guys used to be all over Texas and they're making a comeback in these parts. They're pretty cool. If you catch one, you can flip them over and give them a tummy rub."

"Really?" Garrett didn't look convinced. "He's awful spiky."

"It makes him look fierce." He nodded. "But it's all for show. It does help prevent them from getting eaten by hawks and such. Sometimes."

Garrett studied the taxidermized specimen as if he was taking in what Buzz had said.

"It's getting late, Garrett." Jenna's hand rested on the boy's shoulder. "It's been a long day. And I'm sure Buzz is tired, too."

Buzz wasn't the least bit tired. Wound up tight was more like it. And there wasn't a damn thing he could do about it. As far as days went, today had been a humdinger. Gingham. The Fernandezs. Jenna. A hell of a day. The only good thing was Shaggy finding a home—hopefully. "I am."

Garrett looked at him, his forehead creased. "You okay, Dr. Buzz?"

"It's been a rough day is all." Buzz winked.

"I get that. I had a lot of rough days." Garrett nodded. "The day my dad died, my mom got unhappy and stayed that way. That was hard. And then she died, too." He sounded like a boy then, young and vulnerable. "A lot of rough days." He sighed, pushing his glasses up. "It's only started to get better now that we're with Jenna."

Buzz swallowed. "Well, hell, Garrett. I'm feeling pretty ashamed of myself right about now." He shook his head, studying the boy. Garrett Norris was an impressive little guy. Tough as nails and smart as all get-out *and* he'd been through more than any eight-year-old should have to. Here, Buzz was feeling sorry for himself because he'd been rejected and this boy had been to hell and back and somehow managed to smile. "My bad day isn't looking all that bad."

"Jenna says when things get bad, that's when you look for the good. You'll always find something. I know I'm lucky to have Monica, Biddy…even Frannie." Garrett smiled up at his sister. "We have Jenna and she loves us like our mom did. She takes care of us. She's letting me get a dog." He was grinning. "And she's not sad."

"*Might* get a dog." But Jenna's tone told them all Shaggy was theirs.

Buzz knew better, but he looked at Jenna. The tears in her eyes almost had him reaching for her. She was taking care of her siblings, giving them love and a family—but who was there for her? *Not my job.* Even if he'd wanted it, which he didn't, she'd made it clear she wasn't interested. She wasn't letting him close. With Britney—Lisa and Cameron's mom—he hadn't stopped to think. She was alone and struggling and Buzz had become *her rock*. He'd done everything he could to make her and her kids feel safe and loved and loved doing it, too. But it—he—hadn't been enough to make her stay.

Jenna's gaze darted his way, then back to her brother. "I'm sorry you had a rough day, Buzz." She took Garrett's hand and led them to the school's front doors. "And thank you for letting Garrett visit."

"And the ice cream," Garrett added.

"The ice cream was the best part." Buzz chuckled. "Even if you did wind up wearing one scoop."

"Good night," Jenna said, sparing him a passing glance.

"Night, Jenna." Her name put a lump in the middle of this throat.

"Bye." Garrett waved, following Jenna across the parking lot to their red minivan.

Buzz stopped himself from following, but it wasn't easy. Why, he didn't know. They'd said all that needed saying. This was it. *So why the hell does it feel unfinished? So wrong?* By the time he'd climbed into his truck, he was more out of sorts than ever. He pressed a button on his phone and waited, the ringing of the phone filtering through the truck's radio speakers.

"Hey, Buzz," Kyle answered quick. "What's up?"

"I need a beer." Buzz turned onto the country road that led from all three of Granite Falls schools back to Main Street. "Maybe some pool… And a few more beers."

"Bad day?" Kyle asked.

"Yeah." He sighed. "And I *don't* want to talk about it.

"Fine. Okay if John tags along?" Kyle asked. "Hayden just found out Lizzie is expecting, so I don't see him leaving her side for the next year or so." He chuckled.

"Sure. Tell Hayden and Lizzie congrats." He turned right, heading to the Bear's House. "Bear's House?"

"See you in a few." Kyle hung up.

He parked in the gravel lot, turned off the ignition, and sat—his mind spinning. After learning what Jenna had endured, what the Norris kids had been through, he was feeling like a bastard. He'd been plying her with kisses and hoping she'd fall into his bed with an eager smile. A part of him still wanted that. But there was no way he'd let that happen now.

He should be thankful. She'd shut him down, no discussion. Her "no, thank you" was across the board. No relationship—of any kind. Period. Normally, the very thought triggered an ice-cold panic that shook him to the core. Instead, he was angry she'd been so quick to dismiss the idea of the two of them together. He could picture it. And it was one hell of a pretty picture. A smart man would try to win Jenna Norris's heart and make her family his own. But if he did just that and it didn't work out? His stomach roiled, twisting and churning until his throat burned with bile. He'd be even more broken this time. *Not an option.*

Jenna Norris deserved a good man. *A man that's not me.* He knew that, accepted it. She'd said she wasn't interested in a relationship but that really meant she wasn't interested in a relationship with him. She'd find someone and be happy. As she should be. Someone decent, like Luis Benavidez—who'd clearly been interested. *Why wouldn't he be?* Jenna was… Jenna. But thinking about Luis Benavidez with Jenna had Buzz gripping the steering wheel with a white-knuckled hold.

He climbed out of his truck, slammed the door and headed for the Bear's House. Inside, a handful of locals were scattered. Some were watching television, a few were playing pool and one or two were chatting up Nat, John's wife, at the bar.

"Hey, Buzz," Nat greeted him. "What are you doing on this side of town?"

The Bear's House was on the outskirts of town, just enough off the beaten path to have fewer tourists and families than the Watering Hole on Main Street. "Beer. And a little peace and quiet."

"You okay?" She pulled an ice-cold longneck from under the bar and handed it to him.

He nodded.

"Right. Peace and quiet." She held up her hands. "I'll leave you to it." With a nod, she went back to straightening behind the counter and talking with a patron at the far end of the bar.

A good ten minutes later, he was on his second beer and John and Kyle arrived.

John, being John, marched around the bar to plant one hell of a kiss on Nat. "Hello, wife," John said, before kissing her again. "How are you this fine evening?"

"Better now." She kissed his cheek. "Go, do your guy stuff."

"Only if I get to walk you home later?" John kissed her again.

"I know." Kyle sat on a stool beside him. "Disgusting, right?"

Buzz shot Kyle a look. "Says you? No offense, Kyle, but I'd say each and every one of you Mitchell boys is whipped, but good." But his mind was still working—going places it shouldn't. *Leave it alone.*

"Damn lucky, wouldn't you say?" Kyle slapped him on the back.

Buzz toasted him with his beer. "You ever think about things not working out with Skylar?" As soon as the words were out, he regretted them. What was the point of him asking when the only reason his mind was sifting through all this crap was because Jenna had given him a hard pass?

Kyle turned, frowning. "What do you mean?"

He waved his hand, dismissive. "Never mind. Forget I asked." *Way to kick up a hornet's nest.*

"Hold up," Kyle thundered. "You can't throw something like that out there. What's going on?"

Buzz shook his head. "Nothing. You and Skylar are solid as a rock. Everyone knows it."

"We are." Kyle was staring at him, eyes narrowed. "But there's a reason you asked. And, from the look on your face, you're not letting go so…talk."

"I'm thinking we need more beer." John slid a beer to Kyle. "What'd I miss?"

"Nothing." Buzz stood. "Pool table's full. Let's play darts."

The three of them carried their beer to the table in front of the dartboard before Kyle said, "I know you, Buzz. Rip off the bandage or you'll wind up picking a fight with someone."

"I haven't fought in years," Buzz pushed back. Right about the time he'd had his heart broken and Britney had made him say goodbye to Cameron and Lisa. He took a swig off his beer and set it on the table—to find both Kyle and John staring at him, waiting. "Fine." *Whatever.* "You asked." He ran a hand along the back of his neck. "Would all this lovey-dovey stuff outweigh the pain if Skylar up and left you tomorrow? You wouldn't only be losing her—you'd be losing Greer, Mya and Brynn, too." They weren't Kyle's biological children. "And—"

"First, that's messed up and I sort of want to punch you in the face for taking me there." Kyle spun his beer bottle. "And second, I won't imagine how that'd feel—like losing an arm or having my lungs shut down—no, I don't want to think about it." He met Buzz's gaze.

"What I was asking was… Would you try again?" He'd already rattled Kyle enough for the night, might as well see it through.

"I'm gonna need another beer." John stood. "When I get back, no more of this serious shit." He was scowling as he headed back to the bar.

"I can't answer that." Kyle was watching him. "If I'm being honest here, I don't know if I'd ever get over her—over them. I don't know if I would try again."

Buzz nodded. He'd been looking for validation and now he had it. What-ifs were dangerous things. What-ifs that included Jenna? *Bad idea.* And pointless. No meant no. She wasn't challenging him; she wasn't interested. He should feel relief, not bone-deep disappointment.

"I'm so excited you're taking him." Cassie Lafferty watched as Garrett ran a brush through Shaggy's coat.

Jenna didn't argue; there was no point. She'd told Garrett they were just visiting today—several times—but it was clear they were all hoping otherwise.

"I can tell he's a very happy pup." Cassie smiled at Frannie.

"He is?" Frannie asked. "How can you tell?"

Cassie laughed. "He looks happy, don't you think?"

Frannie turned her head, giving Shaggy a long serious inspection. "You awe wight. He does look happy."

"We can't take him home yet," Monica said. "Jenna has someone coming over to check the fence first."

"We want to keep him safe." Garrett nodded.

"It's an old house. With an old fence." Jenna sat on the chair opposite Cassie, with Biddy in her lap.

"You're on Cypress Hill? The big blue house?" Cassie asked. "It's a pretty place."

"It met my top requirement. It's big." Jenna smiled. "But there's a lot that needs to be done."

"The pipes gwoan." Frannie made a moaning creak sound.

"And the doors stick," Monica added. "Especially the upstairs bathroom."

"I got stuck." Frannie nodded. "It was scawy."

"I bet." Cassie was all sympathy. "Especially if the pipes were moaning, too."

"Jenna had to take the door off with a screwdriver." Garrett kept brushing Shaggy. "But Frannie was crying by then."

"I was," Frannie affirmed, holding up her forefinger and thumb. "A little. This much."

"She was very brave." Jenna nodded. "I don't think anyone likes being stuck in a room."

"Not me." Cassie shook her head.

Shaggy rolled over, earning a wave of aw's from her three siblings. All three of them crowded around the dog to rub his tummy.

"You have your hands full." Cassie watched the communal tummy rub taking place. "Buzz said you were the industrious sort. You'd have to be to juggle all of them, a job, a fixer-upper house and a dog."

"I'm hoping Shaggy will occupy them." Jenna bounced Biddy on her knee. "Long enough that I can get the odd job done. Though, I admit, there are a few things I don't feel comfortable doing on my own. Like the fence. I don't suppose you know of any reasonably priced handyman?"

"Hmm. Let me think about it. I'll ask Buzz, too. He knows everyone." Cassie rolled her eyes. "Mr. Charming."

Jenna managed a smile. *He's charming, all right.* Charming enough to keep her tossing and turning and aching with regret. His words played over and over until she'd almost convinced herself that she'd made a mistake. The stroke of his hands along her neck. The nip of his mouth on her lower lip. What if no one ever made her feel this desirable? What if no one else's kisses made her burn? And, like he said, she burned for him. Even a cold shower hadn't done much to clear her head. But he'd kept his word today and made himself scarce—which she appreciated.

The exam room door swung open and Skylar backed into the room, a towel-wrapped bundle in her hands. "Oh, hi." She held the towel closer.

"How about we move out of the middle of the floor." Jenna scooched her chair over, waving her sisters and brother to follow. "Shaggy, come." Shaggy popped up and trotted over to her. "Sit." He did, so Jenna gushed, "There's a good boy." She scratched behind his ear.

Cassie sprang up and hurried to Skylar. "Oh, my."

"I know." Skylar set the towel on one of the exam tables.

Frannie was moving, ever so slowly, in the direction of the exam table.

"Frannie." Jenna almost laughed at the way her little sister jumped. "We have to stay out of their way, sweetie. This is where they work. I know you love the animals—I do, too—but let's let Skylar and Cassie take care of them. Okay?"

Frannie nodded, slowly walking back to Shaggy.

The door swung wide and Buzz came through, looking official and doctor-ly in his white coat.

And handsome. Oh, so handsome. Which Jenna

knew already. She also knew that she was exhausted and weak and one blue-eyed look might make her behave...*rashly*.

"What's this?" Buzz asked Skylar, zeroed in on the exam table. "What happened?"

"Mom was...*gone*." Skylar pulled on some blue gloves and glanced at the kids.

"Not coming back?" he asked, intent on his inspection.

"No." Skylar turned on an overhead light and tilted the lamp to the side. "They were found in the grass when the homeowner was about to mow."

"Lucky for you two," Buzz said to the towel, leaning in. "They look good. Tiny. Maybe two or three weeks old? Eyes open. Alert." He pulled on some blue gloves and lifted something in his hand. "You're okay," he crooned. "Don't worry. I won't hurt you." He turned his hand one way, giving Jenna a glimpse of gray fur between his fingers.

"What is it, Doctaw Buzz?" Frannie asked, standing on tiptoe to try to see.

"Frannie?" He'd been so attentive to his latest patients, it was no wonder he looked so surprised. "Well, hello there." He waved her over with his other hand. "Come see for yourself."

"Can I, Jenna?" Frannie asked, already heading toward the exam table.

"Of course." Jenna smiled.

"You're all welcome." Buzz paused, his gaze

skirting around her to land on the dog. "Except you, Shaggy, you stay right where you are."

"Biddy and I will keep you company." Jenna leaned over and patted the dog's side.

"What are they?" Monica asked.

"Baby bunnies." Garrett tilted his head to one side. "They're called kittens, aren't they?"

"They are." Buzz nodded, pushing a wide metal stool close with his foot. "You can stand on that, Frannie."

She scrambled up, her little hands clasping in front of her. "They awe so tiny." She smiled. "Awe they new babies?"

"Dr. Buzz said they were two weeks old." Monica shook her head. "They look like toys. I mean, look at them. They are so, so cute."

"There are bunnies all over the place." Skylar held the other one in her hand, offering Garrett and Frannie a closer peek. "My girls found one in our backyard about a year ago. He was older but his leg was a little twisted so we fed him and kept an eye on him and he's sort of stayed around. Jet, our dog, acts like he's just one of the family."

"People could learn a lot from animals, Biddy." Jenna smiled down at her baby sister.

"That's true," Buzz said.

She'd thought she was quiet, so to hear Buzz agreeing with her was a bit of a surprise. She was proud of herself for not looking at him. That tone had all sorts of warm thoughts and feelings rising up inside her. Now would not be a good time to look up and fall into those blue-blue eyes of his.

"Like how to wun and hide?" Frannie asked. "And how to scwatch ouw eaws with ouw back legs?"

"Can you do that, Frannie?" Cassie asked. "I can't."

"I twy." Frannie shrugged. "And I fall oveh."

"She does." Garrett nodded, then started laughing.

Jenna had been watching the exchange, content. She knew Garrett was impatient with Frannie from time to time, but that was a sibling thing. Moments like this, when they were smiling and laughing together, gave her hope that she wasn't failing as their guardian and giving them a miserable childhood. Granted, theirs was nothing like her own laughter-filled early years...

For a minute, a split second, grief crowded in on her—hard and fast. Snippets of memory. Scents and tastes and sounds that made her heart hurt. Her childhood home with the too-small kitchen and the big corner lot. The smell of her mother's cologne and that way she'd laugh when she burned the Sunday biscuits. She'd always burned them. Her father had said he couldn't eat a biscuit any other way. Her father playing the piano. His hugs—strong enough to chase away all her bad dreams. Her stepfather and his puzzle obsession. After her mother's death, she'd had to get their house ready to sell. Her stepfather's office closet was stacked, floor to ceiling, with unopened puzzle boxes. Jenna had kept a couple for each of her siblings in the hopes that later, it would be a happy reminder.

I'm trying. She pressed a kiss to the top of Biddy's head, willing the memories aside. "I'm trying."

"Jenna?" Buzz had stepped closer and was crouching before her. "Garrett thought you'd want to see one." The kids were helping Skylar and Cassie collect supplies behind him.

She nodded, sniffing. "Of course." She hated how pinched she sounded.

His blue eyes met hers, a deep V forming between his brows.

She cleared her throat. "Allergies," she murmured, hoping it would explain why she dabbed at her eye.

From the expression on his face, he didn't buy it. Of course, if she stopped looking at his face, it wouldn't matter.

"Is it a jackrabbit?" she asked.

"Cottontail." He turned the baby bunny. "Little thing."

"Aren't you supposed to leave baby bunnies in their nest? Doesn't Mom come back?"

"Unless a hawk gets them," Buzz whispered,

glancing at her. "I didn't know how *National Geographic* you wanted us to go in front of the kids."

She smiled. "*National Geographic*?"

"You know... And here you see the majestic water buffalo at the river with its calf—right before the crocodile drags the calf into the river." Buzz was smiling an extremely distracting eye-crinkling smile.

Jenna laughed.

His gaze swept over her face slowly before colliding with hers. "That's better." He said it so softly she couldn't be sure she'd heard correctly.

Either way, the damage was done. She was free-falling into those blue eyes and crashing into a molten fire of throbbing want that had her breathless. It was wrong to crave a person this way, surely. Normal people didn't run around resisting the urge to pounce on one another? Did they? At the moment, Jenna was imagining it. She and Buzz—minus everyone else in the room—alone...

"Jenna." He shook his head. "I can't help being here—I know we agreed to stay apart." He swallowed. "But now you're looking at me that way and I'm sorely tempted to plead my case all over again."

His words only fanned the flames higher.

"Buzz?" Cassie called. "Jenna is looking for a handyman to help out with repair. Could you recommend anyone?"

The muscle in his jaw tightened as he stood, staring down at her. "Maybe. I think Bobby Doherty knows someone. I can find out."

"I'd appreciate it." Jenna stood. "We should probably go. You have your hands full and we should get home." *Calm. Breathe.* So far, the only person giving her an odd look was Buzz. And it wasn't odd so much as yearning. *For me.*

"Do we have to?" Garrett asked. "I finished all my homework."

"I don't have any." Frannie hopped off the stool. "But I am hungwy fow a snack."

"Ugh. I do." Monica sighed. "What about the bunnies? What happens to them now?"

"We bottle feed them until we can get them to the county rehabilitation center. They have the manpower to feed these little guys." Skylar ran a finger along the baby bunny's head. "If they can't be returned to the wild, they'll live at the center—well taken care of."

"That's good. What do they eat? And how often do they eat?" Garrett pushed up his glasses, all enthusiasm. "And—"

"Garrett," Jenna cut him off. "It's time to go."

Garrett slumped. "Okay."

Jenna bit back a laugh.

"He can stay," Skylar offered. "I'll bring him home."

"Fine by me." Buzz nodded, acting cool and calm and not in the least bit rattled.

Jenna was fine with it, too. As long as Skylar was the one to bring him home. "If you're sure he won't get in the way?"

Garrett shot her an offended look.

"And that dropping him off isn't out of your way, Skylar?" She hadn't meant to stress Skylar, but she did and, from the smile on Buzz's face, he'd heard it.

"Not at all." Skylar gave her a thumbs-up. "We'll see you later."

"Bye." Garrett waved, his enthusiasm restored.

Jenna led the way from the clinic, eager to leave before she made a fool out of herself. *I'm tired, that's all.* She wasn't one to get all emotional, so that and Buzz's outrageous handsomeness and the hyper-charged electric current between them must have been exacerbated by her lack of sleep. She'd turn in early and tomorrow she'd be seeing clearly and feeling more like herself. At least, that's what she hoped.

Chapter Eight

Buzz finished feeding the baby bunny and lay it beside its fully fed and contentedly dozing nest mate.

"They don't eat a lot." Garrett watched as Buzz arranged the blankets around the bunny kittens.

"They don't." Buzz washed his hands. "Rabbits are pretty interesting creatures. The mom only feeds them twice a day. When they're this age, they spend most of their time huddled in the nest. When they're about a month or so old, that's when they start exploring outside and getting ready to be on their own."

"That's young." Garrett glanced up at Buzz. "Won't they get eaten and stuff?"

"Some do." While he was tempted to sugarcoat things, Garrett was levelheaded and smart.

"I figured as much. I watched a nature show about baby turtles and it showed them trying to get from their nest to the water…" Garrett shook his head. "It didn't go so well for most of them. Seagulls are jerks."

Buzz laughed. "That's nature. One animal's survival often relies on the death and digestion of another."

"It's nice that these little guys won't get eaten." Garrett ran a finger gently along the bunnies' backs.

"Buzz." Skylar came through the exam room doors, her cell phone in her hand. "Greer has a fever."

Buzz could hear the baby's cries through the phone.

"I know she's teething but Kyle…" She held up the phone, baby Greer's wails increasing. "He can't handle it when the girls are this upset and Jan's with Weston and Lizzie at her doctor's appointment."

"Go." Buzz nodded. "We got this."

Skylar hesitated. "Garrett—"

"Garrett and I will close up and I'll take him home." Buzz winced when Greer's shrieks reached an especially high note. "Go. It's almost closing time, anyway. I'm with Kyle on this one."

"Thank you." Skylar smiled. "Garrett, please tell Jenna I'm sorry."

"She'll get it. Biddy and Greer are a lot alike." Garrett nodded. "Good luck."

The boy was so serious Buzz had to laugh.

Skylar left, waving as she went.

"What now?" Garrett asked.

"Let's see." Buzz turned to the large whiteboard against the far wall. "Looks like we take Shaggy here for a walk and we can close up shop."

"I can help with that." Garrett trailed along behind him. "Anything else?"

Buzz talked him through their nightly cleanup, letting the boy wipe down the exam table and anything else Garrett took an interest to. He rinsed out a kennel, checked the back doors were locked and turned off most of the lights.

"If you were sixteen, I'd give you a job." Buzz handed Garrett the leash. "You're a hard worker."

"My dad always said everyone has their share of work to do to help out in a family. He also said if a man works hard, he'll always be able to put food on the table and a roof over his family's head." Garrett shrugged.

At times, Buzz had a hard time accepting Garrett Norris was eight. If the term *old soul* ever applied to a person, it was this little boy. A little boy Buzz couldn't help but like.

"I'm too young to do *that* but I do try to help out. If Jenna asks me to do something, I do it." Garrett clipped the leash onto Shaggy's collar. "Except eat spinach. I try to hide it in my napkin." He made a face and stuck his tongue out. "It's gross."

Buzz grinned. "I won't tell, don't worry. For me,

it's asparagus." He held the front door open and let Garrett walk Shaggy out. "Nice evening."

They walked down Main Street to the large lawn surrounding the courthouse. Shaggy sniffed and explored, while the two of them talked about animals and science and what it took to be a veterinarian. As far as Buzz was concerned, Garrett would make a fine veterinarian—if that's what he chose to do.

When they got back to the clinic, Garrett made sure Shaggy had food and plenty of water. "Don't worry, Shaggy, I'll make sure we get our fence fixed so you can come home soon." He gave the dog a hug and closed the kennel door. "You think he knows?"

"That he belongs with you?" Buzz nodded. "I'd say so."

Garrett smiled.

"Let's go." Buzz flipped off the overhead lights and locked the clinic door behind them. "I'd say we get ice cream but you haven't had dinner yet."

"I'm starving, too, so I hope dinner is good." Garrett climbed up and into the back seat of Buzz's diesel truck and buckled up, chattering the whole ride to their big blue house. "You coming in?"

"I should probably head home." He didn't have the energy to resist Jenna. If she started staring at him like she'd been earlier, he'd start pleading his case and make a damn fool out of himself.

"Okay." Garrett climbed down from the car.

"Thanks, Dr. Buzz. I like that you've always got something to teach me."

"I like talking to you, too." He grinned. "How about you call me, Buzz."

"Bye…Buzz." Garrett slammed the truck door and ran across the yard to the front door. He turned the knob but it didn't open. He knocked, but no one answered. He turned, shrugging at Buzz, and knocked again—harder this time.

Buzz turned off his truck and joined Garrett at the front door. "Jenna?" He knocked.

"Maybe the back door?" Garrett was looking worried.

"Sounds good." Buzz patted him on the back. "Lead the way."

They went through the side fence and were half-way to the back door when Buzz heard the screaming. He didn't pause. He took off running, yanked the back door open and raced inside. "Jenna?" he called out. The screaming kept going, with the occasional sob thrown in. "Jenna?"

"Buzz?" Jenna's voice was barely audible over all the commotion. "Upstairs."

Buzz took the stairs two at a time to find Jenna, crouched on the floor. "The door is stuck and Biddy and Frannie are inside." She stared up at him. "I was getting ready for their bath and I left for a clean towel and the door shut."

"I want out," Frannie howled. "Now."

Biddy was keeping up a steady wail.

"I took off the screws last time but I guess I stripped them when I screwed them back in?" Jenna stood, running trembling hands over her jean-clad thighs.

Buzz took a quick look at the door frame and door. "How attached are you to that doorknob?" How something so little could create so much noise was a mystery. But Biddy wasn't letting up. As far as he could tell, she hadn't paused long enough to take a breath.

"I'm not." Jenna stood, glancing at the doorknob.

"Can I borrow your hammer, real quick?"

"If I had one." Jenna swallowed, her eyes welling with tears. "My collection of tools went with my bastard of a… I don't have them."

"Jenna! Jenna!" Frannie sobbed, rattling the handle and sounding so frantic Buzz couldn't bear it. "Let me out!"

Biddy's wails went up an octave.

"Garrett?" Buzz turned to find the boy at the top of the stairs. "Can you run out to my truck and get my toolbox? You can't miss it. Bright orange—right in the bed of the truck."

Garrett took off running.

"Hey, hey, Frannie." Buzz tapped on the door. "Are you in there?"

"I am, I am," Frannie sobbed. "Doctaw Buzz, I'm stuck."

"I know, hon. I'm gonna get you out but there will be a loud bang, okay?" He paused. "Can you be real brave for me?"

"O-okay." Frannie hiccupped.

"Can you tell Biddy it'll be okay?" He rested his hand on the door, anxious for Garrett's return. "She'll believe you—you being her big sister and all."

"O-okay." Frannie sniffed. "But she doesn't listen to me much."

Buzz grinned and glanced at Jenna…who was crying. "It's going to be okay." He looked Jenna in the eye. "You hear me?"

Jenna nodded.

He winked.

"Yes, I heaw you." Frannie sniffled. "Huwwy please. Biddy is cwying and it makes me scawed and I cwy, too."

Garrett came back, out of breath, the large orange metal toolbox clutched to his chest. "Here."

"Thank you, Garrett." Buzz nodded, crouching to open the toolbox and do a quick rummage. He pulled out his heavier hammer—more like a mini-sledgehammer. "You ready?" he asked Frannie. "Garrett got my big hammer and I'm gonna have to hit the doorknob to break it loose, okay?"

"Okay." Frannie seemed calmer now.

"Stand back, Frannie," Jenna said. "Hold Biddy all the way over by the bathtub, okay."

"But she's scweaming," Frannie moaned. "Weal loud."

"I know, honey." Jenna took a deep breath. "But I need you to do it, anyway."

Biddy's cries stopped instantly.

"I'm holding her," Frannie yelled. "And she has a stinky diapeh, Jenna. Huwwy."

Buzz shook his head, grinning. "Count to three with me?" He paused. "One. Two. Three." He brought the hammer down with all the force he could muster. The doorknob fell to the floor and Buzz reached into the hole, knocked the tongue from the groove, and pushed the other side out and onto the bathroom floor. "Almost there," he said, getting as firm a grip as he could on the hole and tugged.

The door slipped, then stopped, the alignment off just enough to make him work to pull it open.

"Doctaw Buzz." Frannie sat in the corner, Biddy half in her lap, with tear streaks down her bright cheeks. "You saved us. Just like you saved the baby bobcat."

Buzz grinned, standing aside for Jenna.

Jenna grabbed her little sisters in her arms and gave them both a long hard squeeze. "I'm so sorry, Frannie. You, too, Biddy. I thought I'd propped that bad old door open."

"It's okay." Frannie pressed a big kiss against her cheek. "Except Biddy smells, pee-ew."

"You're right, she does." Jenna scooped up Biddy. "I'd have been screaming my head off, too. Let's get you all cleaned up." She stood, Biddy held close. "And then we'll have that bath."

Buzz watched the siblings, and a heavy warmth started in his chest and slowly spread. For the first time in a long time, he didn't feel alone. Seeing Frannie smile at him when he'd opened the door—he'd almost felt like Santa Claus. And now, with Jenna rocking Biddy, as she and Garrett listened to Frannie tell them how horrible it had been trapped in the bathroom, Buzz felt like he was part of something.

His chest deflated, pressing in on him until he had no choice but to accept what was happening. Even in the midst of chaos and one stinky diaper, there was no place he'd rather be.

Realizing that was like a solid knock to the head.

Jarring. Painful. And hella unnerving.

Frannie's arms wrapped around his legs. "Thank you, Doctaw Buzz. So, so much."

He reached down to pat her back, his throat too tight for him to speak.

"What happened?" They all turned to find Monica, a headset around her neck, staring at them in shock. "Is everyone okay? Jenna, are you crying?"

"No." Jenna laughed. "No. Of course not."

"I guess your noise-canceling headphones work." Garrett smiled.

Buzz laughed, easing the tightness if not his panic. "I'd say so."

"You need to leave a review, Monica," Garrett went on. "Seriously. Five stars."

Monica crossed her arms over her chest. "Seriously. What happened?"

"Come help me with Biddy and I'll tell you. Let's pick out some pj's for you, okay, Frannie?" But then Jenna paused. "Buzz—"

"I'll clean up this mess and go." He nodded, needing a quick escape.

"Stay." Jenna smiled. "Please. I have homemade lasagna in the oven. After I get these two to bed, we could eat? If you're hungry? My rolls are nowhere near as good as Lizzie's but they're edible."

He nodded. "With an offer like that, how can I refuse?"

"I'm starving," Garrett said.

"I'll feed you," Monica murmured, hooking arms with her brother. "You go on, Jenna."

"I'll eat with Jenna and Buzz." Garrett tried to pull his arm free.

Monica glanced in the direction Jenna had gone before whispering, "It's already past your bedtime and I know you have homework you didn't tell Jenna about so you could stay at the veterinary clinic, so you're going to eat now." She smiled sweetly at Buzz before dragging Garrett down the stairs.

He'd grown up with a sister; they were mysterious creatures. Knowing that, he couldn't help but think Monica was up to something. She'd had the same expression Cassie had had a time or two growing up. Buzz had learned early on that when Cassie looked like that, she was up to something.

But he had enough to worry about as it was. He packed up his toolbox, threw the old pieces of the doorknob away and took a deep breath. *Dinner. With Jenna. Alone.* He should have turned her down and left, that was the smart thing to do. The safe thing to do. He could still back out. Monica would pass the message along and he could go. *It was the smart thing to do.* He carried his toolbox downstairs and headed for the front door.

"That was a fast bath." Frannie sat, tucked into her small bed. "I'm glad. I'm tiwed."

"Me, too, Frannie." Jenna stooped and pressed a kiss to her forehead. "You had a big day—full of adventures. I bet you'll sleep good."

"Like a log?" Frannie grinned.

"Yep, you'll sleep like a big old log." She kissed her again.

"Will you tell Doctaw Buzz thank you again?" Frannie hugged Clarence the giraffe, her favorite stuffed animal. "Big, big thank you? And a hug? Fwum me?"

"I will tell him." She tapped Frannie on the nose. "You get some sleep and have beautiful dreams."

"Okay," Frannie said, yawning widely as she flopped back against her pillows.

Jenna paused in the doorway and turned off the overhead light. Frannie's nightlight clicked on, projecting a slowly spinning starburst on the opposite wall. "Night," she said again, leaving the door barely cracked.

Jenna peeked in on Biddy, too. Her baby sister had kicked off her blankets and was sound asleep—with her little arms thrown over her head. She blew her a kiss and tiptoed from the room, pulling the door shut behind her.

Then she froze.

Buzz was downstairs.

Monica and Garrett were upstairs getting ready for bed.

Meaning...she'd be alone with Buzz. Alone-alone. She shook her head, staring up at the ceiling overhead. *We can have dinner and a conversation, like two normal people.* That was the key. Conversation. If they were talking—and eating—they'd be too occupied to get caught up in the staring...and other stuff. *Right. Sure. Who am I kidding?*

She'd invited him to dinner. After everything he'd done tonight, it was the least she could do. Hiding up here was...cowardly. *I'm no coward.* She forced herself downstairs and into the kitchen. Where she froze. "What happened?" Candles were lit, sitting in their crystal candlesticks, in the middle of the table. The table had been covered in a clean non-plastic kid-friendly tablecloth and had two places set—with her mother's fine china.

Buzz had been studying the photos covering the front of her refrigerator but he turned now, shrugging. "This wasn't your idea?"

She stared at him. "A romantic candlelight dinner?" Was he serious? No. He couldn't be. "Are you serious? I'm pretty good at multitasking but I'm not sure how I would have managed this and bath time and Biddy and Frannie's bedtime routine."

He grinned. "So far, you've managed to make the impossible look easy so…"

Jenna smiled in spite of herself. "Thank you but this is all Monica." Just when she thought she and her sister had finally reached an understanding, she went and did…this. She took a minute, assessing Monica's work. "I'm impressed." She had to admit, Monica had done well. "Where are the rest of the chairs?" She frowned at the two chairs. "How could anyone comfortably eat that close?" The chairs were squished together, no space between them.

Buzz kept on grinning. "You do have more than two? I was thinking that would make things awful inconvenient at mealtime."

"Eight, total." She really wished he'd stop grinning that way. "I'm sorry about this. Monica watches a lot of those reality matchmaking shows." Too many.

"I'd say she's picked up a few things. It looks nice." Buzz chuckled. His chuckle had a lovely gravelly edge to it.

Jenna swallowed hard and headed for the oven. If she was going to fixate on his crooked grin or his husky laugh or how snugly his pale blue checked button-up shirt fit his broad chest, the likelihood of them having a civilized meal together was slim. "Feel free to turn on the lights." She pulled out the lasagna from the oven and set it on the stovetop.

"It doesn't bother me." Buzz leaned against the kitchen counter beside her. "That's quite a picture gallery." He pointed at the refrigerator.

"I don't want them to forget. Our parents." She shrugged, slicing the lasagna. "I know they miss them." She slid a huge piece onto a plate for him and a smaller piece for her. "With the move, I worry they've lost all sense of stability and normalcy—"

"You worry a lot, you know that?" Buzz faced her, his tone gentle. "I'm sure they miss them, that's normal. You do, too. But what's happening here is nothing but good."

She glanced at him. "I mess up all the time. I've put two different shoes on Frannie, sent Garrett to school with an empty lunch box, missed the deadline to sign the permission form for Monica's class trip and I carry Biddy around like a purse because I'm afraid she's going to hurt herself—trying to walk." She shook her head, surprised at everything she'd just dumped on him. "Sorry. Wow, that came out of nowhere."

"Don't apologize, Jenna."

The deep warmth of his voice when he said her name almost made her drop the rolls she was moving from the tray to the bread basket. If he noticed her hand was shaking, he didn't comment.

"Can I help?" he asked.

"You already have." She looked at him. "I can't thank you enough for tonight, Buzz… I knew they were fine but not being able to get to them? Not knowing what to do? I like to think I'd have figured it out and kept a level head but I let fear get the best of me instead." She shook her head, not wanting to think about it.

"I heard the girls crying and came running—because I was scared out of my mind." He tilted her chin back so she had no choice but to look at him. "It seems to me you're hard on yourself as a rule. I wish you could see yourself like…" He paused. "Like the rest of the world does. Then you'd see the hardworking, determined, can-do, selfless woman we all see. Your brother and sisters are lucky to have you. Garrett sees it. Monica does, too, otherwise she wouldn't be trying to make you happy like this." He let his hand drop, his gaze briefly sweeping over her mouth. "Biddy and Frannie are too young to understand—but they love you and they're happy."

By the time he was done, Jenna was a tangle of

emotions. He had no reason to listen to her whine, but he was. It wasn't his job to cheer her up, either, but he was trying. It was sweet. He was sweet. Which reminded her. "Frannie asked me to give you a big, big thank-you from her. And a hug, too."

Buzz's brows rose, watching her closely. "She did, huh?"

"She did." It was a whisper. There was no way she was hugging Buzz. She couldn't. Once she wrapped her arms around him, she wouldn't let go. She didn't move or breathe.

He grinned. "No hugs necessary, Jenna."

Jenna sighed.

"You don't have to sound that relieved." But he was laughing.

"Sorry." But she was laughing, too. "How about we eat?" She moved the chairs farther apart. "Are you sure about the lights?"

"Monica did go through a whole lot of effort." He shrugged and sat in a chair, his crooked grin back and more tantalizing than ever. He took two rolls for his plate. "Thank you. Smells good."

"Thank *you*. Again." She picked a roll, the sudden quiet of the kitchen calming. They ate, in companionable silence, before Jenna realized this was a first. "You know..." She broke off, shaking her head.

"What?" He waited. "What were you going to say?"

"This is the first time I've had a meal, alone, with another adult in...months." She shrugged.

"Makes sense. You're getting settled, wrangling kids... That's a lot." He tore his roll in two. "I know we've covered this but you should give yourself some credit, Jenna."

"It's just... I know I could do better." She shook her head. He was right—they had covered this. She used to be good at conversation but she wasn't sure where to start with Buzz. "So, you... What made you become a veterinarian?"

"I love animals. Period. That's it." Buzz grinned. "And, now, I love my job."

"We both love what we do. That makes us lucky." Jenna nodded. "Between work and the kids, it's more than enough." Most of the time. "Monica might disagree, but I can't imagine trying to fit in a relationship, too." If that was the case, why had she been so quick to push Buzz away? A no-strings relationship wasn't a relationship, was it? It was all about fun? *Why am I thinking about this now?*

"I feel the same." He chuckled. "Kyle's like Monica—trying to fix me up."

Jenna laughed. "Like you would need to be fixed up."

"Meaning?" He shook his head.

"Meaning you could have your pick, if you wanted." She pointed at him with her fork. "Don't try to tell me you don't know that, because I won't believe you."

His eyes met hers. "We know that's not the case."

It was suddenly very hard to breathe. "I… I was hoping for a nice, civilized grown-up meal with harmless conversation."

"Versus?" He waited, the candlelight changing his eyes to a deep blue.

Jenna blinked. "You—you know. What's happening now." She focused on her lasagna, cutting it into teeny-tiny pieces but not taking a single bite. "You. Me. *This…*"

"No. We've settled all that." His voice was gruff. "Haven't we?"

"I… We had." She stood, carrying her plate to the sink. "I don't even know how we got here."

"It's fine." Buzz didn't sound fine. He sounded irritated. "You didn't eat much."

"I'm not hungry." In fact, her stomach was in knots.

Buzz stood, carrying his plate to the sink. "Thank you for the dinner, Jenna."

She nodded, rinsing her plate and reaching for his.

But he held on to the plate. "Did I say something to upset you?"

Don't look at him. "No." She pulled but he still wouldn't let go. "Buzz." She'd intended to glare at him, to brush him off and act like her thoughts weren't consumed by…him. But they were. She was. Now that he was close enough for her to touch, that's all she wanted to do. "You should probably go."

"Okay." He frowned but let go of the plate.

She listened as he pushed in his chair, the fall of his boots across the floor as he left the kitchen and headed down the hall to the front door. The farther away he got, the harder it was to breathe.

Let him go.

If he stayed, she'd tell him the truth and then… What? What would happen? She could almost feel his lips against hers, firm and warm and devouring her. That was what would happen. *That's what I want.* The plate rattled in the sink as she let it go and turned, hurrying down the hall after him. "Buzz…"

His hand rested on the doorknob, but he looked back.

"I lied." She hugged herself.

"I know." He frowned. "Whatever I said, I didn't mean to rile you up."

"No." She shook her head. "Not that. You didn't… This is all me. It's just, I… I can't stop thinking about…what's *happened* between us." Her gaze locked with his. "Or what you said to me."

He stared back at her, the muscle in his jaw flexed. "I said a lot of things."

"I know." She swallowed, her nerves strung painfully tight. "I remember. All of them. Most nights, I lay in bed and hear you saying them over and over again." *And now there's no going back.*

His jaw clenched tight. "You said you didn't want *anything* to happen between us, Jenna—"

"Because I was scared," she murmured. "I've been kissed before, Buzz Lafferty, but not the way you kissed me. When you kiss me, nothing else matters—and it makes me nervous." She swallowed. "But I like it. I like the way you make me feel."

His hand fell from the doorknob and he set his toolbox on the floor with great care. When his hand rested against her cheek, his eyes were blazing. "Just so there's no misunderstanding what you want, Jenna—"

"I want you, Buzz. No relationships, no strings, no expectations, just this..." She slid her arms around his waist and erased any space between them. "I want you."

Chapter Nine

Buzz wasn't sure if he was dreaming or not. After all the hours wishing and dreaming of this happening, it seemed too easy. But the feel of her, warm and soft and pressed tight against him, was real enough. Hell, nothing compared to having Jenna in his arms.

He didn't linger over the fact that he doubted what she'd said. Not the part where *she* was okay with a no-strings arrangement, but that he was. He knew better. He wouldn't let himself get too attached. He wouldn't…

Right now, he had more important matters to handle. And, oh, was he looking forward to it.

"What's wong?" Frannie's voice jolted the two of them apart. "You have something in youw eye, Jenna?" Frannie walked down the hall, a stuffed giraffe tucked into the corner of her arm and her brown hair a mess. "That huwts. I got an eyelash in my eye and it huwt awful bad."

"Yes." Jenna nodded. "That's it." She glanced his way, smiling. "Thanks, Buzz."

"Happy to help. Anytime." Sooner would be preferred.

"Anytime?" Jenna asked, biting into her lower lip.

His gaze locked on that lip, his insides tightening. *Now* she was going to *tease*. He nodded. "*Any*time." Two can play that game. "I'll be ready and waiting."

Jenna looked just a flushed and rattled as he felt. *Good.*

"Can you help me get some watah?" Frannie asked. "Evewything is too tall." She took his hand and led him back down the hall to the kitchen.

"Too tall, huh?" He walked with her. "Sounds like you need a ladder."

"I can get it, Frannie." Jenna sighed, following. "I'm sure Buzz has things to do," she said, once they were inside the kitchen.

"I was just about to get started." He was smiling like a fool when Jenna's cheeks turned the prettiest shade of pink. "No rush, though."

"Wushing is bad." Frannie hopped onto a chair.

"You make mowe mistakes when you wush." She frowned. "Whewe awe all the chaiws, Jenna?"

Buzz had to laugh over Frannie's concern.

"That's a good question." Jenna pulled a plastic cup from the kitchen counter and filled it with water. "One I plan on asking Monica." She handed the cup to Frannie. "Drink up."

"Why did Monica move the chaiws?" Frannie asked, taking a sip. "Now thewe's not enough foh us. And Doctaw Buzz, too, when he comes to visit." She took another sip. "Monica is silly."

"She is." Jenna nodded.

"Why awe thewe candles? Did the lights bweak?" She sat on her knees and blew out the candles. "It's so dawk."

Buzz flipped on the overhead lights.

"Yay, that's bettah." Frannie yawned.

"Jenna?" Garrett peeked around the door. "Monica told me not to come downstairs but I can't figure out this problem."

"Why on earth did she tell you that?" But then Jenna stopped and sighed. "I thought you didn't have homework?"

"I forgot." Garrett shrugged, his face bright red.

"Did you wush?" Frannie asked, then turned to Buzz. "I bet he was wushing and that's why he fohgot."

"Aren't you supposed to be in bed?" Garrett asked.

“I needed watah.” Frannie help up her cup. “And I was gonna help Doctaw Buzz get an eyelash out of Jenna’s eye, too.”

“All gone.” Jenna patted Frannie on the shoulder. “Why don’t you get your homework set up and we can take a look at it.” She turned. “Chairs…”

“We stacked them on the back porch,” Garrett said, sliding his book onto the table.

“Of course.” Jenna held up a finger and headed for the back door. “Where else would they be?”

“Monica was acting really weird,” Garrett went on. “Maybe she needs to go to the doctor.”

Buzz was having a hell of a time not laughing at the whole exchange. He eyed the open back door and went after Jenna. “If this is what it’s like every night, I’m amazed you get anything—”

Jenna was against the wall right outside the door. As soon as he stepped out, she grabbed him by the belt at his waist and tugged him close. “No talking.”

“Yes, ma’am.” He brushed the lightest of kisses—that was all it took. She was clinging to him and he was hard pressed not to push her back against the wall. But…kissing Jenna was no little thing. If he let himself go, the two of them would have a lot of explaining to do when Garrett and Frannie walked outside. He rested his forehead against hers and whispered, “As much as I wanna keep doing this, I’m not so sure Garrett will buy the whole eyelash thing.”

Her hands eased from his back and she stepped away. "You're right." But the disappointed little sound she made had him eager for all Norris siblings' bedtime. All except Jenna, of course.

"My watah is finished," Frannie called out.

Jenna gave his belt a final tug. "I'm coming." She carried a chair with her.

Buzz lifted two chairs and headed back inside to find Jenna and Frannie gone.

"Jenna had to put Frannie to bed because Frannie is scared of the dark." Garrett scratched his head, his pencil tapping his papers.

"I was. Aren't most kids?" Buzz put the two chairs at the table and went out for more.

"You were?" Garrett asked when he came back.

"Sure." Buzz nodded, closed the back door and sat next to Garrett. "It didn't help that my sister would hide under my bed and, right when I was climbing up to get in, she'd grab my ankle and pull." He grinned, remembering how hard Cassie had laughed and laughed.

"Did she get in trouble? If I did that to Frannie, I'd get in trouble." But Garrett was smiling.

"Sometimes." Buzz smiled in return. "If I told on her. Sometimes, she'd give me candy so I wouldn't tell." He looked at the papers Garrett had spread across the table. "What are we working on?"

"Advanced math. They teach it funny." He pointed

at the row after row of numbers. "It's more work for the same answer."

"Why would anyone make math take longer?" Buzz read over the problem.

There were footsteps on the stairs, followed by Monica saying, "I'm sorry."

"You've said that before but if you mean it, this wouldn't have happened again." Jenna's tone didn't hold that much bark.

"I can't help it, Jenna. I just think you and Buzz are too cute—and totally perfect for each other. Plus, he likes all of us so maybe he won't run off like—"

"Buzz has no interest in a family."

That wasn't exactly true. Buzz wanted a family. He didn't want the complications and heartbreak a family could lead to.

"He can be our friend." Jenna paused. "We all need friends."

"Whatever." Monica snorted. "You think he's hot."

Buzz grinned. He liked hearing that.

"I can have a hot friend." Jenna laughed.

"The whole hallway is like that," Garrett said. "You can hear everything. It's like a whisper chamber."

Buzz didn't know what a whisper chamber was but there was no denying they could hear everything Jenna and Monica were saying.

"What about Alonzo's dad?" Monica asked.

Buzz perked up. What about Alonzo's dad? Luis was a good guy but… No, he and Jenna were no-strings. If she wanted to date Luis, she could. *Does she want to date him?*

"Can we change the subject?" Jenna walked into the kitchen.

"We can, in a minute." Monica waved at him. "You know Alonzo's dad, don't you, Dr. Buzz?"

He nodded. "He's a nice guy, right?" Monica waited for him to nod. "Then tell Jenna she should give him a chance. He's interested. Alonzo said so. He said he thought the two of you were together—I don't know why. Anyway, I told Alonzo you were only friends and he said his dad said he was going to officially ask you to some river festival or something?"

"It's Labor Day. Weekend after next." Buzz nodded. "The Granite Falls River Festival. Music and booths and all sorts of fun set up along the shores of the river in the state park. Everyone goes. Well, most families do."

"See. We're a family." Monica nodded. "And Alonzo's dad has a family."

"His name is Luis," Jenna interrupted.

"Is he asking you to ask Jenna out?" Buzz sat back in the chair, arms crossed. "That's a little weird, isn't it?"

"No. No way. He just wanted to make sure Jenna

was available before asking her. Which, I think, is totally cool since he didn't want to like break a bro code or something." Monica got herself a glass of water. "You know?"

"Bro code?" Jenna asked.

"You know, a guy doesn't ask a girl out if his friend is interested in her sort of thing." Monica finished her water. "Right?" she asked him.

"Right." Buzz grinned. "The bro code."

Garrett was giggling.

"Why are you laughing?" Monica put her cup in the dishwasher.

"You're weird." Garrett said it like it was the most obvious thing in the world. "All the time. Romance and love and all that junk." He pushed up his glasses. "Alonzo this and Alonzo that. The only reason she wants you to date Alonzo's dad is so she can hang out with Alonzo."

Monica turned a bright shade of red. "Not cool, Garrett. Not. Cool."

"Calm." Jenna put a hand on Monica's shoulder. "Do you like this boy?"

Monica sighed. "Yes."

"Then we'll go to the river thingy?" Jenna looked at him. "What's it called?"

"Granite Falls River Festival." Buzz nodded.

"Really, Jenna?" Monica went from red-faced and sullen to beaming and excited in seconds. "I hope you'll give Alonzo's dad a chance—"

"Or we could go, just us," Jenna suggested. "Besides, Luis hasn't asked—"

"He will." Monica hugged her. "Thank you. Love you. Night." And she sprinted from the kitchen.

"Puberty." Garrett turned back to his work.

Buzz burst out laughing, so did Jenna.

"Am I wrong?" Garrett peered at them over the top of his glasses. "I researched it. She's got it."

Jenna was still laughing when she sat opposite Garrett. "How old are you again?"

"Old enough." Garrett pushed the paper to her. "I finished while you put Frannie to bed. Why are we doing it this way?"

Jenna's face cleared as she stared at the math problems. "I know, Garrett. Texas curriculum is different than ours. They think doing it this way means fewer mistakes for kids that can't do it in their head."

"I can do it in my head," Garrett grumbled.

"I know." Jenna frowned and slid the paper back. "And those are all correct, too. Excellent job."

"You're saying I have to do it this way?" Garrett stared at the paper.

Jenna nodded. "I'm sorry."

"It's stupid." Garrett stacked up his papers, neat and tidy. "I know what I'm doing so why do I have to do all the extra work?" He shrugged. "Fine. I'll do it." He looked at Jenna. "Can we get the fence fixed? Soon?"

She nodded. "As soon as I can get someone over here to fix it."

"You've got all the tools, Buzz." Garrett turned toward him. "You've got even more in your truck. I bet you could fix the fence."

"No, no." Jenna put her hand on Garrett's. "Garrett, Buzz has a job. I'll find someone, okay?"

"Okay. Night." Garrett nodded. "I don't want to go to the river thing." He stood, his posture droopy, and shuffled from the room. Even from the kitchen, Garrett's slow heavy steps and multiple sighs were audible.

"Think he'll be okay?" Buzz asked, standing.

"He will." Jenna moved toward him. "He really, really wants Shaggy here."

"Then maybe I should fix the fence." He pulled her into his arms.

"Buzz, no. You do have a job—"

"It'd give me an excuse to be here." He ran his nose along the curve of her ear.

"Oh." She swayed into him. "True… But—"

"I'm sure Garrett will help." He nuzzled behind her ear. "And then I might stay for dinner a time or two."

"That…" She gasped as he drew her earlobe into his mouth. "Can be…arranged." Her arms slid around his waist.

He smoothed her long brown hair from her shoulder and pressed a row of kisses downward to her collarbone. "You smell good." Her scent was light and sweet and very Jenna.

There was the distant thump of a door.

Jenna stiffened in his arms, leaning away from him. "Hear that?" The disappointment on her face was heartfelt.

"I don't hear a thing." His mouth was a hairsbreadth from hers when he heard it, too. "Biddy?" He smiled.

"Biddy." She shook head. "You should go, Buzz. It takes forever to get her back to sleep."

He didn't want to go. He wanted to stay right here.

"It's late and we both have work tomorrow." Her hand took his and led him down the hall to the front door.

"Trying to get rid of me?" he teased, giving her a wink.

"For now." She winked back. "Thanks for breaking the bathroom door."

"Thanks for feeding me dinner and…" He squeezed her hand and opened the door, leaving the sentence to hang there, unfinished.

"Miss Norris, you don't look so good." The school nurse, Anna Arnold, was assessing her with a critical eye. "Are you feeling alright?"

"Tired." Jenna smiled. "That's it."

"I've sent thirteen kids home with what I suspect is strep throat." Anna perched on the edge of her desk. "Seven of them came through your class this morning."

"Thirteen? That's a lot." Jenna chugged down some water, certain the tickling in her throat was the result of Anna's announcement—not any germs she'd come into contact with.

Anna reached over and pressed the back of her hand against her forehead. "How about you come with me to the clinic."

"Now?" Jenna glanced at the clock. "I only have eight minutes left on my conference period."

"It won't take that long. And, if you are sick, you have no business exposing your students." Anna's smile was sympathetic. "Come on."

She made Anna take her temperature twice. She couldn't be sick. It wasn't about missing work—it was about life. If she was sick, who would take care of her brother and sisters? Worse, she could give it to them.

"Don't look so panicked." Anna patted her on the shoulder. "We have a huge pool of substitutes. It's already Thursday so you'll probably be fever-free and able to come back on Monday."

Three days. How was she going to manage three days?

"I've sent a message to the science team lead and they're going to all watch a movie on photosynthesis in their classroom. Which is good— I'll make sure your class is thoroughly disinfected. All you have to do is get your stuff, make a doctor's appointment and head home." Anna grinned. "Oh, and try to touch as little as possible."

An hour later, she was leaving the doctor with a prescription for antibiotics and anti-inflammatories—and no idea what to do. She hated to ask for help, but what choice did she have.

She pulled out her phone and pressed Lizzie's name in Contacts. "Lizzie?"

"Jenna?" Lizzie paused. "Are you okay? You sound funny."

"It's because I'm trying not to cry." She sat in her minivan with the AC on max. "I need you to talk me through this, as a mom. I can do this, I can."

"Okay." Lizzie didn't sound so sure. "What's up?"

"I have strep. And… I just need you to tell me that I can take care of them, wash my hands and spray everything down with antibacterial spray, and they won't get it and it's not a big deal."

Lizzie was quiet and whatever she was saying was muffled.

"Lizzie?" Jenna backed out of the parking lot and headed to the pharmacy next door to the grocery store.

"You're on Speaker," Lizzie said. "You might be okay doing those things."

"Okay, good." She took a deep breath.

"It's Skylar, Jenna. Listen, it would probably be better if you didn't. You need to rest and take care of yourself—and you can't do that and take care of the kids, too."

"I feel fine," Jenna argued. "Just tired." Of course, the doctor did say they'd gotten lucky to catch it so quick. "He prescribed meds and I'm sure I'll feel better very soon. And I won't be contagious after twenty-four hours so—"

"Don't worry about a thing, Jenna honey," came Jan's voice. "I'll pick up your medicine. All you need to do is sleep. We will help, so you relax. Of course you can count on us. That's what family and friends do. Don't you fret now."

"Where are you?" Lizzie asked.

"I had a doctor's appointment so I left school early so I can pick up Monica and Garrett. Just text their teachers and let them know."

"And I'll get Biddy and Frannie," Skylar volunteered. "Just ask Klara if they can stay until five thirty, when I'm off work."

"I'm heading to your place as soon as we hang up. Hayden and Kyle can do daddy duty and I'll come take care of you. Oops, it's me, Jan, again."

Jenna wanted to laugh and cry all at once. "I can't ask you all to do this."

"You didn't, Jenna. We volunteered." Lizzie sighed. "Now, go home, go to bed. We've got this covered. Okay?"

Jenna nodded, her eyes stinging.

"Jenna?" Lizzie repeated.

"Right, you can't see me nodding." Jenna sniffed. "I don't know what to say. Or how to thank you."

"No need for thanks, Jenna." It was Skylar. "I've been in your shoes. I know how hard it is. But you're not on your own, okay?"

Jenna nodded, then laughed. "I'm nodding again."

They all laughed.

"Now, Jan here. Off to bed. I'll come straight over. You leave the door unlocked and I'll let myself in. Bye now."

"Thank you, all." The call disconnected and Jenna turned her car in the direction of home, wiping tears so she could see where she was going. She parked, went inside and found a bottle of antibacterial spray to spritz down everything she could remember touching. Afterward, she headed upstairs for a shower. By then, the pain in her throat was more than a tickle. She stood under steaming hot water until she was relaxed, tugged on her comfy pajamas and climbed into her bed. But laying in bed, with the sunlight spilling in around her curtains, felt wrong. She rolled over onto her side. The clock said 4:12. Between the ache in her head, the throat that was on fire and the weight of her eyelids, Jenna fell into a deep sleep.

At some point, Jan brought her pills and a glass

of water. She tucked Jenna in, got her more water and left without saying a word.

Or maybe Jenna dreamed it. Several times.

When she did wake up, she was achy and disoriented. Her throat. Ouch. It was thick and hot and raw feeling.

"Jenna. Wakey, wakey." It was Frannie. "Open youw little peepahs."

Jenna smiled, turning her head on the pillow to see all four of her siblings peeking in the door. She realized she'd slept the entire day and night and it was the next morning. "What are you up to?"

"They wanted to check in on you before they went to school." Skylar waved, Biddy on her hip.

Seeing Biddy wave and reach out for her with both arms tugged at Jenna's heart. "Hi, Biddy."

"You can cuddle her later, Miss Biddy." Skylar bounced her. "But she doesn't want to share her germs with any of you."

"I don't." Jenna shook her head. "I feel pretty nasty."

"That's why we made you something." Frannie rocked up onto her toes.

"You did?" Jenna rolled onto her side.

"A card." Garrett pulled something from behind his back. "And some flowers."

"Oh, wow." Jenna propped herself up on her elbow. "They're beautiful. That was so sweet of you. It'll make me smile all day."

"That's what Mrs. Mitchell said." Monica smiled. "Flowers make a room happy."

"She's right." Skylar nodded. "We'll get them into a vase, won't we?"

"You look tired, Jenna. Are you sure you're okay? It's just strep?" Monica's voice wobbled the slightest bit. "I mean, I know you're fine but we—" she pointed at Frannie and Garrett "—just wanted to make sure you were feeling a little better."

That's when she realized how worried they all were. Mom had gone to bed with a headache, suffered a stroke and never woke up. It took effort but Jenna sat up, plumped her pillows and leaned propped up against them. "I'm *so* much better today." She forced a smile. "Everyone has been taking care of me—and you all, too. Thank you, Skylar."

"Miss Mitchell says you awe a good patient and you took your medicine." Frannie gave her a thumbs-up. "Does it taste nasty?"

Jenna shrugged, her memories of it hazy. "I slept so hard, Frannie, I thought it was a dream."

"Will you be better after school?" Garrett crossed his arms over his chest. "In case I need help with homework or something."

"I can help you." Monica nudged him. "Jenna should rest until tomorrow. Remember what Buzz said yesterday?"

Buzz?

Garrett nodded.

"I should be up for making pancakes tomorrow morning." Jenna shook her head. "Actually, I'll be up for supervising you make the pancakes."

"Yay, cooking!" Frannie clapped her hands.

Garrett sighed but he was smiling. "I'll help but I'm not cleaning up any messes you make, Frannie."

Jenna smiled. "I can't wait."

"All right, everyone." Skylar glanced at her watch. "It's time to load up and move 'em out. And, Jenna, you chill out and relax. I'll let Jan know you're up."

"Bye, Jenna." Frannie waved. "Sleep tight and don't let the bed bugs bite."

Jenna blew kisses, her heart breaking at the sound of Biddy crying once the door closed.

"I know," Monica said. "It's okay, Biddy."

"I bet Jenna will give you extwa hugs," Frannie added. "When *all* the gewms awe gone."

After the receding thundering of footsteps was followed by the slamming of the front door, Jenna slumped back against her pillows. She'd almost dozed off when there was a soft knock on the door.

"Jenna?" Jan Mitchell opened the door. "How are you feeling?" She set a saucer with pills on her bedside table with a fresh glass of water. "Are you hungry?"

Jenna sighed. "I'm not sure." She smiled. "My

throat is killing me and all I want to do is sleep. How is that possible?"

"Strep is no laughing matter, hon." Jan shook her head. "If you need to sleep, you sleep. Or I can see about getting you a smoothie or milkshake for you first?"

She perked up a little. "I'm not going to lie, Jan. That sounds good."

The older woman grinned. "I'm always in the mood for a milkshake myself." She waited for Jenna to take her pills, then collected the saucer. "I'll see what I can do." With a wink, she left.

Jenna forced herself up for a shower but only managed five minutes before weakness kicked in. She wrapped herself up in a towel, shuffled back to bed and climbed under the covers, tugging up the extra quilt to stop her shivering. She lay on her back, threw her arm over her face and moaned loudly.

There was another knock.

"Come in," Jenna called, not moving. "The shower was a bad idea. Now I'm cold and tired."

"Does that mean I can have your milkshake?" Buzz chuckled.

She lifted her arm. "No." She tugged the quilts up to her neck. "What are you doing here?"

"I'm your friendly neighborhood milkshake delivery guy." He set the extra-large to-go cup on her bedside. "Finding a place willing to make a milkshake at this time of the morning is no easy feat."

"With all that charm and good looks?" She shook her head.

"Ever think you're the only one that finds me charming? And, what did Monica say? Oh, wait, hot." He nodded.

She pulled her blankets over her head. "You could leave the milkshake and go, you know. Since I'm sick and need to rest."

"I'm teasing you, Jenna." His knee nudged the bed. "It's what I do. You know, part of that charm you were talking about."

"Mm-hmm," she murmured, not moving. "Charming."

Buzz chuckled. "How are you feeling?"

"I'm tired. And achy." She peeked over the edge of her blanket. "My throat hurts."

His smile faded, an entirely different expression on his face. "I'm sorry you're hurting." He shoved his hands in his pockets. "What can I do?"

She shook her head. "Skylar and Lizzie and Jan—"

"And Cassie."

She closed her eyes. "I feel horrible."

"It'll take a while for the medicine to kick in, is all." He patted the quilt.

"No… I mean, yes. But I was talking about all the bother. I feel bad that everyone is being so inconvenienced by me."

"Well stop it." Buzz scowled at her, his hands on

his hips. "You didn't ask anyone. You're not making anyone. They want to do it, so stop feeling guilty and start getting better." He pointed at the side table. "And drink that. It'll feel good on your throat."

Beneath her blankets, Jenna was smiling.

"I can tell you're smiling." He shook his head.

"I am not." But she was giggling.

"What's so funny?" He wasn't smiling.

"I've never seen you so…so bossy before." She slid the blanket down a little. "Is it hot?"

His gaze had shifted and was now glued to her bare shoulder. "It's getting there."

She was laughing again. "Now you're just being silly. I know what I look like and it's—"

"Beautiful." He shook his head again. "Even with a puffed-up nose and red eyes and pale lips, you're just about the prettiest thing I've ever seen, Jenna Norris." He swallowed. "And if I knew your middle name, I'd use it so you'd know I'm dead serious."

"Marie," she whispered, more than a little dazed. She blinked, her lungs so tight she couldn't breathe. He'd been teasing but…he was also serious. *Middle name serious.* He thought she was beautiful? And hearing him say it—and her name—triggered the now-familiar spark and hunger, even with her throat on fire. But there was more this time. It wasn't just her body that ached for him—it was something else. She could try to deny it, but there was no point. When she'd told him theirs would be a no-strings agreement, she'd meant it. But that was before her fool heart had decided to give itself to Buzz. Now that it had, there was no way for Jenna to get it back.

Chapter Ten

Buzz looked up from the counter to see John and Kyle walking through the clinic door. “What’s the problem?” He pulled his cell phone from his pocket. “If you called, I didn’t get it.”

“Nothing veterinary related.” Kyle held up three large brown paper bags. “More like lunch.”

“Skylar’s already left. It’s her half day.” Buzz reminded him.

“For you.” Kyle sat on one of the lobby chairs. “Unless you’re busy?”

Buzz glanced back and forth between them. “I don’t know. Considering you’ve never brought me lunch in…ever, I can’t deny I’m a little freaked out.”

John chuckled. “I figured.” He shrugged. “This is all Skylar’s idea. And Lizzie. And Jan.”

“Not Nat?” Buzz asked, coming around the counter and sitting opposite them.

“Nah, my wife prefers to let things work out on their own.” John took a sip from his to-go cup. “Smart woman. One of the reasons I married her.”

“How about we get this out of the way and we can just eat?” Kyle asked, bracing his hands on his knees, and looking every bit as uncomfortable as Buzz was feeling.

“Fine by me.” John grabbed one of the sacks and started eating French fries. “I’m only here for the food.”

Kyle chuckled. “Lemme start off by saying Skylar loves you.” He paused. “Most of the time, anyway.” He took a sip of his drink. “You know Skylar was on her own when I met her?”

“Living in a hell of a place with a bastard of an uncle or cousin or something?” Buzz took the bag John offered him. “You might have mentioned it a time or two.”

Kyle nodded. “I think that’s why she feels she and Jenna are kindred spirits.”

Jenna? This was about Jenna. He hadn’t stopped thinking about her since he’d left her house this morning. “Jenna is—”

“The whole single-mom thing probably helps.”

Kyle hadn't heard him. "I know Jenna's not their mom but—"

"She might as well be." John pointed with a fry. "She's got four. Skylar only had three."

"Not sure how that helps." Kyle shot his brother a narrow-eyed look.

John held up his hands in surrender. "I'll be over here eating my food."

Buzz laughed. "I know where this is going but—"

"I tell Skylar pretty much everything so she might know about Britney." Kyle was a man on a mission, head down, words coming, not paying attention to a single thing Buzz was saying. "And I might have mentioned you've sworn off women with kids—no exceptions—"

"Mentioned once or twice," John murmured, wincing when Kyle punched him in the arm.

Buzz didn't laugh this time but he did smile. He knew what was coming.

"Maybe, if that's still the case, Jenna isn't a good idea. I get that the two of you have something going on but that doesn't mean you have to do anything about it. I mean, it's not just about you and her when there are kids involved."

"I know." Buzz nodded. "You think I don't know that?" He'd asked Britney to marry him. He'd wanted the whole package but she hadn't. She'd had a whole slew of reasons for leaving him but it'd been a kick to the gut when she said she couldn't stay with someone who loved her kids more than he loved her. At first, he'd denied it. But the sad thing was she'd been right. When she'd left, he'd missed Cameron and Lisa. Britney? Not near as much.

Jenna wasn't Britney. There was no comparing them—or the way he felt about either of them.

"I do." Kyle sat back. "And I know what happened with Britney was bad. I was there."

Buzz nodded again. Kyle had stood by him. When Buzz drank too much, Kyle drove him home. When Buzz threatened to go after her and her new boyfriend, Kyle was the one to talk him down. When Buzz couldn't get Cameron and Lisa out of his mind and he started picking fights, Kyle was the one to break things up before it got too serious—and tend to any wounds he might have.

"The other night, you were asking about giving things a second chance so I was hoping that meant, maybe, Jenna changed your mind?" Kyle shrugged.

"It's not that easy." Buzz propped his elbows on his knees and rested his head in his hands. "Even if I had changed my mind, Jenna might laugh in my face." Her face appeared, peering over her quilt—looking too frail for his liking. He hadn't wanted to leave… And it scared the shit out of him.

"Nobody said it was." John shook his head. "Dating. Commitment. Marriage."

"Love," Kyle cut in.

"That, too." John shrugged. "I didn't want it.

I fought it—Nat deserved better, we all know that. But she loved me, anyway. My daughter? Poor kid. But at least she's got Nat as her mom. And I've got them." He stopped eating and looked at Buzz. "What are you waiting for? Shit happens. We get hurt. People come in and out of our lives—sometimes expected, sometimes not. You can't live your life worrying about what might happen." John ate another fry. "I like her. Not that it makes a difference. But if you're wanting input or taking a vote or something. I say yes."

Kyle punched him again and they all laughed.

"Thanks for the vote." Buzz took a sip of his iced tea and glanced up to find both Mitchell brothers looking at him. "You've got more to say?"

"If we're putting it all out there…" Kyle took a deep breath. "You and I both know no two people are the same."

Buzz nodded.

"Truth." John pointed back and forth between him and Kyle. "And we're brothers."

Kyle rolled his eyes. "So why are you so hell bent on believing Jenna's going to leave you like Britney did? This might sound harsh but, it's an excuse—an easy way out for you."

Buzz sat back then, an edge to his laughter. "You're saying I'm a dumb-ass who's screwing things up."

"Basically, yeah." John shrugged. "But don't

worry. I was a much bigger dumb-ass and things turned out great for me."

"This was one hell of a pep-talk." Buzz dropped his fry back into the bag. "One I didn't need." He sat back and crossed his arms over his chest. "Now, can you shut up long enough for me to talk?"

Kyle and John exchanged a look, then nodded.

"I know Jenna's not Britney. There's no comparison. Not to mention I don't want to compare the two of them." He stood, running a hand along the back of his neck. "Jenna… Well, I knew she was trouble when I found her crawling around on the side of the road. I've tried to keep my distance because of that but that didn't last for long." He shook his head. "Every time I turn around, she's there. Or something that makes me think of her. And now she's sick… So, this morning, I took her a milkshake—since her throat is hurting her—and I didn't want to leave. I wanted to stay and…take care of her."

"I bet that scared the shit out of you." John chuckled.

"Damn straight," Buzz agreed.

"You care about her, Buzz. You care about the kids." Kyle shrugged. "I see no problems here."

He glanced at them. "We've sort of come to an… understanding."

The brothers exchanged another look.

"Like?" Kyle frowned.

"Like a no-strings, no-expectations sort of understanding." Buzz sighed. "Because I'm a bastard."

John started laughing.

"Huh." Kyle's brows rose high, almost into his hairline.

"She doesn't want a relationship." He cleared his throat. "She point-blank said so."

John was still laughing.

"Huh," Kyle said again.

"Neither one of you are helping." Buzz shook his head. "Not that I'm thinking there's much either one of you can do."

"Nope." John shook his head. "This is all you. Though I wouldn't mind being a fly on the wall when you do decide to try to change up this understanding of yours."

"If that's what you want?" Kyle asked. "'Cuz you still haven't said what, exactly, you want."

"I don't know." He sat again. "One minute, I'm thinking Jenna and I… It might work. The next, I'm thinking she'll decide to up and move someplace without snakes and poison oak and fire ants, and where does that leave me?"

"You know, there are veterinarian clinics in places outside of Granite Falls, Buzz." John reached for Buzz's bag. "You going to eat those fries?"

"Yes." Buzz grabbed the bag. "You're both missing the important part here."

"Which is?" John sat back, arms crossed over

his chest. "Besides the fact that your food's getting cold."

"She said she doesn't want a relationship." Buzz offered the bag to John, who snatched it. "I'm sitting here, listening to you two yahoos trying to convince me to try again with Jenna when she's already shut me down."

Both of them fell silent. John ate Buzz's French fries while Kyle looked thoughtful.

"Skylar would say you two need to sit down and talk." Kyle shrugged.

"Nat's all about talking stuff out." John shuddered. "Thankfully, we understand one another, so that doesn't have to happen too often."

Buzz glanced at his watch. "Yeah, well, as much as I appreciate this talk, I've got a conference call with the teaching hospital in Bryan–College Station I need to get set up for."

"Look at you, sounding all important on your conference call." John handed him back the bag and stood. "I didn't eat your burger."

Buzz peered into the bag. "But you did eat all the fries."

"Hey, I'm only human." John paused. "Good luck with the *talk*."

Kyle stood, too. "You good?"

Buzz shot him a look.

"Okay." Kyle sighed. "Guess we didn't help much."

"You brought me food." Buzz grinned. He waved

them off and carried his burger into his office. It'd been a while since he'd talked to his old classmate Benji Rashim, so he figured getting online early might be in order. Ben wasn't one to keep his stories short and he always had stories to tell. It'd be nice to spend a little time thinking about something other than Jenna, the kids…

He glanced at the wall, remembering he'd offered to pick up Garrett and Monica from school. He set an alarm on his clock. *If I pick them up and head straight to the Hill Country Farming Supplies, I can pick up the wood needed to replace the rotten boards along Jenna's back porch.* If he got that done, with Garrett's help, Shaggy might just be able to spend his first night with his new family.

Buzz headed into the back, opened Shaggy's kennel and the two of them headed into his office. Shaggy sat, his big brown eyes glued to the brown paper bag Buzz had placed on his desk.

"I'll share." He sat, pulling the burger out, unwrapping it and tearing it in two. "See."

He glanced at the clock again. Ten minutes before he needed to be online.

"Might as well call and make sure they have everything we need, don't you think?" Buzz asked, offering the dog a piece of the burger.

Shaggy took the burger, swallowing it in one bite.

"I'll take that as a yes." He put the rest of the burger on the floor, wiped his hands off with an antiseptic wipe and reached for his phone. “I might not know what to do to make things right between Jenna and me, but I can get you and Garrett squared away and happy easy enough.” And that, right now, seemed like a good place to start.

“How are you?” Cassie asked, carrying in a bowl of soup. “Jan made it, don’t worry.”

Jenna smiled. “I’m sure it’d be just as delicious if you’d made it.” She stretched. “Honestly, I’d really love to get out of bed.”

“I don’t blame you.” Cassie frowned. “I’d be all twitchy after being in bed this long, too. Also, I’m guessing that means you’re feel better?”

“Almost human. Antibiotics are a wonderful thing.” Jenna stood, running a hand over her hair. “If you can stand it, I’ll clean up after. I’m starving.”

“I think I can stand it. Let’s have your afternoon snack in the kitchen.” Cassie laughed. “Besides, those pj’s are super cute.”

“From Garrett for Christmas last year.” She smiled down at her periodic-table-print pajamas and followed Cassie down the stairs. “He’s all about the science.” As soon as she took in the state of her kitchen, she froze. “Holy moly. How long was I asleep?” Jenna prided herself on keeping a clean house but it looked especially spotless. “Did you do this?”

"Not guilty." Cassie shook her head. "My guess is Jan. I don't know where she gets all that energy."

Jenna nodded and sat, smiling her thanks as Cassie put the bowl on the table. "You've all been so amazing. I was so out of it, I don't even know who's done what or how I'd have managed the last eighteen or so hours without you."

"Consider it a perk of small-town living. We look out for each other." Cassie shrugged. "Between Jan and Skylar, plans were made and set in motion. Skylar dropped off all the kids this morning."

Jenna nodded, her first spoonful of Jan's chicken-and-dumpling soup all sorts of comforting.

"Buzz is picking up the big kids after school—he said he and Garrett were going to fix the fence and this would be Shaggy's first night here, in his new forever home. I can't help but think he's doing it more for Garrett than Shaggy, though." Cassie sat, glancing at Jenna. "He's really fond of Garrett." She paused, grinning. "I think Buzz sees a lot of himself in your brother. Not that Buzz was ever shy—he was the class clown, of course. But the studiousness and love of science and curiosity. That's Buzz all over. Still is, for the most part."

Jenna could easily imagine this younger version of Buzz. He'd have been the sort of student that made excellent grades but would be a handful in the classroom, all the same. She smiled, thinking about it. "I'm fairly certain Garrett has a full-blown case of hero worship for Buzz." Not that Jenna was complaining. He was a boy who didn't have a male role model in his life. If Buzz was willing to step in and be that person now and then, Jenna wouldn't stop him. Of course, if he wanted to do so more than now and then, she'd be fine with that, too. She swallowed, the yearning ache that stirred whenever she thought of Buzz too long filling her chest.

"I won't tell Buzz. He already has a pretty high opinion of himself. Let's not add to it." Cassie stood, pulling two glasses from the kitchen counter.

Jenna laughed. "Deal."

Cassie put the glasses on the counter and pulled out a pitcher of iced tea.

Iced tea? She didn't know how to make iced tea. More of Jan's magic?

"Too bad Buzz has vowed never to get involved with another woman with kids—I think you two would suit pretty well." Cassie shook her head, her sigh long-suffering. "I'd like to think he'd change his mind but it's been a long time and he's showing no signs of budging on this. As his sister, I think I'm qualified to say he's too pigheaded for his own good."

Jenna managed to swallow without choking. Words like *vow* and *never* and *again* echoing in her mind. At first, she couldn't get beyond what Cassie had said—how she'd thrown it out there like it wasn't a big deal.

But...it was.

At the same time, why was she surprised? She'd seen his initial reaction when he'd learned she and the kids were a package deal. He'd been shocked and panicked. But then he'd seemed to calm down. He'd even seemed to take an interest in the kids. And recently she'd thought…she'd hoped…

What? What had she hoped for? *What did I think would happen?* Their agreement—an agreement she'd prompted and spelled out—was no strings or expectations. At the time, it had seemed like a good idea but then… *No. Just because I've gone and fallen in love with him doesn't change a thing.* For the most part, anyway. She still didn't have time for a relationship. She still felt like she was spread too thin. She didn't want a relationship… Wrong. She *hadn't.* Now? A relationship with Buzz was exactly what she *did* want.

"Jenna?"

Jenna turned, Cassie's question pulling her from her thoughts. "I'm sorry, Cassie. What was that?"

"You okay?" Cassie asked, sliding a glass of iced tea onto the table. "You look a little…" She shrugged.

"I guess I'm still a little foggy." She sipped her tea. Now was not the time to get sucked into a what-if vortex of despair. If anything, she should be relieved. Thanks to Cassie, she could accept that her newfound affection for the man was a dead end and attempt to redirect her focus elsewhere. Right. So. Focus. "What were you saying?"

"I was just saying I noticed you need a new bathroom handle upstairs." Cassie was watching her closely.

"I do." She nodded, shoving aside any and all memories of that night. "It's on my list." She nodded at the magnetic backed tablet she had affixed to the side of the refrigerator.

Cassie peered at it. "Land sakes, that looks like some list."

"It is," Jenna agreed. "It would have been lovely to find someplace a little more turnkey but there wasn't time and Lizzie was so wonderful to find a place big enough for us. Of course, she was just as wonderful when we were in high school together, years ago. She went off to art school and I pursued my teaching degree but we kept up when we could. She's one of those people you can go years without seeing but you'll pick up right where you left off, you know?"

"Lizzie is pretty wonderful." Cassie grinned. "I like her. And Skylar. In a way, they don't feel like they're newcomers to Granite Falls. But a lot of that is thanks to Jan, I think. If she takes you under her wing, you're a Mitchell—and part of the Granite Falls family." She patted her hand. "That applies to you and your siblings, too."

"I don't know how we would have managed without you all…" Jenna's throat felt tight, emotion welling up. *Emotion I do not have the energy for right now.* "I think I'd better drag myself back upstairs and take that shower before I run out of steam."

"Good idea." Cassie nodded. "You shouldn't push too hard, too fast. Jan said your fever was pretty high."

It was after she'd gone back to her room, taken her clean clothes into her bathroom, and closed the door behind her that she considered allowing herself a little cry. *Just a little one.* Honestly, she'd earned it. In all the time since her mother's death, she'd kept her chin up and been strong. She'd had to. She couldn't even cry herself to sleep for fear Frannie would slip into bed with her, or Garrett would drag his blanket into her room and camp out on the floor next to her… It happened—often. But now she was alone and tired and Cassie's hope-crushing announcement had been the final domino in a long feelings-to-be-avoided chain of dominoes.

A little cry.

But the tears wouldn't come. The sting was there, hot and frustrating, until she was sure the tears would come. Not a single tear.

Instead, she scrubbed herself clean, dressed in some cotton pajama pants covered in beakers and theorems and an oversize T-shirt that said Science—Like Magic, But Real, and picked up a book on how to create a more engaging and accessible classroom.

She flopped into the large overstuffed chair she'd placed in front of the window and sat, hoping some inspirational reading would perk her up. After reading the same sentence a handful of times, she closed the book, rested her head along the back of the chair and willed herself to think happy thoughts.

Downstairs, the door opened.

"Hey, sis." Buzz's voice rolled up the stairs. "Got Garrett and Monica. Garrett and I are going to get started on the fence."

"Sounds good," Cassie answered. "Monica, you can help me figure out dinner?"

The conversation grew more muffled and the front door closed.

Jenna relaxed against the chair, contemplating her options. If she went downstairs, she'd have to keep up a conversation and she wasn't up to it. She was feeling better, loads, but she was tired and bruised feeling—like all the unshed tears had gathered right beneath the surface and could break through at any moment for a potential tear monsoon.

Or stay here and keep an eye on things. From her comfy chair, she could ensure Garrett didn't maim himself, Shaggy or Buzz without having to interact with… *Buzz*. No sooner had she thought his name than he appeared. Garrett, three dogs and Buzz all came through the backyard's side gate. Three dogs? She recognized the two from the first day she'd met Buzz. From the looks of it, the three dogs weren't strangers. They ran all over, Garrett following, tails wagging, pouncing and all-around general merriment.

She was still smiling when her attention wandered to Buzz, a stack of replacement privacy fence pickets balanced on his shoulder.

His broad shoulder.

Held in place by his well-muscled arm.

An arm encased in a skintight gray T-shirt.

Her gaze wandered—revealing that the shirt wasn't just tight on his arm but his back, too. From the looks of it, Buzz's back was just as impressively sculpted as his arm. All those muscles were… She swallowed, zeroing in on the man in her yard.

He was the most manly man she'd ever seen. In real life, anyway. It wasn't just the ridiculous physique or timber of his voice, it was the confidence he radiated. The fact that she had no control over the visceral response her body had to him was something she still hadn't come to terms with. It—he—was an anomaly.

When Cassie had shared Buzz's vow, she'd said *again*. *Again*, meaning Buzz had been involved with a woman with children. Whatever happened had to have been pretty horrible for Buzz to make such a promise to himself.

Oh, stop. Now that she knew where he stood on the relationship thing and she'd had time to stop and clear her head and he wasn't standing five feet from her too tempting to deny, she realized she couldn't go through with this agreement of hers. If she did, it would take that much longer to get over him.

She shook her head. After the fence-building and dinner thing, she'd talk to him. Get it out in the air and over with.

Buzz was laughing at something Garrett had said, one hand on his hip, the other tipping his straw cowboy hat back enough so that Jenna could see his face. And, oh, what a face. *Right. Enough. No more looking.*

Dog or no dog, it would be nice to have a usable space where Frannie and Biddy could play. Assuming there were no fire ants or poison oak or snakes or scorpions or… She was out of her chair and down the stairs before she'd thought things through. She hurried down the hallway.

"Hey, Jenna." Monica was in the kitchen, her backpack on the kitchen table. "You're up. How are you feeling?"

"Oh, those pajamas are just as cute as the last ones." Cassie smiled.

"Almost human." She smiled, holding up her finger as she crossed to the back door. "Give me a sec and I'll come back and you can tell me all about your day?"

"Sure." Monica nodded, her brow furrowed.

Jenna opened the back door and stood, barefoot and with wet shower hair, on the wooden porch.

"Hi," she called out, shielding her eyes from the sun. "You two look like you're about to get things done."

"That's the plan." Buzz was smiling at her, the sort of smile that had his charm-o-meter off the charts. "You look…good." He chuckled. "Nice pants."

Nice shirt. She swallowed. "I'm sick. I'm allowed to wear pj's." She waved him over. "Can I talk to you for a minute?"

"Yep." He laid the board he'd had propped up onto its side and walked her way, those blue eyes of his locked on her. "It's nice to see you—up and around and not peeking over your blanket at me."

She smiled. "Yes, well… I don't know if I said thank you for the milkshake?" She shrugged. "But thank you." She stepped a little closer, lowering her voice. "Is there anything I need to worry about? Is it safe? Nothing rotten or poisonous or…*dangerous*?"

"We're not talking about the milkshake anymore, are we?" He grinned.

"No." She was capable of putting together a perfect sentence. She knew it. He knew it. But… *Stop smiling like that so I'm not babbling.* "I'm talking about the fence and the yard." She pointed at the large lot. "Out here. Is it dangerous?"

His gaze wandered. "Nice shirt."

"Buzz." She sighed. "I'm talking about bobcats and coyotes and fire ants and scorpions and poison oak—"

"Don't forget cactus and ticks, armadillos and skunks, brown recluse spiders and chiggers, too."

She blinked, frozen in place. "Are you trying to get me to pack up and go pack to Kansas?" She was only partly joking.

He frowned, taking the steps two at a time until they were face-to-face. "Hell, no." His voice was pitched low and earnest. "I'm sorry. I was teasing—"

His response rattled her all the more. She hugged herself, wishing he'd step back—or wrap her up in those strong arms and pull her close. *No.* She stepped back, tearing her gaze from him to watch Garrett and the dogs running around the yard.

He stepped forward. "I get that you're worried but you know as well as I do that it's a fence not a forcefield." He sighed, shoving his hands into his pockets. "There are some tricks to keeping most things out and away I can help out with—"

"I don't want to keep relying on you, Buzz." She took a deep breath. *I can't.* The kids were doing well. She didn't want to confuse them with another man they thought they could rely on leaving them. It had taken her weeks to convince them her and Hugh's breakup wasn't their fault. If it happened again, it would be harder for them—she knew it.

He studied her for a long time.

"What?" she asked, pretending like the intensity

in those blue eyes hadn't flipped her upside down and her heart into overdrive.

"You look sad. A little riled up." He frowned. "Like something's wrong." The concern in his voice rolled over her.

Dammit, no. Hold it together. But that look, that voice had the first domino in her emotional domino chair teetering. She swallowed. *No. Oh, no.* She was not going to erupt into her tear monsoon right here. "Fine." But it came out garbled so she cleared her throat. "I'm fine."

He reached up, pressed the back of his hand to her forehead and frowned again. "You sure?"

She nodded. "I need reassurances about…this." She pointed into the yard. "Right now, I need a sense of control over things—even if I don't have any. And this stupid fence is impacting my emotional state far more than I'd like." The fence was a grasp at just that—surrounding herself and her brother and sisters with the illusion of safety and control. *Control—the one thing I don't seem to have when you're around.*

"I'll make it as solid as I can." He nodded. "And we will get the bugs and everything else figured out, too, I promise."

She didn't miss that he said *we*. Or that hearing him say *we* had her heart painfully twisting inside her chest.

"Jenna?" Cassie called from the kitchen. "Is

pizza okay for dinner? I volunteered to cook and I don't cook so—"

"Pizza would be amazing." Monica's voice spilled out onto the back porch. "We haven't had pizza in forever. Since before we moved here so, yeah, like forever."

"Pizza is good," Jenna croaked.

"She said yes," Buzz answered for her before he took a deep sigh and said, "You know you can cut through the bullshit and say whatever it is that's troubling you. Whatever it is has you down here versus resting in your bed."

"Maybe I don't want to tell you. Maybe..." Why would she share anything with him? They were friends, sort of, but not the kind that would pour their hearts out to one another, that's for sure. "I can't." She shook her head, angry at him, this situation and her fool heart for loving him. If they'd had a little more privacy, now would be the perfect time to tell him she was calling off their agreement.

But Garrett was close and anyone could come walking out of the kitchen. "Ever think that *you're* what's troubling me, Buzz Lafferty?" She spun on her foot, pleaded a headache and headed straight for her room—where she stayed until Buzz and his smile and his charm had left. Unfortunately, the ache in her heart didn't leave with him.

Chapter Eleven

Buzz had done his best to be his normal self all afternoon. Lucky for him, Garrett and Shaggy were too excited to pick up on his moodiness. But, dammit all, he couldn't figure out what Jenna meant. Only one thing was certain—she'd spit it out like it left a bad taste in her mouth, so he was pretty sure it wasn't good.

Ever think that you're what's troubling me?

What had he done? As far as he was concerned, he'd done everything she asked. She wanted him to back off—he had. Garrett had wanted to stay at the clinic—he'd brought him to Jenna's class later. She changed her mind and wanted a casual arrangement—he agreed. She'd wanted a milkshake—he got her one. Her brother and sister needed picking up—he'd been ready and waiting. Her fence needed fixing—he was fixing it.

After he was done scrolling through everything he'd done or said, something else had become certain. He could no longer say a word about Kyle doing things for Skylar. All this time, he'd been teasing his best friend, saying he was beaten. That wasn't the truth of it. Kyle did it because he wanted to make Skylar happy. The same reason Buzz had done everything he had.

Plus, the kids were pretty damn adorable. Even though every damn thing about the situation with Britney and her kids and Jenna and her kids was different, they had that one thing in common. He loved the kids.

"I think we did a great job." Garrett stood back, the hammer in his hand, admiring his handiwork.

"It couldn't get any straighter, that's for sure." Buzz nodded, tilting his hat forward. "I don't know, Garrett, if you decide veterinary medicine isn't your thing, you could also go into engineering. You've got quite an attention to detail." He stood, hand on Garrett's shoulder, to survey their work. "I'm pretty sure the fence guy Bobby told me about couldn't have done it any better."

Garrett smiled up at him, the tip of his nose and his cheeks red.

"You know, Garrett, we need to get you a cap or a cowboy hat so you don't burn your face. The Texas sun is nothing to play around with." Buzz was pretty sure he had an old one he could pass along to the boy for times like this.

Garrett nodded, glancing from the fence to Shaggy, Roscoe and Scooter—sleeping in the sun—to the fence again. "You sure Shaggy can't get out."

"I'm sure." Buzz gave the boy's shoulder a light squeeze. Even if Shaggy did manage to dig his way out, Buzz didn't get the feeling Shaggy would wander all that far. The dog was smitten with Garrett. As soon as he heard the little boy's voice, Shaggy's tail was wagging and he was up and waiting for Garrett to get to him.

"I hope not. I know he's only been my dog for an hour but...he's my dog, you know?" Garrett glanced up at him, all serious and one hell of a cute kid.

"I do." Buzz nodded. And it was plain to see that Shaggy knew Garrett was his. *As it should be.*

"Looks good," Jan Mitchell called from the back porch. "You two must have worked up quite an appetite." She carried a tray with two tall glasses of lemonade out to them.

"Thank you." Garrett took the glass. "Do you think it's straight enough, Miss Mitchell?"

"I should say so." She nodded. "I saw you with that level, Garrett. I've always appreciated someone who rechecks their work before they hammer in that first nail. That way you don't have to go back and fix it all over again."

Garrett stood a little taller from the woman's praise.

"You two have done some good work. Come on in and wash up. I'm sure Cassie will have something whipped up for dinner shortly." Jan took their glasses and carried the tray back inside.

"Are you staying for dinner, Buzz?" Garrett asked, walking at his side.

Good question. Initially, he'd been planning on it. But that had been before Jenna got sick and the two of them were planning on enjoying some time together after the kids had gone to bed. Clearly, that wasn't happening now. If he stayed, there was the chance they'd talk but she was still recuperating so it was probably best for her if he didn't. "Probably not."

"Oh." Garrett drooped.

Buzz grinned, clapping Garrett on the back and holding the back door wide. "There will be other times." Maybe. Hopefully.

A quick sweep of the kitchen and there was no sign of Jenna.

"She's not feeling well," Monica offered before he could ask.

Buzz nodded. So much for being discreet.

"She's really hiding from you." Monica sighed

and shook her head. "Why do grown-ups make everything so hard?"

Buzz wasn't going to argue. Thirteen or not, Monica had a point.

"I mean, it's not that hard. Can't you just say, 'Hey, Jenna, I like you.' And Jenna won't say anything because Hugh made her think that no guy would want to marry her because of us so, yeah..." Monica stopped talking and blinked. "You did know about Hugh, though, right? I mean, I didn't totally just dump Jenna's stuff out there. I did, didn't I? Oh, no, I can't believe I just did that."

Buzz wasn't exactly sure who Hugh was but he was certain he didn't like the man.

"Why would they have talked about Hugh?" Garrett was glaring up at her. "Why do you have to keep making this weird? What's wrong with you? They can just be friends. *You* should stop trying to fix up Jenna. She's happy with us. And we're happy with her and that's enough." Garrett stomped out of the kitchen, up the stairs and slammed the door right about the time Skylar came into the kitchen with Biddy and Frannie.

"Everything okay?" Skylar asked, glancing between them all.

"I messed up." Monica sniffed. "Again. It's my fault." She tried to smile. "I can't help it, okay? I guess I worry. A lot, okay? Like, all the time. And it's stupid, I get it, but my mom was fine until Dad died. She was like, totally happy. Always. Then he died and she was always *unhappy* and…and she died." She blinked rapidly, the end of her nose going red. "I mean, I know it's stupid, I do, but… I just want Jenna to be happy. Like *really* happy. And, even though I didn't like him, she did seem happy with Hugh until we came into the picture." She shook her head. "You're a boy, Buzz. Is Garrett right? Is there something wrong with me?"

He shook his head, his throat too tight to speak. After everything she'd just shared, he was hurting for the girl.

Frannie let go of Skylar's hand and hugged her sister. "You awe pewfect, Monica. I love you all the way to the moon—"

"And back," Monica said, scooping up her sister and holding her close. "And I love you, Frannie-Banannny."

"Don't cwy." Frannie's lower lip flipped out. "Please don't cwy, Monica."

Buzz wanted to say the same thing. He'd no doubt they'd cried enough. Losing their father and their mother… He couldn't begin to imagine the grief they'd endured. Feeling hurt and loss was normal, but that didn't make it easy for him to stand there doing nothing. They were hurting, here and now. Awkward or not, he was going to offer them comfort.

"Frannie's right." Buzz rested his hand on Monica's shoulder and gave Frannie a wink. "There's no reason to cry. There's not a thing wrong with you, Monica. You're trying to take care of your sister. I know that can be challenging." He grinned, giving Monica's shoulder a light squeeze.

"Hey, I heard that," Cassie called back, but she was smiling.

"I know." Buzz was relieved to see Monica smiling now. "I think, in his own way, Garrett's trying to do the same." He cleared his throat, knowing full well all three women in the room were watching and listening. "I'll tell you something important, something I know for a fact. Jenna is happy. When the right fella comes along, he'll fit in and add to that happiness. But, until then, you don't want her wasting time on someone like…"

"Hugh." Frannie made a monster face. "Garrett calls him Hugh the poo," she whispered, giggling. "Hugh the poo."

Buzz had to laugh—partly from the insult and partly from Frannie's contagious giggle. "Oh, really?"

Monica nodded. "It's probably the worst thing Garrett's ever called anyone. *Ever*. But he did dump Jenna. Who does that? She's…awesome." She rolled her eyed. "He is *totally* poo."

Buzz couldn't have said it better himself. Not that he'd have used *poo*, but close enough. "And you don't want any more of those for Jenna. Might be part of the reason she doesn't want to be fixed up?" Buzz shrugged.

"I guess that makes sense." But Monica didn't look fully convinced yet.

"Your heart is in the right place." Cassie slid her arm around Monica. "I can't tell you how many times I've tried to fix up my brother—Buzz here—with someone." She sighed. "It's never worked."

Skylar laughed.

"These things just…happen." Jan Mitchell sounded off. "Though I can see why you'd think Buzz and your sister would get on, Monica. They have a whole lot in common, it seems. I'd say it's a smart match."

"Right?" Monica nodded. "That's what I thought. They both like animals and kids and science and all that. And Jenna said—" She stopped. "Whoa, I can't believe I almost said that. If I finished that sentence, she'd be so mad at me."

Frannie covered Monica's mouth. "Don't say it, Monica."

Everyone laughed—except Buzz. He knew what Jenna had said. He was hot. Not that she liked him or wanted to get to know him, just that he was hot. It used to be enough. But now he wanted her to think he was hot, plus care about him. No, more than that. He wanted her to be as in love with him as he was with her.

"Let's get you changed, shall we?" Skylar said

to Biddy. "Then we can come down and help out with dinner."

"Pizza." Monica was delighted. "Cassie's treat."

"What?" Cassie shrugged as both women turned her way. "You know I don't cook, and they were so excited."

Skylar grinned. "I'll be back in a minute."

Monica and Frannie were calm now but he couldn't bring himself to leave until he knew Garrett was okay, too. "I'll go up with you and check on Garrett." He called Shaggy inside to follow him and headed for the stairs.

Skylar didn't say a thing all the way up the stairs, but when they reached the landing, she faced him.

He could tell she was about to say something from the way she was looking at him. "What?"

Skylar bounced Biddy on her hip. "You know what I think?"

"That's a rhetorical question, right? It's not like I can say no and walk away." He and Shaggy waited.

"I guess you could but that would be rude." Skylar sighed. "I think Jan's right. And Monica, too. You have a chance at real happiness here, Buzz Lafferty. If you play your cards right. In time, of course."

"Yeah, yeah. I'm glad you've all got my personal life sorted for me." He rolled his eyes, ignoring her laughter, and walked down the hall to the door covered with stickers. From alien movies to solar system stickers to silly science phrases to a sign that read Scientist At Work, there was no mistaking whose room this was. He knocked. "Garrett?"

He opened his door, red-faced and his hair on end. "You can come in." He instantly perked up at the sight of Shaggy. "Hey, Shaggy. Come in, boy." Shaggy trotted in and instantly leaped up onto Garrett's bed. "Good boy."

Buzz did a slow turn to take in the boy's room. "That's quite a few models. All spacecrafts? Is that Apollo 13?" He saw the boy nod. "You thinking about becoming an astronaut?"

"My dad and I made them together." Garrett shrugged. "I used to. I don't know. I'm still considering my options."

"Good idea." Buzz chuckled. "I wanted to make sure you were okay."

Garrett sat on his bed, looking up at him. "You have a sister. Are they always like that? Make you mad like that?"

"Oh, Cassie and I don't always see eye to eye, that's for sure." Buzz sat in the desk chair, rested his elbows on his knees and sighed. "I do think Monica and Cassie are a lot alike. They have big loving hearts but sometimes they do or say things on impulse. Never out of meanness, normally it's 'cuz they're trying to help." Buzz shrugged. "I'm pretty sure Monica's trying to do something to make her worry less about Jenna."

"I'm worried, too." Garrett's voice shook. "She's sick." He blinked. "She never gets sick." He cleared his throat. "And she's sad. She hides it but she is. Mom died and Jenna's boyfriend dumps her because of us. She has to be sad, doesn't she?"

What? Buzz knew he was entering dangerous territory here. "She and Hugh broke up after your mom died?"

Garrett nodded. "He said he wasn't ready for kids and if he was ever going to have them, he wanted them to be *his* kids." He shrugged, looking uncomfortable. "Monica and I…sort of listened through the door."

He'd been having a hard time picturing Jenna sharing her private and adult conversation with them so this made sense. "I can't tell you how many times I did that to Cassie." Buzz admitted, laughing.

Garrett relaxed then, grinning. "Yeah, Monica said we needed to know so we could help since Jenna's trying to do everything on her own." He scratched Shaggy's stomach. "Jenna said it was okay and that they were still friends but he doesn't call and he never came by to see her again." Garrett looked at him, frowning. "They used to talk about their life *after* they got married a lot. He had a plan—for his whole life. He talked about it a lot. He said he was a planner. Monica said he was a stick in the mud."

Buzz tried to cover his laugh with a cough.

"Sounds like it might be a good thing it didn't work out?"

Garrett shrugged. "Sometimes I wonder if we'd liked him and been nicer to him, maybe he wouldn't have minded us? Maybe he and Jenna would be together and happy now?"

"I tell you, Garrett, you've got a good head on your shoulders. If he couldn't see that, he's not worth your or Jenna's time." Buzz hoped like hell he was saying the right thing.

Garrett paused mid-tummy rub. "Do you think… Do you think you could ever like Jenna that way? Like Hugh?"

Buzz nodded.

Garrett nodded.

"You'd be okay with that?" Buzz wasn't sure why he was asking, but it was important to him. If Garrett told him no, then Buzz would respect that. Of course, he was hoping pretty damn hard Garrett wouldn't say *no.*

Garrett looked at him for a long time. "I think so. As long as you didn't leave." He squared his shoulders. "She deserves better. I might be little but I won't let anyone hurt her, you know?"

"I do." Buzz fought the urge to hug the boy tight. He was eight, and small for his age, but he was letting Buzz know he'd defend his sister if it came to that. He was quite a little man. "I feel the same about, Cassie. I've chased one or two bad apples off, let me tell you."

"I might have to ask you for advice. I think Monica might have a bad apple or two that needs chasing off." Garrett sighed his world-weary sigh.

"Happy to help." Buzz stood, damn near choked up over the look on Garrett's face. The boy looked at him like he was something special. Like he was important to Garrett. It filled his heart and scared him to his core all at once. "I should head out."

"I said I'd feed you dinner." Jenna stood in the door, with her hair in a ponytail, wearing a shirt and leggings. "Just like you, I honor my promises."

He had no idea how long she'd been there or what she'd overheard. Had she heard the part where he'd said he could be interested in her? Did she care? Her near blank face didn't tip him off one way or the other. But she was asking and after all the back and forth tonight, he had questions and he might as well stick around to get some answers. "In that case, I accept."

Jenna had taken one look at Buzz and Garrett and known she wouldn't make it through dinner without making a fool of herself. Walking into Garrett's room to find her little brother and Buzz in hushed conversation had Jenna's insides melting. It wasn't that Garrett didn't talk to her; he didn't really talk to anyone. He was on the shy side. Reserved. Cautious. But, from the looks of it, he and Buzz had been having a pretty intense conversation.

Jenna hadn't given herself a second to consider this could be a glimpse into her future—no matter how tempting the idea was. Buzz didn't want a woman with kids. She had kids. He was being awful sweet to Garrett now but Buzz would find someone, settle down and have a family of his own. Once that happened, the likelihood of him still having the time or inclination for her brother was slim.

She knew that but it didn't stop her heart from wishing things were different.

It was her heart that had her hide in her room through dinner—only emerging when Buzz's voice was no longer audible and the house was mostly quiet. Monica and Jan were washing dishes, talking and laughing, without a care in the world.

"Can I do anything?" she asked.

"I thought you were sleeping." Jan turned, wiping her hands on a dish towel.

"I was," she lied. "But I felt bad for not checking on things so—"

"Everything's cool, Jenna." Monica nodded. "Skylar put the girls to bed and Garrett pretty much wore Shaggy out playing in the backyard so he went to bed, too."

"This one here stayed to help me clean up." Jan gave Jenna a once-over. "You're looking a little less pale. But you shouldn't push it. My boys are going to take your brother and sisters on a trail ride tomorrow—to get them out of your hair so you can have a little more time to yourself."

"Oh, Jan, I couldn't." Jenna shook her head. "You've done too much as it is. I shouldn't be contagious anymore—I'm probably not now—we'll be fine."

"I'm sure you would be." Jan nodded. "But the kids would be disappointed. Skylar got them all excited over riding the trails and seeing the ranch." She crossed the room and pressed her hand to Jenna's head.

Monica was nodding. "It does sound like fun."

Jan was studying her. "You're still a little warm, Jenna. Why don't you sit and let me warm up some soup?" Jan pointed at one of the kitchen chairs. "I won't push, but think about it. I'm thinking you could use another day of rest."

Monica was making her pleading face, hands pressed together and overexaggerated frown.

"Okay, fine." Jenna sighed.

Monica clapped her hands. "Yay."

Monica chattered away while Jenna had her dinner. Cheerleading tryouts, learning how to play cornhole, and some boy named Greg were all covered thoroughly. Monica wasn't sure she wanted to try out but didn't see why not. Cornhole was a beanbag toss game and she didn't understand why it was called cornhole. And Greg was some cute guy in her history class. *I wonder what happened to Alonzo. At least she wouldn't have to worry about more setups with Alonzo's dad.*

Jan finished disinfecting every inch of the kitchen, waited for Jenna to finish her soup, then cleaned up after Jenna, too. "I guess that's it. I'll see you in the morning." She gave Monica a hug.

"Night." Monica blew Jenna a kiss and ran up the stairs, her door closing quietly.

"She's a good girl." Jan smiled. "You've got yourself quite a troop, haven't you?"

Jenna nodded. "I'm lucky and I know it. Being a teacher, I know not all kids are as well-mannered and considerate as they are."

"That's the sad truth." Jen sighed. "Now, Jenna, you're still running a fever. I know you don't want to worry your siblings but you need to try to get some sleep, you hear me? You can't take care of anyone if you're not well."

Jenna nodded, the sting of tears back and in full force. It wasn't just that Jan was right; it was that she sounded so much like Jenna's mom.

"You okay? Did I say something?" Jan's forehead creased.

"No." Jenna shook her head. "It's just... That was such a mom thing to say." She swallowed. "Sometimes I miss her, you know?"

Jan nodded. "I do, honey. I do." She squeezed

Jenna's shoulder. "Don't make me use my mom voice again, now. You go on up to bed and sleep."

Jenna went up to bed, but she didn't sleep. She tossed and turned and stared up at the ceiling but her mind wouldn't shut off. Next week's lesson plans. Buzz laughing. Frannie on a horse. Buzz and his crooked grin. Taking the minivan in for a tune-up. Buzz's eyes right before he'd kissed her. If she was going to tell Buzz their deal was off, she needed to stop letting her imagination get the best of her.

She was dozing off right about the time sunlight was spilling in under her curtains. Skylar and Kyle peeked in on her, told her to go back to sleep, but every noise was amplified. From Biddy's happy squeals to Frannie telling Kyle she could tie her shoes to the thunder of footsteps down the stairs and the gentle click of the front door closing. Jenna heard it all.

She was sitting on the edge of her bed, contemplating coffee, when she heard the front door open. A few minutes passed and she heard the thump and creak of footsteps on the stairs. She was torn between calling out and hiding under her bed.

Considering the crime rate in Granite Falls was almost nonexistent and she'd had an endless stream of people coming in and out of her house for the last two days, it didn't make sense for her to be worried. But she was. Jan, Skylar and Cassie all announced their arrival. This person, whoever it was, hadn't made a peep.

She stood, her gaze sweeping the room for any useful item to help defend herself—if necessary. The only thing close was her hairbrush. She grabbed it and waited, her heart hammering. When the handle on her door turned and the door slowly opened, she panicked and lobbed the brush with all her might.

"Ow, damn, ow." Buzz stumbled into the room, his hand pressed to his temple. "What the hell?"

"Buzz. Oh, I'm so sorry." She ran forward, her heart in her throat. She'd played softball in high school and her throwing arm packed a punch. "Are you bleeding? Did I hurt you?"

"Well, it didn't feel good." He took his hand away. "That's some throwing arm you've got there."

"How many fingers am I holding up?" she asked, holding up her hand.

"I don't have a concussion, Jenna." He chuckled. "What did I do to earn that?"

"I didn't know who was coming up the stairs." Jenna shook her head. "I heard the door open and no one said anything." She frowned at him. "I'm not used to people just walking into my house—not without any advance notice that they're coming. A normal person would have called out or said something—"

"A normal person might have worried he was

waking up the patient and didn't want to do that."

Buzz stared down at her. "From the looks of it, that's what happened." He swallowed, the muscle of his jaw clenching tight.

"I wasn't sleeping." She crossed her arms over her chest.

Buzz's nostrils flared just a bit.

"I'm sorry. I'm sorry I hit you in the head with my hairbrush." She frowned. "Don't be mad, please. It was an accident."

"It's not my head," he bit out, staring up at the ceiling. "How about you go get back into bed."

She paused. What was wrong? She'd never thought of her long-sleeved floor-length white cotton nightgown as attractive, but it wasn't that hideous. Okay, Monica did call it her granny gown but she was thirteen, what did she know about comfy nighties? "What?" She glanced down and froze. "Oh."

It wasn't her nightgown so much as the direct stream of sunlight where she was standing and the sheerness of her gown. Crossing her arms had only pressed her breasts up for his inspection. That's why he was staring at the ceiling with his jaw clenched tight.

She ran to her bed. "Clear."

He grinned, shaking his head. "You sure? That's the sort of thing that can give a man a heart attack."

"What does that mean?" She sat up. "Should I be offended?"

Buzz was looking at her then and the fire in his gaze left no room for misinterpretation.

"Oh." She couldn't breathe but that didn't stop her from smiling.

"Oh, is right." His voice was gruff enough to send a shudder running down her spine. "I figured you might want this?" He offered her an extra-large to-go cup.

"A milkshake?" She couldn't stop smiling. "That's why you're here."

"One of the reasons. I'll be honest and say I might have reconsidered my decision had I known about the brush." He sat in the chair at her bedside. "Where is everyone? It's oddly quiet."

"Jan arranged a trail ride for them. She said I needed more rest." She shrugged. "I was still running a fever last night."

"And here I thought you were just avoiding me." His brows rose.

"Why on earth would I be avoiding you?" She tried to sound amused but it was more pinched than anything. She took a long sip of her milkshake.

"That's the other reason I'm here. To find out." He nodded at the milkshake. "And to bring you that."

She shrugged, continuing to swallow down large amounts of the ice-cold drink.

"You keep that up and you'll get a headache." His blue eyes traveled over her face. "If you're trying to stall in the hopes that I'm leaving, you're out of luck."

She stopped drinking, cradling the cup in both hands. "Okay." She cleared her throat. Now was as good a time as any. "I want to back out of our agreement."

There was silence.

"I… I think it'd be best if you didn't spend as much time around here, too." She glanced his way, wishing she could read his thoughts.

"The fence is done." He nodded, his tone sharp.

She was so stunned all she could do was stare.

"I'm sorry." He ran a hand over his face. "That was mean."

"It was," she whispered.

He stood, pacing. "You don't want me anymore, fine, but why cut me out of your life. Garrett and I get on—"

"I know. That's what worries me." She pushed back her blankets.

"That I'm friends with your little brother?" He frowned. "That's a bad thing?"

"I don't want him to rely on you." She shrugged.

"Why?" His frown grew. "What did I do to make you think I'm unreliable? I don't understand any of this, Jenna."

"I have my reasons." *I love you and you being here makes me want all the things I can't have.*

"Reasons you're not going to share with me?" He was angry now. "He's a good boy."

"I know that." She stood, angry at the accusation on his face. "I know he's this wonderful sweet boy with a huge heart and big emotions he tries to hide. But he's lost so much—"

"You all have." His scowl deepened. "You're already counting on me leaving?" He stared down at her, his gaze sweeping over her face. "I'm not Hugh, Jenna. I make a commitment. I stand by it. Call me old-fashioned, but keeping my word matters. It's who I am."

How did he know about Hugh? And why? It's not like this was the sort of thing that came up in casual conversation. "Who told you about him?"

"Does it matter?"

"Yes, it matters." She shook her head. "Of course, it does. It had to be Monica or Garrett and if they're still talking about it..." She pressed her eyes closed, pressure—like a rock—landed square in the middle of her chest. "They don't blame themselves? Do they? I told them it wasn't their fault but they can't understand. To them, love makes everything better. So, when the person who is supposed to love you best doesn't love you enough to stay when you need them most, it doesn't make sense."

"It doesn't make sense. And if you'll excuse my

language, he sounds like a rat bastard to me." His tone was soothing. "They love you so much, Jenna. They worry about you being happy."

She nodded, but refused to open her eyes. "They worry too much for their age." Dammit, the stinging was back, the horrible weight behind her eyes—all the tears rising to spill out. "Buzz..." She took a deep breath. "I need you to leave." *I will not cry in front of you.*

"Why?" His hands landed on her shoulders. "Why are you so bound and determined to keep me out? Open your eyes, Jenna."

She shook her head. "No." She squeezed her eyes shut. "I won't. Now go." Her voice broke. "Please, Buzz, please."

His hands lifted and she was pulled into his arms.

He felt so good that a strangled little moan slipped from her lips. "I don't want to cry," she whispered, terrified of what was about to happen.

"I don't want you to cry." He was gruff again, hoarse. "But let it out. I've got you."

She didn't know when the tears had started, but her cheeks were already wet. The force of her sorrow tore away all the control and restraints she'd put in place to shelter her siblings. They needed her strength so that's what she gave them. Her body was wracked with sobs, so hard she held on to Buzz like the anchor he was. She needed this; she needed him. And, for now, she'd give in.

Chapter Twelve

At some point, she'd dozed off against him. He'd carried her to the big overstuffed chair in the corner and rocked her until she'd gone limp and her tears had finally stopped. He didn't know what to do or say but leaving her wasn't an option. So, he sat, his head resting against the back of the chair and let the feel of her deep even breathing steady him.

Was she fighting him because of Hugh? Had Hugh really convinced her she wasn't enough? The bastard had left her because of her siblings. It was a lot, he'd give the guy that. But you don't leave. You don't bail on the person you've promised to stand by. They might not have been engaged, he wasn't sure of that, but Garrett had said more than enough. If they'd talked about their life after they were married, expectations had been set.

Did she think he'd do the same? That he'd leave her high and dry to pick up the pieces all over again? After taking on so much on her own, why risk it being torn down by someone else? It was a big risk.

He understood all about taking big risks. *But you're worth it.* He pressed a kiss to her temple.

There was another option but it was too bleak to consider. If she was that set against having him in her life, there wasn't much he could do about it.

How do I make you fall in love with me? That was the real question. How did he show her he wasn't like Hugh? That, despite his initial reaction, he'd come around to realizing the only future that got him excited was one with her in it.

She murmured something in her sleep, shifted just enough to make him tighten his hold and buried her face against his chest.

He could handle several dozen decades of this. Well, maybe not the crying part. He smoothed the hair from her forehead so he could study her. She had to be tuckered out. She'd cried and cried until he worried she'd make herself sick all over again.

The distant sound of a car door, followed by a bark, had him gently carrying her to her bed. He was careful, smoothing the blankets over her, turning off the side table lamp and slipping from the bedroom. He was standing in the hallway when the front door swung wide.

"Told you it was his truck," Hayden said, walking inside with Biddy in his arms. "Evening, Buzz."

Biddy waved.

"Hey, Buzz." Garrett came in, a too-big cowboy hat on his head. "Look what John gave me. It's nice, isn't it?" He paused and tipped his hat.

"The one I have for you is better." Buzz winked.

"What are you doing here?" John asked, a grin on his face. "And where is Jenna?"

Hayden nudged John on one side. Kyle nudged him hard on the other side.

"Ow. Ow." John stepped away. "What?"

"Hey, Buzz." Frannie came running to him. "We ate passghetti for dinnew and it was yummy."

"It was." Kyle patted his stomach. "We brought some home for Jenna. Mom figured it wouldn't be too hard on her throat."

Buzz nodded. Jan Mitchell was a thoughtful woman.

"Hey, Buzz." Monica didn't seem the least bit surprised to see him. "John said we were going to make s'mores." She carried the brown paper bag into the kitchen. "I've never made them on an open fire before."

"Skylar mentioned there was a firepit out back?" Kyle asked.

"I'm gonna take Shaggy out." Garrett ran into the kitchen.

"Wait fow me, Gawwett. Wait." Frannie ran after her brother, the back door slamming shut.

They all winced.

"Do I want to know how you all ended up on kid duty?" Buzz whispered to Kyle.

"What, we're all dads. We know the drill. Lizzie can't help out, being pregnant, and Jenna has strep. And I figured Skylar and Jan might want to hang with their grandkids at home so…the dad brigade to the rescue." Kyle's side-eyed glance spoke volumes. "What brings you over?"

"A milkshake for Jenna." Buzz shrugged. "She's sleeping but I figure she'll appreciate it when she wakes up."

"That was really sweet, Buzz." Monica took the baby from Hayden. "Don't worry. I know the drill. I helped my mom out all the time." Monica carried Biddy upstairs. "And I'm babysitter-certified. I know CPR and everything." She made a funny face at Biddy. "Don't I? We'll let Jenna sleep, too. No fusses."

"Fusses?" Buzz asked, praying Biddy wasn't getting sick. They'd all been so careful. Jan had the whole house smelling like bleach and disinfectant.

"Mom said something about Biddy teething." John shrugged. "Wait, did she say she's babysitter-certified? Jackpot. Hello, date night with my beautiful wife."

Kyle chuckled. "Greer's teething, too." Kyle winced. "It ain't pretty. I put a teething ring in the refrigerator, in case you need it."

Meaning Biddy might wake up screaming and Jenna'd be left to take care of her little sister. Jan had spent both nights in the guest room—in case Biddy needed anything. Jenna had put her foot down and refused to let Jan stay another night. But then, she hadn't planned on crying her eyes out, either.

"You really think s'mores is a good idea this late?" Buzz glanced at the clock. It was eight thirty-two.

All three of the Mitchell brothers looked at him, then started laughing.

"It's Saturday." Hayden shrugged, carrying the bag out the back door.

"We have to keep them occupied somehow," John explained. "Nat gave me some movie with talking troll things but I'd rather eat s'mores."

"The movie with the trolls that sing?" Kyle shook his head. "Not again. Please. I've seen that thing more times than is right. My girls love it."

Frannie and Garrett helped find kindling in the fading Texas summer sun. By the time it was dark, the firepit was crackling and the s'mores were being assembled—and devoured.

Frannie had crawled into Buzz's lap the minute he sat down and now the two of them were wearing a good amount of melted chocolate and marshmallow.

"Yummy," Frannie said, biting into her second s'more. "These awe delicious," she said around a mouthful of goo.

Buzz chuckled. "Careful or you'll wind up wearing more than you eat."

Frannie smiled. "Okay."

An hour later, Buzz had Frannie sitting on the bathroom counter while he scrubbed off the evidence of their evening's activities. "Might be easier to just spray you down with a hose."

Frannie giggled, then yawned.

Buzz did the best he could before tucking her into her little pink bed.

Garrett was next. He'd passed out in the yard, half on and half off Shaggy. Luckily, he wasn't covered in s'mores. Unluckily, it was impossible to get Garrett to stay awake long enough to get him upstairs and into his bed. Buzz carried Garrett up, taking off his shoes and sliding him into bed—with Shaggy sprawling across the floor like a canine area rug.

"You don't have to carry me," Monica said as they passed on the stairs. "I'm going to take a shower and read."

"What are you reading?" Buzz asked. What did a thirteen-year-old read?

"Don't tell Garrett but it's one of his science fiction novels." She shrugged. "What can I say? I'm a science geek, too. Thanks for tonight—taking care of Jenna, I mean. I know, I know, just as friends. I figure she could use those, too. And, you know, friends make you happy."

"They do." Buzz nodded and made his way back downstairs and outside. "Did I miss anyone?" he asked, sliding into his chair. "Don't anybody help or anything."

"You had it covered." Hayden toasted him. "You're a pro."

Kyle chuckled. "I wouldn't go that far."

"She's got a nice little setup here." John inspected the backyard. "I'm not sure all your animals will fit, though."

Buzz didn't take the bait.

"There's plenty of room for Jenna and the kids out at his place." Kyle leaned back in his chair, enjoying another s'more.

"How are things going?" Hayden asked.

"With what?" Buzz leaned forward, his skewer full of marshmallows.

"You're hilarious." John chuckled.

"You don't want to talk about it?" Kyle asked.

"It?" Buzz watched the marshmallows turn a nice golden brown. "My personal life, you mean? In the backyard of the woman who has no idea how I feel about her?"

"Got it." Hayden nodded.

"How does she still not know?" John sighed. "You were here, alone, just the two of you and a milkshake." He grinned. "That sounds like a fun afternoon."

Buzz shook his head but he was laughing. "Minus the whole strep thing."

"Got a text." Kyle was reading his phone. "Time to head out."

"Everything okay?" Hayden asked, standing.

"Yup. My wife said the kids are asleep and to come home." Kyle stood. "Let's go."

Buzz waved them off and sat outside, making himself a stack of s'mores and eating them all, before dousing the firepit and carrying the remaining s'mores supplies back inside. He was getting settled in on the couch when Biddy's cries reached him. He kicked off his boots, grabbed the teething ring from the refrigerator and took the stairs two at a time.

"Hey there, darlin'." Buzz reached into her crib and scooped her up. "I don't know what I'm doing here so bear with me."

Biddy blinked, her big eyes staring at him in the night-light's glow.

"Diaper. Right?" Buzz had worked with diapers before. There were a whole lot of Mitchell babies. And every now and then, an animal would require one. All he needed was a diaper. "We got this." He opened drawers until he saw the neat stack of diapers in a storage cube next to the changing table.

"Lookie there, Biddy. If I mess this one up, we've got extras. You take this." He handed her the teething ring, which she promptly started gnawing on.

His first attempt was inside out but he got it right the second time.

"Better?" he asked Biddy.

Biddy just stared at him, still chewing the teething ring.

"You know, there's a lot to be said for not speaking unless you've got something important to say but I bet you've got something to say." He waited, smiling when she yawned. "Yeah, me, too." He tossed a large stuffed panda from the rocking chair and sat. "Let's see if we can't get you back to sleep." He patted her little back. "Let those sleepy little eyes close now." He used a soft voice.

Biddy relaxed against him, her teething ring clasped in both hands and her heavy-lidded eyes fixed on his face.

"We're just chilling out, little girl." Buzz grinned. "No big plans or anything. Just me and you and this rocking chair."

Biddy yawned, resting her cheek against his chest, but her eyes never left his face.

"That's right. You rest a while." He patted her back, yawning himself. "Let's just rock a while." He rocked until her eyes finally closed and her teething ring slid from her little hands. And then, he rocked some more.

* * *

Jenna poured hot water over her peppermint tea bag. She knew the dull throb in her head wasn't from strep. It was from the gallons of tears she'd cried—all over Buzz Lafferty. She shook her head, refusing to think about that part. She'd sit, enjoy her tea, consider taking a long bubble bath and try to get some more sleep. She drew in a deep breath, the refreshing mint scent flooding her nostrils.

Perfect.

But she almost lost her tea and her teacup when she tripped over something on the floor by the couch. She flipped on the lamp and froze.

Boots.

And the throw blanket that normally draped over the back of the couch was spread across the thickly cushioned seat.

Further inspection of the boots confirmed they were Buzz's.

Unless he went home barefoot, he's still here.

She set her tea on the end table and crept up the stairs, going room by room. Monica was asleep. Garrett was sleeping on the floor by Shaggy—who wagged his tail in greeting but didn't move. Frannie was asleep in her inchworm pose, with her heinie sticking up and her face smashed into her mattress. Jenna smoothed Frannie's blankets and headed for the nursery.

Her breath caught.

There was something about a man with a baby—at least Jenna had always found it endearing. But Buzz Lafferty, sound asleep, holding Biddy? That was a whole different thing. Just when she didn't think he could be any more handsome, she was proven wrong. All the wants and hopes he stirred came rushing forward. Little impossibilities like this: having him here; having him as part of her daily life, of the kids' lives.

Oh, stop it, Jenna. For her own self-preservation, she needed him to leave. She didn't have the energy for this. As lovely a picture as this was, it hurt. The sooner he left, the better.

"Buzz," she whispered, crossing the room. "Buzz."

He looked so peaceful. Long dark eyelashes resting against his cheek. A dark stubble lining his jaw. She bent forward to whisper—doing her best not to wake Biddy. At least, that was her excuse for leaning this close to him.

He blinked once, then again, realization dawning on his face. She should step back—he was awake now. But the flicker of emotion on his face reached inside her chest and grabbed ahold of her heart.

He stared at her so long Jenna had to step back for fear of climbing into his lap. He stood, carefully carrying Biddy across the nursery and putting her into her crib. In his skintight shirt, it was hard not to notice the way his muscles shifted as he patted Biddy's back. He paused, searching for something.

He crossed back to the rocker, picked up a teething ring and put it into the crib beside Biddy.

Stop. Please. Do something, anything, to make yourself less appealing.

She pulled the door closed behind them, hurrying down the stairs and waving him downstairs after her. It was only when they were in the living room, and Jenna was standing on the far side of the room, that she said, "Where is Jan or Skylar or Cassie?"

"Basically, anyone but me?" The corner of his mouth kicked up. "The boys and I made s'mores with the kids and then I did the whole bedtime routine and must have dozed off."

Because she'd told Jan she'd be fine tonight. And she was—well, she didn't feel sick anymore. "Well…thank you…for everything." She didn't elaborate on the *for everything.* She hoped neither of them would ever mention her tantrum. "I'm sure you're anxious to get home."

Buzz sat, rubbed his eyes and yawned.

"Right. It's late." She almost choked on her peppermint tea when Buzz stretched and the hem of his tight shirt rose enough to reveal a golden expanse of skin and muscles. "Bedtime."

Buzz looked at her.

"I mean, you should go home—to your bed." She swallowed, wishing he'd tug his shirt down so she could pretend he wasn't fully aware of how distracted she was by his stomach.

He glanced down at his stomach, then back at her, and her mind came to a complete stop.

When he looked at her like that, she felt desirable in a way she'd never experienced before. Fire. Hunger. Need. She didn't doubt that he wanted her. It was *possible* his want was as great as hers. And when he stood up and closed the distance between them, she was drowning in him.

"Jenna." Her name. Rough and broken and sexier than it should be.

Her breathing was rapid and erratic—talking was definitely out.

"I want to stay." His hand rested against her cheek. "With you."

She was having a hard time breathing at all now.

"But if you tell me to go, I will." His words were a whisper.

The throb of her heart was quickly outpaced by the throb of her body. She wanted Buzz to stay, too. She wanted him to kiss her breathless… She wanted him. All of him.

He took her teacup and put it on the coffee table. "I'm going to kiss you." He bent his head, his lips sweeping across hers.

It was featherlight, but it was enough. She moaned, her arms twining around his neck.

His hands slid down her back, holding her against him. The thin weight of her cotton gown did nothing to cool the heat of his touch. His lips nipped and pulled, devouring her mouth until she was panting for breath. Then, his tongue swept along her lower lip and she was lost.

Jenna's hand slipped beneath the hem of his shirt to slide across the skin, firm with muscle.

Buzz reached up and tugged his shirt over his head.

For a minute, all she could do was stare. This was Buzz. This funny, kind, playful man was also this ripped, gorgeous, sensual man she very much wanted in her bed. "We can't do this—"

"Okay." Buzz was breathing hard but he stepped back, stooping to collect his shirt.

She grabbed the shirt from his hands. "Here." She pointed around them. "Not here."

"Okay." He was grinning then, holding on to her hand as they tiptoed up the stairs and to her room. "Better?" he asked, closing the door behind them.

She nodded, shaking with anticipation. "This is it, Buzz. Just this. Once." She said it for herself—to remind herself that this wouldn't change anything.

"If that's what you want." He kissed her, his hand twining in her hair. "I'm not going to argue." He kissed her again, pushing the neckline of her nightie aside to nuzzle along her collarbone. "But I'm sort of hoping I'll change your mind."

She said something or made a noise. She didn't know what it was because his lips were traveling up her throat and that was the only thing that mattered. Until his fingers worked the buttons down the front of her nightgown free.

"You sure?" he asked, tilting her head up to look at him.

She nodded. "I can't breathe and my heart might just pound out of my chest but yes. I'm sure." She'd said more than she should but she seemed to have no more control over her what she was saying or what her hands were doing. At the moment, she'd unbuckled his belt and was sliding the wide leather strap free.

"I'm glad to hear it." He was kissing her, spinning her, guiding her back to her bed. "Because I want you so bad I hurt, Jenna."

She'd never been so happy to be naked. Ever. If she hadn't been naked, she wouldn't be able to feel how glorious it was to be pressed up against him. And Buzz naked was beyond her wildest dreams. He wasn't shy about exploring each and every one of her curves. She was too eager to enjoy every inch of him to feel inhibited.

The feel of his body filling hers made her cry out—but Buzz caught the sound with his kiss. He was smiling, broadly, but she was, too. And when he'd found his rhythm, Jenna arched to meet him. It was the strain on his face as he fought for control that triggered her climax. She grabbed him to her and kissed him to muffle her moans as her body came apart. Seconds later, he followed, his body tensing and his eyes blazing into hers. His kiss was soft and clinging, his hands coming up to gently cradle her face.

When he rolled to her side, the first flush of shyness rolled over her.

"Are you blushing?" he asked, propping himself up on one elbow.

She shook her head, slowly tugging up the sheet.

He chuckled. "You've got nothing to hide, Jenna Norris. You're beautiful."

Jenna stared at him, her heart in her throat. What had she done?

His smile faded. "What is it?" He reached up to smooth the hair from her shoulder.

"I..." *I love you and this was a mistake.* Now when she lay in bed thinking about him, she'd know how incredible it was between them. She'd know and miss him. Not the idea of him, but the real him.

"Whatever you're thinking, say it." He searched her eyes.

She shook her head.

"Why?" He rolled onto his stomach, studying her. "What's holding you back?"

"I already cried myself to sleep on you once today. I'd rather not do it again." She tugged the sheet up.

"I'd rather you didn't cry again, either." His brows rose. "But if you're not done crying yourself out, I'll manage."

"That's not what you're supposed to say." She stared up at the ceiling overhead. "You're supposed to say something that makes me like you less and then you leave."

"Hold on. What?" He shook his head, looking confused. "You don't want to like me?"

"Of course I don't want to like you." She sat up, holding the sheet to her chest. "We… This… It would be easier if, for me, if you could stop being nice." She tugged, uncovering Buzz and making her stare back up at the ceiling.

"I guarantee you nothing has changed since you last saw me." Buzz chuckled.

"Everything has changed." She scooted toward the edge of the bed. "We agreed to no strings. But you've been taking care of me, taking care of the kids… This has to be it. It has to. Before things get twisted up and people get hurt." Namely, herself.

"You already broke that agreement." He slid across the bed, sitting behind her and pulling her against his chest. "Maybe it's okay to like me?"

She stood, her heart breaking. "No, Buzz, it's not. What good would it do me? You've probably noticed I have kids—siblings—and a lot of them." She swallowed. "And we, they, are getting fond of you. You know that."

"And that's a bad thing?"

"Yes." She didn't understand why he was pushing back like this. "I'm giving you what you want,

Buzz. I'm ending this before it…it becomes something that will only hurt us both."

"I never said a damn thing. You were the one that said you didn't want a relationship." Buzz was frowning now. "Are you telling me that's changed?"

"No. Definitely not. If I did, it would be stupid of me to pick you, knowing how you feel about my situation. I don't feel that way about you, Buzz. This is…was it." She had to force each word out. If she didn't send him away, she'd only prolong her heartbreak. She'd let too much happen already. She had to put a stop to it. "I'll be fine but, if this drags out, I'm putting the kids through pain they don't need. I can't risk that."

"So that's it. You've got it all figured out and that's that?" he asked, watching her. "Walk away now and no one gets hurt?"

She nodded and stood, silently, watching him get dressed. What was she supposed to say? Was there anything left to say? She'd been harsh, yes, but she had to. He couldn't love her because of the hurt he'd endured. If she told him she loved him, that wouldn't change.

When he was dressed, he hesitated, then pulled her close and kissed her. "You're a damn stubborn woman, Jenna. But I hear you. I've been listening to you the whole time. If this is what you want, I'll do my damndest to stay away." He rested his forehead against hers. "But you should know, it's too late for me. I was willing to risk it. Leaving here tonight, I'm hurting." His blue gaze searched hers before he turned and left.

Jenna stared after him, too startled to move or call him back. He was hurting. He'd been willing to risk it. Did he…did he care about her? How could he? And why hadn't she stopped talking long enough to listen to what he had to say. She'd been so determined to protect the kids and protect herself. In the process, she'd shut him out before she'd given him a chance. Her eyes were burning but she shut them down. No more tears. She'd said some horrible things tonight. But, somehow, she had to find the courage to tell him the truth—that she loved him—even if she had to beg him to listen.

Chapter Thirteen

Buzz wiped his forehead with his frayed bandanna and slipped it back around his neck. It didn't matter that it was after five o'clock, the air rippling from the heat. He downed more of his water bottle and walked the perimeter of his chicken coop. Lucky for him, the dogs had chased the fox off before it had taken off with any of his chickens. But it couldn't hurt to make sure the coop was sound and there were no gaps in the fence. And he'd do just about anything to keep his mind busy.

Roscoe and Scooter sat in the shade of a large Spanish oak, panting hard and barely moving.

"You two hot?" He pulled a bowl from his horse's

saddlebag, filled it with the remainder of his water bottle and set it on the ground between the dogs. “Here you go.”

The dogs both stood, draining the water bowl within seconds.

“Guess so.” He packed the dish back up and patted his horse, Scout, on the flank. “You two stay here.” He pulled himself into the saddle, tipped his hat forward to shade his eyes and steered Scout along the path that circled his property. He’d gotten word that some feral hogs had been spotted not too far from his place. While they could be a threat to animals, they were more a nuisance than anything. They’d tear up the soil, destroying fences and—depending on how big their herd was—wipe out a whole store feed for livestock.

A couple of hours later, he’d found no sign that the pigs had been through his property so he circled back around and was heading home through the north pasture, when he saw Cassie riding up. It wasn’t that he didn’t adore his sister, he did. But he wasn’t in the mood for one of her pep talks. Hell, he wasn’t in the mood to talk period.

“Hey.” She waved, guiding her black-and-white mare his way.

Buzz drew Scout to a stop. “What’s up?”

“Can’t a sister go on a leisurely horseback ride with her brother?”

Buzz shot her a disbelieving look and nudged Scout forward.

"Just because we haven't done it in a long time, doesn't mean we shouldn't start doing it." Cassie shrugged.

"A long time?" Buzz shook his head. "Try never."

Cassie sighed. "So…"

"So…" He shot her another glance. "If you've come out here to try to have some sort of healing talk, let me stop you now."

"What do you mean, *healing talk*?" Cassie nudged her horse closer to his. "I didn't think *we* had any healing to do. Are you mad at me?" She smiled, all feigned innocence.

"Not yet." It was Buzz's turn to sigh. "But if you mention Jenna or the kids, that could change." He'd done all he could to avoid any talk and sight of the Norris family for the last week. Considering how small Granite Falls was, that was no easy task. If he was going anywhere in town, he drove right past her street. All he had to do was look and, boom, there was her house. The fence he'd built with Garrett. And the family he wanted to call his own.

"I wasn't going to mention them so much as check in on you." Cassie's teasing gave way to true concern. "You're not usually the brooding type. But you've been a downright grump for the last few days."

Buzz let Scout make his way down a slight incline before he answered, “I’ll work on it.”

“That’s not what I meant and you know it.” Cassie steered her horse closer. “I’m worried about you.”

“Don’t.” Buzz tried to smile.

“Yeah, sure. Now that you’ve told me not to, I’ll totally stop.” Cassie shook her head, all irritation. “You’re hurting. You’re my brother.”

He didn’t argue. He was hurting. He had a searing hot knife stuck in his chest. It was there every second of every day—a constant reminder. No one could see it, but he’d felt it digging deeper every day since he’d left Jenna’s bedroom. “I’ll survive.”

“Buzz.” A hint of impatience hardened Cassie’s voice as she grabbed Scout’s reins. “You don’t have to suffer through this alone, you know?”

“Maybe I’m not suffering. Maybe I’m taking time to figure things out.” He sighed.

“What, exactly, are you figuring out?” Cassie’s brow creased. “You never know, maybe talking to me could help.”

“I appreciate it, Cass, I do.” The slightest pressure of his knees had Scout trotting. “But there’s nothing to talk about. It’s a me thing—in my head. Letting go. Moving on. All that.”

“You can be a stubborn ass, you know that, right?” Cassie waved, her horse going from a trot to a gallop as she flew by him.

He laughed and followed, slowing as he spied

Kyle Mitchell's truck and glanced Cassie's way. "Call in some reinforcements?"

She shrugged, already dismounting and leading her horse into the barn.

Buzz took his time putting his saddle away, brushing out and feeding Scout. When he finally turned Scout out into the corral, he spied Kyle, John and Hayden on the porch, waiting.

"Took you long enough." John was sitting on the back porch step. "Anyone ever tell you you've got like a Doctor Dolittle thing going on around here?" He pointed. "When the hell did you get a llama?"

"It's an alpaca." Buzz shrugged.

"Whatever." John shook his head. "You've got your own little zoo out here."

"If they've got no place else to go…" Buzz grumbled.

"My brother is a big ol' softy when it comes to animals," Cassie called out from inside. "There's pizza and beer and cupcakes. I bought it all so it should be edible." She stepped out onto the back porch. "You boys have fun." She winked at Buzz, heading for her car.

Buzz frowned. "Anyone want to clue me in on what's going on?"

Kyle held up his finger, shushing Buzz. "Hold up," he murmured.

Cassie climbed into her car, slammed the door shut and turned on the engine.

"Now?" Buzz asked.

"She was freaking out. Which got Skyler worrying—then Lizzie and Jan and..." Kyle gave him a once-over. "You do look a little worse for wear."

"Thanks." Buzz headed inside to find the table set up. "Poker?" He hung his cowboy hat on the hat tree to the right of the door.

"Poker." Hayden clapped him on the shoulder. "Unless you want to have some heart-to-heart talk?"

"Poker it is." Buzz grinned. "I'm surprised you came. I guess Lizzie made you?"

Hayden shrugged. "I will neither confirm or deny that." But John and Kyle were both nodding and giving Buzz the thumbs-up.

"You hear about the McCarrick place?" John asked, grabbing a piece of pizza.

Buzz nodded. "That's why I was out, taking a look around. So far, it doesn't look like the hogs have found their way onto my property."

"Angus was all bent out of shape over the fences they took down. Broke down one of the retaining walls of a tank, too. Water everywhere..." Kyle shook his head. "Damn things are hard to get a handle on."

"They're wild animals." Buzz shrugged. "They're doing what they do."

"Being damn pests?" John nodded. "Guess so."

"Lemme wash up." Buzz headed down the hall to his bedroom. He kicked off his dust-covered boots, shrugged out of his jeans and shirt, and left them on the ground. He hadn't exactly been wanting company, but since they were here, he might as well enjoy himself—and take all their money.

Ten minutes later, they were sitting around the table. The pizza was gone and so were most of the cupcakes, but there was still plenty of beer when Hayden took a deep breath and said, "Before I whoop y'all's butts at poker, might as well get this out of the way." He took another deep breath.

"Here we go." Buzz took a long sip off his longneck and leaned back in his chair.

"I need you all to promise me, if Lizzie is having a little girl..." Hayden shook his head. "If she's having a little girl, I'm going to need backup. I'm not sure how I'd hold up."

They all laughed at that.

"Listening to Lizzie and Jenna talking about Monica makes my stomach hurt."

What about Monica?

"Teenagers." John sighed. "I like to pretend my baby girl won't pull any of that stuff. But I'm not going to worry about it until Leslie's walking and talking and out of diapers."

What stuff? Buzz finished off his beer and went for another.

"I think they're blowing it out of proportion." Kyle rubbed his hand along the back of his neck. "It's not that big a deal."

"Anyone want another beer?" Buzz asked, staring into this mostly empty refrigerator—his heart in his throat.

All three Mitchell brothers held up their hands.

"She's disappointed. I think that's all there is to it." Kyle took the beer Buzz handed him.

Buzz handed out the rest of the bottles and sat. Try as he might, there was no way he could stop himself from asking, "What's going on with Monica?"

"Oh." Kyle winced. "Right, sorry. We weren't going to talk about Jenna."

"Way to go." John hauled off and punched Kyle in the arm.

"He started it." Kyle rubbed his arm and nodded at Hayden.

"I don't give a damn who started it." Buzz's control was slipping. "What the hell is going on with Monica?"

All three Mitchell brothers were staring at him now.

"She didn't make the cheerleading squad." Kyle shrugged.

As far as Buzz knew, she hadn't been all that interested in being a cheerleader. "That's all?" The way the three of them were talking, he'd worried something was truly wrong.

"Jenna's pretty sure there's more to it—she doesn't know what, exactly." Kyle shrugged. "She's been crying a lot. Staying in her room. Monica, that is." His voice lowered. "She's not talking to anyone."

Buzz frowned. Monica loved to talk. All the time. "Nothing happened?"

"Not that we can figure." Kyle was watching him.

He remembered the last conversation he'd had with the girl all too clearly. How she'd worried there was something wrong with her—that she'd chased off Hugh. She bears her heart to him and then what does he do? Up and disappear on her, too. He didn't like the guilt that reached inside his chest to squeeze against his already wounded heart. "How are the others?"

"They're fine." John popped the lid of his beer. "And they're not your problem."

Buzz couldn't stop himself from glaring at John. True or not, Buzz didn't want to hear it.

"Dammit." Hayden shook his head. "I was worrying about something years down the road—I wasn't thinking about now. I'm sorry, Buzz."

Buzz shook his head. "You don't need to apologize. Just because she's not interested in me, doesn't mean I stopped caring about them." And Monica not talking to anyone, crying, worried him. A hell of a lot. That wasn't like her.

The table fell silent.

"Garrett's been missing you," John murmured. "He came out the other day and wanted to show you a new trick he'd taught Shaggy."

Buzz smiled. He could only imagine Garrett with Shaggy. What was it Jenna had said? How the boy would hold on to something until he was an expert at it. That would be the best-trained dog in all of Granite Falls by the time Garrett was done.

"Next time they come out, I could call you?" Kyle offered.

Buzz shook his head. As much as he wanted to see the kids, and he did, he knew it'd be that much harder when he said goodbye. The truth of the matter was he didn't know if he was strong enough for that. "I think that would only make things worse."

"For them? Or for you?" Hayden reached for one of the card decks. "Maybe you should talk to her again?"

"I did." Buzz watched Hayden deal out the cards to each of them. "I told her how I felt, told her what I wanted and she sent me on my way." He shrugged, trying to keep his tone light. "I guess it's karma? All those years of swearing I'd never get involved with a woman with kids and then I go and fall, hard, for one."

"How many times has he thrown up?" Jenna asked, tilting Shaggy's head one way, then the other. The dog, usually all tail wags, slumped into her hand.

"Too many times." Garrett was frightened.

Garrett, frightened, was enough for Jenna. "Okay."

She stared around the table at her siblings, feeling sick inside. The last thing they needed was for Shaggy to get sick—or worse. "I guess you all want to go?"

"We have to." Frannie's big eyes were full of tears. "Shaggy needs us."

Garrett swallowed. "Can we go? Now?"

Jenna stood.

"I can stay with Biddy." Monica didn't look up from her plate or the peas she kept poking with her fork.

"You have to come," Garrett argued. "We all have to."

Monica looked up then, studying her little brother before saying, "Okay."

Jenna got Biddy's diaper changed while the other three put on shoes. She'd worry about the dishes and food later.

"He won't walk, Jenna." Garrett was on the verge of tears. He'd clipped Shaggy's leash onto his collar and was holding it but Shaggy hadn't moved from his spot on the floor.

"Can you get Biddy buckled in?" She handed Biddy to Monica. "He's just tired, Garrett." She managed to scoop the large dog into her arms. "When you get sick, all you want to do is lay around, too. Don't worry. Buzz and Skylar will get him better."

The drive to Buzz's clinic was silent. Even little Biddy wasn't her normal babbling self. Instead, the vehicle was thick with unspoken fears. In the short time Shaggy had been with them, he'd become an important member of their family. Now…

He will be fine. Jenna pulled in front of the vet clinic, her heart in her throat. Everything will be fine. "Garrett and Monica, please get the little ones out and onto the sidewalk. I'll get Shaggy."

"Dr. Buzz!" Garrett pushed the front door open, dragging Frannie behind him. "Please come quick."

Jenna staggered in behind, Shaggy mostly limp in her arms.

When Buzz burst through the exam room doors, Jenna was overcome with relief. She'd always thought the whole knight-in-shining-armor thing was a terrible cliché…but a knight in a white doctor's coat? That seemed about right. She didn't care about anything that had passed between them—not right now. All that mattered was that he'd fix Shaggy. She knew it.

Buzz took one look at her, then Shaggy and hurried to take the dog from her. "Shaggy not feeling well?"

"He's been throwing up," Garrett replied.

"Well, that's no fun." Buzz looked at Shaggy. "He eat anything weird? Get into anything?"

Jenna had been grading papers since she got home. She'd had no idea Shaggy was even sick until Garrett said something. "Not that I know of." *And now I feel like the worst pet owner in the world.*

Buzz looked at Garrett. "When did you notice him feeling bad?" He pushed through the exam room doors with her and the kids on his heels.

"Hi." Skylar followed. "Shaggy under the weather?"

Jenna nodded. "Throwing up and listless."

"We were sitting in my room on the floor." Garrett's face was drawn tight as he considered Buzz's question. "He was okay when I got home but then..." He frowned. "He went out of the room and came back and threw up all over my floor."

"No idea where he went?" Buzz lay Shaggy on the exam table.

Garrett shook his head. "He couldn't have gone too far. He was only gone a second. The only room that was open was the bathroom."

"Bathroom?" Skylar frowned.

Because there was a dozen or more things Shaggy shouldn't ingest in the bathroom. *Wait, no.* She was super careful about locking everything up. "Between Biddy and Frannie, I don't leave anything on the counter—let alone something toxic."

Buzz nodded. "Baby shampoo." He flashed a light in Shaggy's eyes. "I'm betting. It smells sweet—but I can't imagine it tastes all that good." He used his stethoscope to listen to Shaggy's belly.

"Will he be okay?" Garrett placed his hand on Shaggy's side, his hand sinking into the dog's thick coat.

"He will. Shaggy is a big dog—it'd take a whole lot of baby shampoo to make him too sick." Buzz clapped Garrett on the shoulder.

"And we were almost out," Jenna announced. "I'm so happy we didn't get to the grocery store last night." So happy she was on the verge of tears.

The corner of Buzz's mouth cocked up and, for a second, he really looked at her.

"That's good then, right?" Garrett perked up.

"I'm thinking so. We'll get to work on him, okay?" He glanced her way, then. "Jenna, it might be best if you and the kids waited in the waiting room?"

Jenna nodded. "Of course." She took Biddy from Monica. "Let's give Dr. Buzz room to work."

"I could stay and help." Garrett's hand fisted in Shaggy's fur. "I won't get in the way."

"I know that." Buzz smiled at him. "Let me do a few tests first and then we'll see, okay?"

Garrett nodded, his hand sliding from Shaggy's side. He paused, then rushed forward to hug the dog. "You feel better, Shaggy. Let Buzz fix you, please. Please get better."

Jenna was blinking rapidly, trying to hold back the tears. *Please be okay, Shaggy.* Her eyes met Buzz's.

He stared at her, those blue eyes warming her through. Then he blinked. "Skylar will come get you in a few minutes."

Jenna led the kids into the waiting room. The television in the waiting room was on a nature channel. It didn't take long before the older three were reluctantly wrapped up in learning about the meerkat. Biddy, however, wanted to move.

"Okay, Biddy-boo." Jenna sat her little sister on the floor next to her chair, too agitated to do much more than sit and stare anxiously at the exam room doors.

"Na," Biddy announced, standing on her little feet and holding on to Jenna's chair. "Nana." She smiled up at Jenna.

Monica, Garrett and Frannie all turned to stare at their little sister.

"What's that Biddy-boo?" Jenna was too delighted to hear Biddy speak to care what she was saying.

"Nana." Biddy patted Jenna's knee.

"Jenna?" Monica asked. "Is that Jenna?"

Biddy grinned widely, all the while staring up at Jenna. "Nana."

"Biddy said yaw name, Jenna." Frannie slipped out of her chair and came hopping over to Biddy. She hugged her little sister, almost knocking Biddy onto her bum. "Biddy, say my name." She pointed at herself. "Fwannie. Say Fwannie."

"Ni." Biddy giggled when Frannie hugged her close again.

"That's me. I'm Ni." Frannie pointed at herself. "She knows my name and yaw name, Jenna."

Monica and Garrett were quick to jump on board and the meerkat program was forgotten. Biddy's sudden interest in communicating provided the perfect distraction. Jenna was laughing and giving Biddy encouragement just like the rest of them.

"She just needed something to say." Buzz's voice was a surprise. "Guess now she does."

"She does." Frannie grinned. "My name and Jenna's name."

"How is Shaggy?" Garrett was up, taking Buzz's hand in his as if it was the most natural thing in the world.

But it was the way Buzz squeezed Garrett's hand in his that had Jenna's heart thumping and twisting all at the same time. How many times had she reached for the phone? How many times had she imagined dropping by to tell him she loved him? But she couldn't do it. Cassie's words lingered—making her second-guess Buzz's declaration. And she was too afraid to outright ask Buzz.

It was time to stop lying to herself. The real reason she stopped herself from reaching out wasn't Buzz. It was fear. She was scared to give Buzz a chance—to give them a chance—only to have him change his mind or have it all fall apart. Her heart, the kids' hearts, had all been trampled and kicked around so much already...

"He's fine. We're giving him lots of fluid to wash all the soap out of his system. Then we'll give him some pills to stop him from throwing up." Buzz paused. "But I would like to keep him overnight. Just to keep an eye on him. Plus, if he throws up—you or Jenna won't have to clean it up."

Garrett's shoulders slumped but he reluctantly agreed. "If you think he needs to stay over..."

"I do." Buzz nodded. "But you can come get him after school tomorrow?" He glanced her way. "Or I can drop him by?" He waited, his blue eyes searching hers.

She nodded—then shook her head. It wasn't right to have him drop off Shaggy—he was just as busy as she was. Taking advantage of his kindness was wrong. "We will come get him, tomorrow. But thank you, so much, for everything."

The muscle in Buzz's jaw clenched tight. "It's my job."

"He's too busy." Monica's tone was brittle. "We should go." She took Frannie's hand and led her across the lobby and out the front door before Frannie could say goodbye.

Buzz frowned, once more looking at Jenna. All Jenna could do was shrug. If she knew why Monica was acting this way, she could fix it. But Monica wasn't talking—to anyone.

"She's acting weird again." Garrett shrugged. "Don't take it personally."

"Is there anything I can do?" Buzz's gaze was trained on the glass door of the clinic. He was watching Monica, holding Frannie's hand, looking strained and tense.

"She thinks you're not coming around because we talked to you about…well, you know." Garrett glanced back and forth between her and Buzz.

Buzz's brows rose. "You tell Monica that Jenna and I are friends. That's all. Nothing anyone said will change that." He looked at her, then. "Right?"

The lump in Jenna's throat made it hard for her to say, "Right." And they'd stay friends because she was too afraid to give them both a chance at happiness. It was wrong. It hurt—horribly. Every day, she woke up hopeful and went to bed defeated. She'd never wanted anyone as much as she wanted Buzz. She'd never imagined a future so full of laughter and love. If she'd take a leap, trust in him, then there'd be nothing stopping them.

"I've got to get back to work." Buzz patted Garrett on the shoulder. "Jenna." His smile was tight.

"Thank you, again." She stepped forward and froze.

Buzz had reached out for her. One hand, toward her face. She knew it would be warm and strong against her cheek. But he stopped himself from touching her, shoved his hand into his pocket and nodded. "We'll take good care of Shaggy."

Jenna watched as he disappeared through the

exam room doors, her heart screaming at her to do something—anything. Instead, she shifted Biddy to her other hip, took Garrett's hand and led them outside to the van. But even hours later, as she stared up at her bedroom ceiling, her heart wouldn't stop screaming for Buzz. *What am I doing?* She had a chance at happiness and love. He'd offered it up, freely… It—he—was everything she wanted. She loved him. Her love for him was stronger than her fear. Jenna knew, no matter how scary it might be, it was time to listen to her heart. It might be risky but Buzz was worth it.

Chapter Fourteen

"You owe me," Buzz said into the phone. Could this Monday get any worse?

"Gosh, thanks, boss." Skylar sighed. "It's not like I wanted strep throat."

Buzz sighed, ran a hand over his face and stared at the school. "I still don't understand why I'm here. Surely, there was someone, anyone, who could have filled this spot."

"I told you they wanted someone in veterinary medicine." She said something, but it was muffled. "I have to go, lie down, be sick, that sort of thing."

"Fine." But Buzz heard her laughing before he hung up. His fingers flexed on the steering wheel and he took a deep breath. "Career Day." Skylar did these sorts of things. But Skylar was sick and here he was. "Let's get this over with."

He stepped out of his truck, slipped on his white coat and went around to the rear of his truck. He didn't know if he'd have Garrett, but he'd brought something special just in case the boy was in one of his groups. He'd had to go out on a call when they came to get Shaggy and he'd hated missing them. In the days since he'd left Jenna's room, the hollow ache in his chest had only gotten bigger.

Enough of that. He'd get in, get out and find something to keep his brain busy. *Yeah, right.* He stacked up a couple of plastic tubs onto a wheeled cart and pulled it across the parking lot to the front doors. Banners hung from the ceiling and decorated the walls, welcoming their career-day guests. Buzz was impressed by some of the artwork. One of the perks of a small town was days like today. The middle and elementary school kids were both able to participate—being right across the street from one another.

"Good morning, Dr. Lafferty." The principal, Mary Jenkins, greeted him. "Thanks so much for stepping in this morning. Let me show you where you'll be setting up."

Buzz walked with her, his stomach churning when he realized he'd be in the room right next-door to Jenna.

"There's a projector and television for your use, as well." She glanced at the clock. "You have a bit of time as the bell doesn't ring for another eleven minutes. Feel free to set up and test out the equipment."

Buzz unloaded the three small cages he'd brought with him, then pulled out his laptop. Skylar had given him a thumb drive to use so he plugged it in, connected his computer to the projector and stared up at the presentation Skylar had provided.

There was a knock on the door, so Buzz hit pause and turned. "Jenna." He cleared his throat. Beautiful or not, he wouldn't stare or trip over his words or make an ass out of himself. He'd done that enough already.

"Buzz." She smiled. "Skylar called me. She thought you might have left your phone in the truck?"

He patted his coat pocket and sighed. "It would appear so." Skylar could have called the school—anyone. She didn't know the details of what had happened between them, only that he was trying to keep some distance between him and Jenna. And yet, here she was. Smiling at him. Looking beautiful and calm while his insides were inside out and his heart felt sliced open.

"She said there were two presentations on the thumb drive and to play the second one." She shrugged.

Buzz clicked on the thumb drive. A long list of documents with meaningless titles appeared.

"She said it was called presentation two." Jenna stepped forward. "Do you need any help with the technology? Sometimes these projectors can be glitchy."

He didn't need help. He needed space. She was close enough to smell the citrus scent of her soap. "I've got it." He took a deep breath, his eyes fixed on the computer screen.

"Okay." She nodded. "If you change your mind, I'm right next door."

"I know." He made the mistake of glancing her way.

She walked away, looking…*sad.*

As far as he was concerned, she had no right to be sad. He was the one whose heart had been stomped on. *Fool that I am.* He scrolled through the list, found presentation two and hit play.

A slide popped up that read, *Fight or Flight…*

What the hell was he presenting? He'd assumed it would be a day-in-the-life sort of thing.

Animals, like humans, rely on their instincts for survival. A video played of a gazelle gracefully sidestepping and escaping a lion.

Buzz shook his head. "Not exactly scientific genius."

The world is full of dangers, and animals of prey must stay on constant alert. But sometimes, the need for self-preservation can make an animal, or per-

son, miss important clues that are vital to their well-being.

Buzz ran a hand over his face. What was he supposed to do with this?

Impulses such as the fight-or-flight are often employed. Some species, like the chameleon, can camouflage themselves to protect themselves. Humans cannot.

No shit. What was Skylar thinking?

But humans, unlike animals, can communicate by the use of words. When used incorrectly, tragedy can strike. A silent video played. A man was walking toward a door when another man yelled for him to stop. The first man didn't stop but opened the door—only to have a bucket full of paint fall and cover him from head to toe.

Worse, humans can let fear prevent them from hearing correctly.

Buzz gave up trying to make sense of what he was watching.

At this time, humans can use their words to ask for a clarification. An apology is often used at the beginning or ending of such a clarification.

The presentation ended, the screen went white and Buzz was beyond confused.

There was a knock on the door again.

Buzz turned, hands on hips, to see Jenna peering inside. "Sorry to interrupt but Skylar called and said she was wrong and it's presentation number one."

"Thanks." He tore his gaze from hers, closed the presentation and scrolled through the list for presentation one. When he glanced back up, she was gone. *Good. That's good.* The hurt was a little too new for him to be immune to her.

This one was exactly what he'd expected. A day in the life.

The bell rang and the first class came in. The kids were curious, he got a few good questions and he was actually looking forward to his last group. Until Jenna's class came in—and Jenna stayed.

Dammit all.

He knew what she was doing through his entire presentation. How she perched on one of the lab tables. The whole time he was talking, she swung her legs, back and forth. She was wearing black-and-white flats with bows on top. And when a good portion of her students' arms shot up to ask questions, she smiled.

It was a hell of a smile. The sort of smile that landed a hard kick to the chest and left him rattled.

By the time the bell rang, Buzz was a ball of tension.

"I thought I'd stay and lend a hand," Jenna offered. "It's my conference period—"

"No, thank you." Buzz didn't look at her. "I think it's best if you…stay in your room and I'll stay here." He waited, hoping she'd go. If she didn't, there was a high likelihood he'd leave everything here and get Cassie to come pack it all up later.

"Buzz—"

"Jenna, I'm asking." He looked her in the eye, hoping like hell he wouldn't have to beg.

This was not going well. Not at all. The video had been a terrible idea. She'd known it as they were making it but she'd done it, anyway. "You didn't like my PowerPoint?" Jenna asked.

"What PowerPoint?" He was on edge, angry. With her.

"Presentation two..." She cleared her throat. "I'm sorry, Buzz."

He stared at the screen.

"It was stupid—I was trying to be funny. Just forget about it, please." She hurried on, wishing she hadn't listened to Monica. "Monica thought it was cute. She said you'd laugh and think it was funny and I... I don't know why I believed her. It wasn't. Obviously. I couldn't come up with a way to do this without babbling like this or crying right away."

He was staring at her now. "You lost me."

"No." She shook her head, desperate. "Don't say that. Please." She grabbed his hand with both of hers. "You were right. I should have listened to you. I should have asked you about the whole vow thing but I didn't. I was scared. If Cassie was right, then we didn't stand a chance. If Cassie was wrong, then

I'd have to put my heart on the line and risk getting it discarded. I let my fear scare me. I was a fool. I'm sorry, Buzz. I am." She took a deep breath and kept going. "I said horrible things. Mean things. But I had to make you leave, don't you see. I was scared. I knew how I felt and knew you didn't, couldn't feel the same, so… I knew if you stayed, then I'd just drag out the inevitable—you leaving."

"I'd never leave." His gaze trailed over her face. "If you were mine, I'd never leave your side."

She could breathe. "I am yours, Buzz. Always." It was hard not to grab him then. "Just tell me I haven't lost you."

"You haven't. You won't. You're here. I'm not going anywhere." The corner of his mouth kicked up. "Am I the lion?"

"What?" Now she was confused, ridiculously happy, but confused.

"The first video." He was smiling now. "The gazelle, dodging the lion. I figure there's some sort of symbolism going on there?"

"Nope. Garrett told me I'd need an action element to hold your attention." Jenna shook her head, threading her fingers with his. "Yes, my thirteen-year-old sister and my eight-year-old brother helped me." She shook her head. "Turns out Monica was mad at me. It was only when I asked for her help to…win you back that she told me the truth. She said I was giving up on something—like our mother.

I already knew I wanted you—I was prepared to grovel—but her words drove it all home. I won't give up on us." She paused, staring into his blue eyes until he was smiling. "As far as siblings go, I think mine are pretty amazing."

"Because they want you to be happy." He rested a hand against her cheek. "Just so there's no more misunderstanding here, I make you happy?"

"You do." She leaned into his hand. "Most definitely." She covered his hand with hers.

"And you're not going to hightail it out of here for someplace more exciting when I'm ready to put a ring on your finger?" He wasn't smiling now.

"More exciting?" She slid her arms around his waist. "There is nothing more exciting than you, Dr. Lafferty." She loved the feel of his lips against hers, how they fit together. *Like we are meant to be.* "Plus, there's all the skunks and fire ants and possums and poison oak around—I think we've got exciting covered."

"Don't forget the snakes and scorpions." He pulled her closer.

"No way." She stroked her fingers along his jaw. "As far as the whole ring thing—"

"Garrett's already given me his blessing." He smiled, leaning forward to kiss her again. "All we need is the ring," he said against her mouth.

"You're sounding awful confident, Dr. Lafferty."

"I'm wearing my doctor's coat. When I'm wearing it, whatever I say is true. It's a doctor thing." He stared into her eyes. "I love you."

Jenna's lungs emptied but her heart was oh, so full. "I might need to hear that again. Just to be sure I heard that correctly."

"I love you." He brushed his lips to hers. "Don't worry, you'll be hearing it at least once a day from here on out."

"You are wearing the coat, so I guess I'll believe you." She stood on tiptoe. "And I love you."

He checked the clock on the wall. "When does school let out, Miss Norris? I'd like to celebrate this properly and I'm pretty sure there are things involved that your principal might not approve of."

Jenna laughed. "Assuming we find time to celebrate when Biddy and Frannie and Garrett and Monica aren't around, that is."

"If something's important, Jenna, you make time for it." He was so intent and serious her bones went soft.

"I can do that." She nodded. "I will do that for us."

"For us." He rested his forehead against hers. "Always."

* * * * *

COMING NEXT MONTH FROM

HARLEQUIN

SPECIAL EDITION

#2923 THE OTHER HOLLISTER MAN

Men of the West • by Stella Bagwell

Rancher Jack Hollister travels to Arizona to discover if the family on Three Rivers Ranch might possibly be a long-lost relation. He isn't looking for love—until he sees Vanessa Richardson.

#2924 IN THE RING WITH THE MAVERICK

Montana Mavericks: Brothers & Broncos • by Kathy Douglass

Two rodeo riders—cowboy Jack Burris and rodeo queen Audrey Hawkins—compete for the same prize all the while battling their feelings for each other. Sparks fly as they discover that the best prize is the love that grows between them.

#2925 LESSONS IN FATHERHOOD

Home to Oak Hollow • by Makenna Lee

When NIcholas Weller finds a baby in his art gallery, he's shocked to find out the baby is his. Emma Blake agrees to teach this confirmed bachelor how to be a father, but after the loss of her husband and child, can she learn to love again?

#2926 IT STARTED WITH A PUPPY

Furever Yours • by Christy Jeffries

Shy and unobtrusive Elise Mackenzie is finally living life under her own control, while charming and successful Harris Vega has never met a fixer-upper house he couldn't remodel. Elise is finally coming into her own but does Harris see her as just another project—or is there something more between them?

#2927 BE CAREFUL WHAT YOU WISH FOR

Lucky Stars • by Elizabeth Bevarly

When Chance wished for a million dollars as a teenager, he never expected it to come true—especially not via his late brother's twins, who are now his responsibility. Luckily, Poppy Digby has known the twins all their lives and agrees to stay—just for a few days!—but they each find themselves longing for more time...

#2928 EXPECTING HER EX'S BABY

Sutton's Place • by Shannon Stacey

Lane Thompson and Evie Sutton were married once and that didn't work out. But resisting each other hasn't worked out very well, either, and now they're having a baby. Can they make it work this time around? Or will old wounds once again tear them apart?

YOU CAN FIND MORE INFORMATION ON UPCOMING HARLEQUIN TITLES, FREE EXCERPTS AND MORE AT HARLEQUIN.COM.

HSECNM0622

SPECIAL EXCERPT FROM

HQN

Welcome to Honey, Texas, where honey is big business and a way of life. Tansy Hill is fierce when it comes to protecting her family and their bees. When her biggest rival, Dane Knudson, threatens her livelihood, Tansy is ready for battle!

Read on for a sneak preview of The Sweetest Thing, *the first book in the Honey Hill trilogy, by* USA TODAY *bestselling author Sasha Summers.*

"He cannot be serious." Tansy stared at the front page of the local *Hill Country Gazette* in horror. At the far too flattering picture of Dane Knudson. And that smile. That smug, "That's right, I'm superhot and I know it" smile that set her teeth on edge. "What is he thinking?"

"He who?" Tansy's sister, Astrid, sat across the kitchen table with Beeswax, their massive orange cat, occupying her lap.

"Dane." Tansy wiggled the newspaper. "Who else?"

"What did he do now?" Aunt Camellia asked.

"This." Tansy shook the newspaper again. "'While continuing to produce their award-winning clover honey,'" she read, "'Viking Honey will be expanding operations and combining their Viking ancestry and Texas heritage—'"

Aunt Camellia joined them at the table. "All the Viking this and Viking that. That boy is pure Texan."

"The Viking thing is a marketing gimmick," Tansy agreed.

PHSSEXP0622

"A smart one." Astrid winced at the glare Tansy shot her way. "What about this has you so worked up, Tansy?"

"I hadn't gotten there, yet." Tansy held up one finger as she continued, "'Combining their Viking ancestry and Texas heritage for a one-of-a-kind event venue and riverfront cabins ready for nature-loving guests by next fall.'"

All at once, the room froze. *Finally.* She watched as, one by one, they realized why this was a bad thing.

Two years of scorching heat and drought had left Honey Hill Farms' apiaries in a precarious position. Not just the bees—the family farm itself.

"It's almost as if he doesn't understand or…or care about the bees." Astrid looked sincerely crestfallen.

"He *doesn't* care about the bees." Tansy nodded. "If he did, this wouldn't be happening." She scanned the paper again—but not the photo. His smile only added insult to injury.

To Dane, life was a game and toying with people's emotions was all part of it. Over and over again, she'd invested time and energy and hours of hard work, and he'd just sort of winged it. *Always*. As far as Tansy knew, he'd never suffered any consequences for his lackluster efforts. No, the great Dane Knudson could charm his way through pretty much any situation. But what would he know about hard work or facing consequences when his family made a good portion of their income off a stolen Hill Honey recipe?

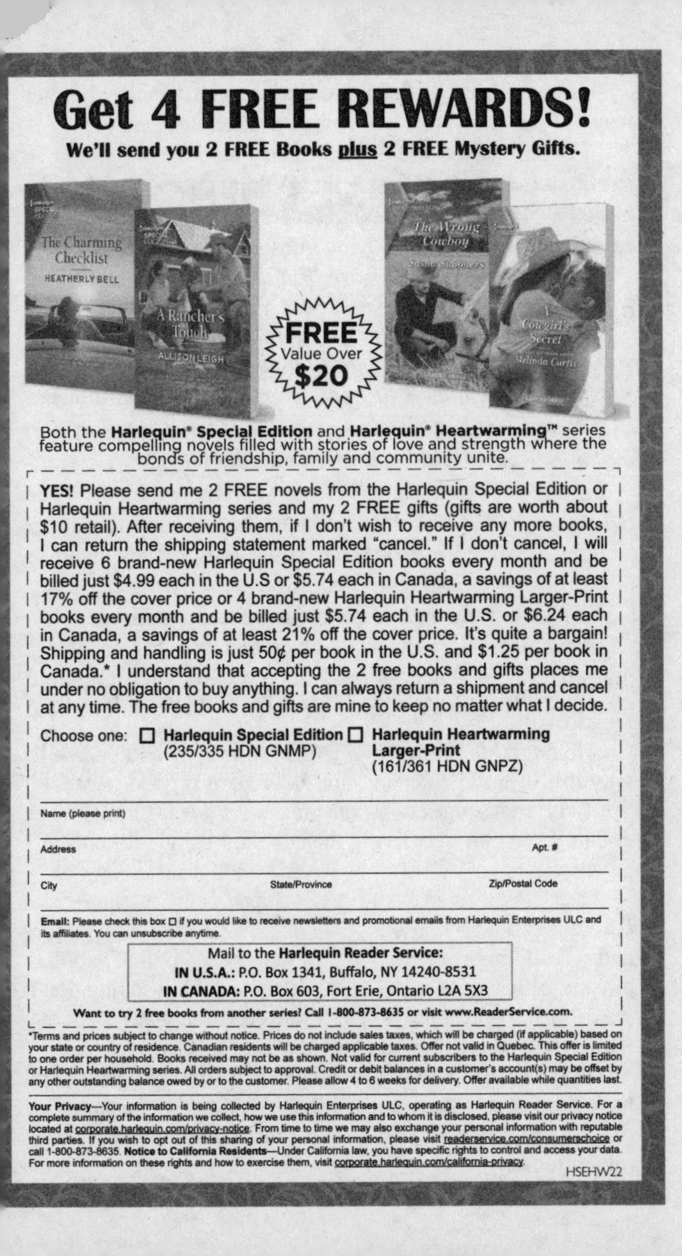

Get 4 FREE REWARDS!
We'll send you 2 FREE Books plus 2 FREE Mystery Gifts.
The Charming Checklist
HEATHERLY BELL
A Rancher's Touch
ALLISON LEIGH
FREE
Value Over
$20
The Wrong Cowboy
A Cowgirl's Secret
Melinda Curtis
Both the Harlequin® Special Edition and Harlequin® Heartwarming™ series feature compelling novels filled with stories of love and strength where the bonds of friendship, family and community unite.
YES! Please send me 2 FREE novels from the Harlequin Special Edition or Harlequin Heartwarming series and my 2 FREE gifts (gifts are worth about $10 retail). After receiving them, if I don't wish to receive any more books, I can return the shipping statement marked "cancel." If I don't cancel, I will receive 6 brand-new Harlequin Special Edition books every month and be billed just $4.99 each in the U.S or $5.74 each in Canada, a savings of at least 17% off the cover price or 4 brand-new Harlequin Heartwarming Larger-Print books every month and be billed just $5.74 each in the U.S. or $6.24 each in Canada, a savings of at least 21% off the cover price. It's quite a bargain! Shipping and handling is just 50¢ per book in the U.S. and $1.25 per book in Canada.* I understand that accepting the 2 free books and gifts places me under no obligation to buy anything. I can always return a shipment and cancel at any time. The free books and gifts are mine to keep no matter what I decide.
Choose one: ☐ Harlequin Special Edition (235/335 HDN GNMP) ☐ Harlequin Heartwarming Larger-Print (161/361 HDN GNPZ)
Name (please print)
Address
Apt. #
City
State/Province
Zip/Postal Code
Email: Please check this box ☐ if you would like to receive newsletters and promotional emails from Harlequin Enterprises ULC and its affiliates. You can unsubscribe anytime.
Mail to the Harlequin Reader Service:
IN U.S.A.: P.O. Box 1341, Buffalo, NY 14240-8531
IN CANADA: P.O. Box 603, Fort Erie, Ontario L2A 5X3
Want to try 2 free books from another series? Call 1-800-873-8635 or visit www.ReaderService.com.
*Terms and prices subject to change without notice. Prices do not include sales taxes, which will be charged (if applicable) based on your state or country of residence. Canadian residents will be charged applicable taxes. Offer not valid in Quebec. This offer is limited to one order per household. Books received may not be as shown. Not valid for current subscribers to the Harlequin Special Edition or Harlequin Heartwarming series. All orders subject to approval. Credit or debit balances in a customer's account(s) may be offset by any other outstanding balance owed by or to the customer. Please allow 4 to 6 weeks for delivery. Offer available while quantities last.
Your Privacy—Your information is being collected by Harlequin Enterprises ULC, operating as Harlequin Reader Service. For a complete summary of the information we collect, how we use this information and to whom it is disclosed, please visit our privacy notice located at corporate.harlequin.com/privacy-notice. From time to time we may also exchange your personal information with reputable third parties. If you wish to opt out of this sharing of your personal information, please visit readerservice.com/consumerschoice or call 1-800-873-8635. Notice to California Residents—Under California law, you have specific rights to control and access your data. For more information on these rights and how to exercise them, visit corporate.harlequin.com/california-privacy.
HSEHW22

SPECIAL EXCERPT FROM

HARLEQUIN

SPECIAL EDITION

When Chance Foley wished for a million dollars as a teenager, he never expected it to come true—especially not via his late brother's twins, who are now his responsibility. Luckily, Poppy Digby has known the twins all their lives and agrees to stay—just for a few days!—but they each find themselves longing for more time...

Read on for a sneak peek at
Be Careful What You Wish For,
the first book in New York Times *bestselling author Elizabeth Bevarly's new Lucky Stars miniseries!*

"Wait, what?" he interrupted again. "Logan worked for a tech firm?"

Although his brother had taught himself to code when he was still in middle school, and he'd been a good hacker of the dirty tricks variety when they were teenagers, Chance couldn't see him ever living the cubicle lifestyle for a steady paycheck.

"Yes," Poppy said. "And he developed a computer program several years ago that allowed companies to legally plunder and sell all kinds of personal information and online habits of anyone who used their websites. It goes without saying that it was worth a gold mine to corporate America. And corporate America paid your brother a gold mine for it."

Okay, that did actually sound like something Logan would have been able to do. Chance probably shouldn't be surprised that his brother would turn his gift for hacking into making a pile of money.

Poppy pulled another piece of paper from the collection in front of her. "I have another statement that's been prepared for your trust, Mr. Foley."

He started to correct Poppy's "Mr. Foley" again, but the other part of her statement sank in too quickly. "What do you mean my trust?"

"I mean your brother and sister-in-law have put funds into a trust for you, as well."

He didn't know what to say. So he said nothing, only gazed back at Poppy, confused as hell.

When he said nothing, she continued. "The children's trust will begin to gradually revert to them when they reach the age of twenty-two. That's when the funds in your trust will revert entirely to you."

Out of nowhere, a thought popped up in the back of Chance's brain, and he was reminded of something he hadn't thought about for a long time—a wish he'd made to a comet when he was fifteen years old. A wish, legend said, that should be coming true about now, since Endicott had been celebrating the "Welcome Back, Bob" comet festival for a few weeks. Something cool and unpleasant wedged into his throat at the memory.

He eyed Poppy warily. "H-how much money is in that trust?"

Her serious green eyes had never looked more serious. "A million dollars, Mr. Foley. Once the children have reached the age of twenty-two, that million dollars will be yours."